The Devil's Promise

Celso Hurtado

Copyright © 2023 Celso Hurtado

Published by Inkshares, Inc., Oakland, California
www.inkshares.com

Edited by Adam Gomolin
Cover design by Tim Barber
Interior design by Kevin G. Summers

ISBN: 9781950301638
e-ISBN: 9781950301645
LCCN: 2023939531

First edition

Printed in the United States of America

To Dad, for the unwavering support, and for making sure
I always had plenty of comic books to read

If ever faced with the Devil, guard your soul with tenacity. For He will endeavor to steal it, whispering pleasant, pretty words while slicing your bruised skin wide open.

—John F. Dubois

CHAPTER 1

THE DEMON WINKED, a mischievous grin plastered on his face as he held out long, veiny arms, open and inviting. Erasmo Cruz shuddered as he caressed the monster, running his fingers over the hard edges of its face and deep folds of its belly, searching for the creature's secrets.

He peered down at the wooden sculpture in his hands, turning it over a few times. There were inconsistencies in the carvings, so it definitely wasn't mass-produced. And the figure didn't look decorative, meant to be placed on a coffee table as a conversation starter, like those bullshit replicas you'd find all over Etsy. No, the detailed rendering of the horns, the nuanced shading of each bulging vein and muscle, the careful thought given to every grotesque proportion. It was exceedingly clear.

This demon was created with love.

He placed it back down with the others. Even in the weak light, he could make out some familiar figures: Malphas, Aamon, Morax, and Baphomet were just a few of the creatures glaring back at him. An interesting assortment to be sure. A Great President, a Grand Marquis, and a Great Earl of Hell, plus a goat-headed deity. It must've taken a great deal of time to carve all of these. Their creator clearly had a fanatical interest in all things demonic.

Erasmo considered going back up the brittle, creaky stairs he'd just descended. This wasn't exactly what he'd been hired for. Ms. Jenkins, the cantankerous old woman who owned the house, was utterly convinced it was haunted. When the two of them had first spoken, she said her family had abandoned the place over twenty years ago. They'd always meant to come back and live here again but somehow never had, and over time the house had fallen into disrepair.

Ms. Jenkins claimed she'd sent her "dumber than rocks" nephews to renovate it so as to sell the property, but they'd gone in for all of ten minutes and now refused to go back. They repeatedly swore up and down that the house didn't want them there. And now she wanted to make sure that whatever might live in these walls wouldn't bother any new residents.

"I've heard all about you," Ms. Jenkins had said on the phone, her fragile, wavering voice still somehow managing to intimidate him. "You're that boy from the Ghost Tracks. You investigate these kinds of things. Get rid of the . . . unnatural. Isn't that right?"

"Well," he'd said, embarrassed at how she'd put it, "I just do my best to try and figure out—"

"You get on down that house and do what you're good at. Don't worry. I'll pay for your services. *If* the job is done satisfactorily."

And before he could muster a response, Ms. Jenkins had hung up on him.

When he arrived, Erasmo had come down to the basement as his first order of business. It was usually in the underbelly of the house where the first seeds of darkness took hold. He again peered down at the group of carved demons he'd stumbled across after descending the stairs.

This, he thought, *is not the type of darkness I expected to find.*

Erasmo ventured farther into the pitch-black basement, looking for any other oddities, listening for the slightest disturbance. Soon, he'd gone so deep into the basement that he could no longer make out the jagged silhouette of the stairs.

A mournful groan floated around him. Erasmo whirled around, frantically aiming his flashlight in every direction. Nothing. He kept waving the weak beam of light around, but saw only stained, dingy walls and moldy boxes. After a long moment, Erasmo finally released his breath. It must've been the wood shifting. This house was old after all. Damn. He knew better than to—

It was then his flashlight passed over the figure standing in the corner. A whimper escaped his lips, and he dropped the flashlight at the shock of what he'd seen. It clacked on the floor, shutting off at impact. The figure had been visible for only a second, but it was more than enough for Erasmo to take in every detail. The towering and thick-set frame, the flowing black robes, its unnatural proportions. But these features were not what caused fear to curl into Erasmo's belly. No. It was something else entirely.

This figure didn't have a human face.

Its skin was scarred and leathery, the shade of dark piss. Thick, ridged horns grew from its furrowed brow, curling to the back of a misshapen skull. The creature's black lips were pulled back, displaying a mouthful of glistening, pointed teeth. But what frightened Erasmo most were the figure's eyes. They didn't share the menace of the rest of its face. Instead, they were warm and inviting.

As if the demon were happy to see him.

He dropped to his knees and desperately searched the floor but felt only dirty concrete underneath his trembling fingertips. Panic seized him as thoughts tumbled together and coalesced in the dark. Ms. Jenkins's nephews said they'd heard noises, had sworn up and down that voices had floated throughout the house. But what they'd heard hadn't been spirits at all. It had been this thing.

But what was it exactly? His brain clicked through the possibilities while he fumbled for the flashlight. A real demon? Impossible. He hadn't seen a summoning circle, or candles, or anointing oils, or anything else that even hinted a conjuring took place. The air smelled musty, but not a hint of sulfur floated around him. And there was no possible reason for a demon to take up residence in an abandoned basement in San Antonio, Texas. That left only one other possibility.

There was a person living down here. Dressed in this grotesque, unnerving costume, passing the time by carving figures of the creatures he adored. And he clearly loved the Devil something fierce.

Erasmo needed to get the hell out of there. Right goddamn now. If he didn't leave soon, this lunatic was going to strangle him or slit his belly open or grab him from behind and—

Breathe. Just focus on getting out of here.

Erasmo continued to frantically reach around for the flashlight, heart pounding. A glimmer of hope arose when the side of his hand brushed cool metal but then vanished with the clacking sound of the flashlight rolling away. He crawled after it, knees digging into the rough concrete, feeling around gently this time so as not to knock it away again.

Finally, right when he was about to give up on finding the flashlight, his hand closed around it and Erasmo almost cried in relief. He jumped to his feet, praying that it hadn't been damaged in the fall. A beam of light shot from his hands, and he immediately waved it around the basement in every direction until it shone weakly on the stairs. Erasmo ran for them, reaching the first step after several lurching strides. He was about to sprint up the steps but paused before climbing them.

If he left now, he'd never know who exactly was standing in that corner, and why. And even though there were multitudes Erasmo didn't understand about himself, there was one thing he knew for certain. If he walked away now, not knowing what this masked, disturbed man was doing down here, the question would forever gnaw a hole in his gut.

Besides, he'd been hired to do a job, hadn't he? Erasmo took in a lungful of musty air and turned to face the room's absolute darkness. Yeah, he had been. And it was time he got on with doing it.

"I'm not scared of you," Erasmo said, taking a hesitant step forward. "I've seen people in horrifying masks before. Even scarier than yours."

The person lurking in the dark corner, sharing the same stale air as him, didn't respond.

Erasmo kept the shaky beam of light trained on the ground in front of him, not wanting to trip on anything and drop the flashlight again. Or perhaps he was lying to himself. Wouldn't be unheard of. Maybe he was really keeping the light away from the corner because he was terrified of seeing that figure again. After all, this was a person squatting in a lightless, abandoned basement, who found it enjoyable to carve intricately detailed homages to lieutenants of Hell. Not to mention he got a kick out of slipping on an unnerving demon's costume to scare whoever might dare disturb his fun.

The more Erasmo thought about this, the more his gut screamed at him to run away. Clearly this person was deranged and could do anything to him down here. He turned and took a hesitant step toward the stairs.

No. Ms. Jenkins would surely send someone else down here, or she might even take a look herself. And who knows what this person would do to her. He had to at least try to get rid of this freak. Better him than her. Erasmo gripped the flashlight, ready to use it as a weapon if he had to.

As he crept nearer to the corner, his heart picked up speed. Soon he'd have to shine the flashlight on this sicko.

"You don't belong here," Erasmo said, his voice wavering. "The woman who owns this place hired me to clear it out. I won't tell anyone that you've been trespassing. Just take your carvings and go. Please." The fear in his voice sounded pathetic even to his own ears.

Erasmo had trouble drawing a full breath, as if the figure's silence were sucking the oxygen out of his burning lungs. He couldn't wait anymore. It was time to aim the light on this strange man playing dress-up, who was trying to scare the hell out of him. To be fair, it was working. But he'd been scared before, hadn't he? And seen terrible, vile things. But also a few wondrous ones, too. These comforting memories emboldened him. The warm, reassuring feeling now coursing over him reached underneath his wrist, caressed it, and slowly lifted his hand.

The beam of light exposed the floor farther ahead of him, revealing a nebulous patch of oil-stained concrete. Wait . . . *was* it oil? Now that he looked closer, the stains were unmistakably a deep shade of maroon.

Jesus.

Erasmo forced himself to keep the shaky circle of light moving forward, until it finally reached a sight that stopped him cold: the figure's feet, standing perfectly still. Except he now saw they weren't feet at all.

They were black hooves, cleaved and jagged.

He forced his trembling hand to slowly raise the flashlight. The hooves were attached to thin, fur-covered legs, like those of a goat, which disappeared into the black robe it wore. After a few moments of shakily rising upward, the light finally reached this creature's grotesque face. Erasmo forced himself to look into its eyes. And when he did, his heart slowed and his nerves calmed, because he finally realized his mistake.

This was neither a person nor a demon. In fact, the figure looming over him wasn't alive at all. It was simply a statue: a more intricate, life-sized version of the carvings he'd already seen. Erasmo cursed himself, as this was something he should've realized right away. He drew closer and inspected the details. This piece was much more convincing than the smaller ones. At six feet tall, the contours under the robe convincingly suggested supple muscles and bizarre proportions.

He dropped to his knees and shone the light over its fur. Amazing. The legs looked incredibly real, the black fur reflecting light in a subdued sheen. Erasmo wondered if these were shavings from a dead goat that had been meticulously glued onto this figure's legs. He tried very hard to push away thoughts of the maroon stains covering the concrete he now knelt on. Unable to stop himself, Erasmo ran his fingers through the fur but immediately drew his hand back, a scream trapped in his clenched throat.

The figure's leg was warm and throbbing.

Erasmo jerked his head upward, desperately attempting to train the flashlight on its chest. He held the beam as steady as he could, but it still wavered, like a drunk attempting to walk a straight line. Still, there was just enough light to make out what he'd wanted to see.

The figure's thick robes were at one moment unmoving, and the next expanding outward, chest muscles underneath rippling. This continued for a few seconds until Erasmo could come to only one inescapable truth.

This creature was breathing.

Erasmo shot up, legs unsteady, and forced himself to look into its eyes. At first glance, they appeared glass-like, large lustrous marbles that had been fashioned with great care to glare fearsomely out into the world. But as he shone the light into them, they now seemed more than that. Their irises glistened, and thin pulsing veins covered each sclera.

He shifted to the creature's side to study its profile, still unable to truly convince himself this was real. How *could* it be? There was no one down here to summon it, no signs that a ceremony had even taken place. None of this made the slightest bit of sense. He directed the light into the side of the creature's eyes, and his breath stopped at how truly alive they looked.

And then, as if the demon had heard this very thought, its eyes turned wetly in their sockets and glared directly at him.

Erasmo shrieked and fell on his ass, again dropping the flashlight. It rolled away behind him, leaving his entire field of vision a wave of darkness. He shoved backward with his hands and feet, desperate to get away from the demon who lurked in the corner. Flashes of movement appeared in front of him, silhouettes of frantic jerks and spasms. He soon realized these motions were his own legs, flailing for purchase against the concrete. But how was it possible to even see this? There was no light in—

Erasmo shifted his gaze upward and saw the demon's eyes now glowing a deep red, casting a crimson light over both the room and its own scarred face. The creature's fiery eyes approached until they loomed directly above him, glaring down. The demon reached for him, its hand resembling a splayed chicken's foot, long black nails curling from each finger.

It was the first caress of this claw against his cheek that made Erasmo shriek again. He closed his eyes, giving himself over to whatever gruesome, unnatural fate was surely about to befall him. Perhaps it was a blessing, and what he truly deserved. This thought, though, did little to lessen the terror that surged through him as the jagged claw reached around his neck and squeezed gently, as if testing how durable he was. Erasmo continued to scream as the pressure around his throat tightened, and soon the world thankfully fell away into a rich, welcome darkness.

CHAPTER 2

ERASMO WOKE TO a sharp jab in his stomach. He tried to look around the room, but his vision was blurred and useless. All he could vaguely make out was a hunched figure looming over him. Before his eyes were able to focus, another painful jab came from above.

"You're not dead . . . are you?" a voice said as the prodding continued. It was a familiar voice, one he'd heard before. "I hired you to do a job, not take a siesta on my property."

Ms. Jenkins. Shit.

"I'm awake," he croaked, holding his hands up, hoping it would prevent another jab to his stomach. His vision finally came into focus, revealing the ancient woman standing over him and the mahogany cane in her gnarled hand she'd been using to poke him. Erasmo slowly got to his feet, head throbbing, as if it were being recklessly inflated and about to burst.

What the hell had happened? He rubbed his right forearm, which hurt like a son of a bitch. He must've landed on it when he fell.

A bright LED lantern Ms. Jenkins held in her non-cane-wielding hand lit up the basement. He made a mental note to get one of those. Well, when he could scrape up some money that wasn't earmarked for his grandmother's treatment.

Erasmo scanned the room as he tried to clear the shroud of fog enveloping his head. None of the carved wooden figures were anywhere to be seen. And of course, no demonic figure lurked in the corner, either. His eyes continued to flit around, searching for something, anything that would help make sense of what he'd seen. Or what he thought he'd seen anyway.

"I would ask if you managed to get rid of whatever lurks in this house," Ms. Jenkins said as he rose unsteadily from the ground, "but I won't bother. From the looks of it, you don't seem to know whether you're coming or going."

Erasmo shuffled over to the corner where the figure had stood. There wasn't a trace of the damn thing. Not an outline against the wall, not a hoofprint on the dirty concrete, not even a goddamn strand of goat fur.

"This old abandoned place is no place to fall asleep. I couldn't believe my eyes when I pulled up and saw your car was still here." The old woman's annoyance was hard to miss. "Can you at least tell me why you stayed all night?"

"I . . . I honestly don't know," he said. And this was the God's honest truth. "Wait, did you say *all night?* What time is it?"

Ms. Jenkins looked bemused. "It's 9:00 a.m., Mr. Cruz."

Christ. Whenever Erasmo was hired for a job, he almost always began at midnight. In his experience, limited as it was, entities seemed more inclined to reveal themselves during the transition from one day to the next. But this meant he'd been down here for nine hours. That was a hell of a lot of time unaccounted for after seeing . . . what exactly?

An incredibly vivid hallucination. Had to have been. And then he'd fainted at the unnerving image his mind had dredged from his subconscious and presented to him.

This was the most likely explanation, given that he'd been burning the candle at both ends lately. Maybe taking every case he could get his hands on hadn't been such a great idea. And he still hadn't shaken whatever bug had been screwing with him lately. Probably just the flu . . . but it'd been wearing him out pretty bad. Whatever was wrong with him, he hoped it ran its course soon so he'd stop feeling like death warmed over.

Between general exhaustion from working too much, and his lethargy from whatever ailed him, it shouldn't come as a shock that he would imagine things that weren't there. Or that his body shut itself down and forced him to do what he'd refused to: get a good night's rest.

"You look a tad piqued, Mr. Cruz," she said, a hint of accusation in her voice. "I hope you're not expecting a handout, since you clearly weren't up for the job I hired you for."

"Sorry about falling asleep," he said. "I didn't encounter any actual spirits last night, so I couldn't get rid of them for you. You're right, though. I'm not really feeling my best, so no charge for the visit."

"Well, that's very respectable of you," the old woman said through pursed lips. "Owning up to your dereliction like that."

Erasmo sighed and took a few steps toward the stairs. He turned to see Ms. Jenkins's tiny eyes, almost completely buried beneath loose, wrinkled flesh, studying his every motion.

"I'd like to come back another time," he said. "Take another shot at it when I'm feeling a little better."

"Perhaps," Ms. Jenkins said, her expression making it clear she found this prospect highly doubtful. "But I'll probably just contact someone else. I'd prefer to let someone who *hasn't* already fallen asleep on the job have a go at it."

Erasmo nodded, a wave of feverish shame spreading through his chest. He turned, still feeling her watchful eyes as he ascended the brittle stairs, not at all ready to face the new day.

Erasmo hated it here. *Hate* was a strong word, but in this case, it wasn't quite strong enough. He could probably make a list of all the things about this place that elicited paralyzing fear and abject revulsion in him, and get to a hundred without even thinking hard. It was a cliché, of course, to hate hospitals. Everyone did. But he hadn't fully understood just how truly wretched an experience this would be.

He stared down at his grandmother's withered body, allowing his tears to flow freely. Sometimes he held them back, even though he wasn't quite sure why. Surely something to do with his inability to process all of this.

Even now, a whisper in the back of his head insisted this wasn't as bad as it seemed, that the doctors were wrong when they'd told him where this was headed. He resisted the allure of the whispers as best he could, but found it increasingly difficult.

If there was one thing Erasmo had learned, it was that he loved to lie to himself. And he was so very good at it.

His grandmother looked horrible, even worse than yesterday. It wasn't because of her skeletal appearance or the breathing tube down her throat—both horrors that usually unnerved him. No, this time it was something different, a new way his grandmother's body had found to make her suffer. When the doctor had mentioned an infection in her gums, Erasmo had paid it little mind. An issue with her mouth seemed trivial when compared to the rest of her body's betrayals. But the grave manner with which the doctor had told him about the infection should've warned him otherwise.

Erasmo studied her again, and this time loud, hitching sobs accompanied his tears. The right side of her face was now swollen to three times the size of her left, rendering it unrecognizable. For the first time, he was grateful his grandmother was unconscious, so she didn't have to endure the agony and humiliation of her body's rapid breakdown.

This particular doctor, young and utterly devoid of bedside manner, had said the infection was a "complication" from her treatment. That was one thing Erasmo had learned about loving someone who was gravely ill. Every day was just lurching from one complication to the next, heart stuck in your throat at each announcement of a new one. When they'd first laid out his grandmother's treatment plan, it had seemed like a straightforward path, from A to B to C. Of course, he was naïve to think it would be that way at all.

As he continued to observe her, a horrifying truth fought its way to the surface: His grandmother might be dead by Christmas. Then he would truly be alone.

Erasmo froze. A sound had escaped his grandmother's lips. A mournful whimper, filled with pain, and fear, and regret. It was a sound Erasmo wished he hadn't been around to hear.

"Grandma? Are you awake?"

But now she was silent again, oblivious to the world around her.

She'd once told him to go out in the world and find a family to make his own. But that's not at all what he wanted. He wanted her. Along with his grandfather, she was the only family he'd ever really known, who'd ever really cared about him. Besides, the idea that anyone would want to throw their lot in with him seemed fantastical at best. Even his own parents hadn't wanted him.

He rose to leave. The nurse would be in to bathe her soon, and Erasmo felt like he'd faint if he didn't get out of here for a

while. After taking one more long look at his suffering grandmother, he turned and shuffled out into the sad, desolate
hallway.

CHAPTER 3

WHEN ERASMO ARRIVED home, he immediately felt an urgent need to leave, to turn right around and seek the mild warmth of the morning sun he'd just abandoned. The house's oppressiveness attacked him, like relentless fire ants swarming over fetid, rotting flesh.

He eyed the ever-growing stack of medical bills as he passed the kitchen counter, a knot forming in his gut. When his grandmother had first gotten sick, he'd made numerous attempts to navigate the insurance minefield. So many hours spent on the phone with the hospital, trying to understand the deluge of eye-popping charges, what the countless medical codes meant, if there were any ways to negotiate lower costs.

But he'd been passed around endlessly, each new person using increasingly confusing terms and citing nonsensical policies. The hospital sent him to the insurance company, who sent him back to the hospital, who sent him back to the insurance company in a maddening, never-ending cycle.

He'd wanted so badly to scream at them. *My grandmother is dying!* he imagined shouting. *Can't you please just help me!* But he couldn't say those words out loud, as that would mean admitting the truth.

Erasmo eyed the lopsided Christmas tree standing in the corner, its sparse ornaments leaving most of the tree undecorated. He'd put it up out of a sense of obligation, knowing his grandmother would've wanted him to. At first, he had fantasies of her coming home before the holidays were over, imagining her beaming with delight at the tree. But putting it up by himself had gutted him, his mind constantly replaying all those years they'd carefully decorated the tree together, full of hope and anticipation. And now it appeared those fantasies of her coming home for the holidays were just that. A fantasy.

He approached his grandmother's threadbare recliner, eying the indentation in its cushion. He'd make certain to go back to the hospital later and spend time with her once his head cleared a little. Erasmo allowed his fingers to graze the rough, aged cloth of the recliner and then forced himself to walk past it.

His room at the back of the house was a sloppily constructed addition built years ago by his great uncle. To Erasmo's exhausted eyes, it looked even more pathetic than usual. The off-kilter angles and uneven proportions, which never bothered him when he was younger, now sent a surge of anxiety coursing through him.

Erasmo maneuvered around the stacks of books rising from the floor like misshapen stalagmites in an ancient cavern. He'd been meaning to get rid of a few but always found it impossible to part with even one. A few of the titles caught his attention as he settled into bed: *Buckland's Complete Book of Witchcraft*, *Secrets to Deliverance: Defeat the Toughest Cases of Demonic Bondage,* and *Dreaming the Future: The Fantastic Story of Prediction*.

He'd found all three thoroughly fascinating, particularly *Dreaming the Future*. The author delved into every method of prognostication possible, ranging from the zodiac all the way to fox's paw prints. While some soothsayers and prophets were debunked in its pages, the author also acknowledged the spiritual side of attempting to peer into the future. It was the rare book for believers and nonbelievers alike. Of course, he'd been fascinated by the subject matter ever since the craziness with Billy, whom he still thought of almost every day.

Erasmo was just about to grab this book off the stack when his phone vibrated, startling him. He glanced down and froze when he saw who it was.

Rat.

He tried to send the call to voicemail, but his finger trembled, and so it required several attempts to finally silence the phone. Did Rat really think he'd talk to him? After the way that son of a bitch had been acting . . . after the accusations he'd made? That guy had some goddamn nerve.

A flurry of knocking erupted from the front door. Erasmo had a sudden, irrational urge to run to the backyard and hide, to wriggle underneath the house and wait for this person to leave, however long it took.

Another burst of knocking, just as urgent. Who the hell could it be? He certainly wasn't expecting anyone. Erasmo glanced down at his phone, its call history still showing Rat's name.

Had he called from outside? Was his former best friend standing out there this very moment, adjusting his thick, smudged glasses as he waited? For some reason, this thought once again made Erasmo want to run away and never come back.

His curiosity got the better of him though. He tiptoed to the living room, and after inhaling a deep breath, peeked through the curtains. Erasmo recognized the car in the driveway, and a tremor of relief swept through him when he saw it wasn't Rat's vehicle.

He walked over to the front door and slowly opened it, unable to muster much enthusiasm for the person occupying his porch.

Andy Gorecki stood there, fidgeting in ill-fitting dress clothes and holding a greasy paper bag. His plump features gave him a friendly, disarming appearance. Despite the cool morning, a light sheen of sweat glistened on his pockmarked skin.

"Hey, man!" Andy said, his enthusiasm already making Erasmo's head hurt even worse. "Just came by to see how everything went last night."

He stared at Andy for a few seconds, unsure how to answer without getting trapped in a long conversation. If Erasmo told Andy about the demon he thought he'd seen, they'd be on this porch all morning.

"You know, at the Jenkins place," Andy prompted.

"Didn't have much luck," Erasmo finally said, deciding to forgo the truth to save time. Andy was the only person he'd ever met, besides Rat, who was as interested in the supernatural as he was. "Spent the whole night there, but nothing out of the ordinary happened."

Andy's face fell at this news, his morning clearly ruined. He ran a hand through his unwashed thicket of black hair, which was speckled with dandruff. "Well, that's a damn shame." He squinted, as if staring into an intense light. "You know . . . if there are any other cases you're working on, I'd really love to join in. I could help out with whatever you need."

Erasmo had liked Andy from the beginning. They'd first met when he and Rat visited the Emily Morgan Hotel a few months ago to rent a room. It had been a source of embarrassment to live so close to a hotel *USA Today* ranked the third most haunted in Americaand to have never stayed even one night in its hallowed walls. They'd tried to rent a room from the portly young man at the front counter—who appeared to be only a few years older than them, and had been taken aback when he'd outright refused.

"Do you know why I work here?" he'd asked them, right eyebrow raised, as if two complete strangers would have the slightest clue. "One day," the clerk had said, glancing around the lobby before returning his eager gaze to them, "I want to do what you do."

Neither of them had spoken, too surprised to respond.

"Yeah . . . I know who you are, Erasmo Cruz. In fact, I knew all about you even before that craziness over the summer. I remember that first incident from down at the Ghost Tracks, the one that was all over the news."

Andy had gone on to staunchly claim that his interest in the paranormal rivaled even theirs, and that he worked there for only one reason: to study and experience firsthand the hotel's many ghosts.

"I'm writing a book on haunted hotels. Pretty obsessed with the subject." He'd glanced around again, as if about to betray a deeply held secret. "Did you know this whole structure served as the city's Medical Arts Building until 1976? There was both a psychiatric ward and a morgue located here. No wonder this place is so damn haunted."

Andy had slid a key card across the desk. "Look, since you guys are kindred spirits, no charge for the room. Just don't tell anyone, okay?"

He and Rat had talked more with him that night, bonding over the Dancing Devil of El Camaroncito. The three of them had such a good time discussing the cloven-hooved figure who danced the night away in a west side nightclub, they'd stayed in touch ever since.

Erasmo appreciated Andy's agreeable nature and liked to bounce ideas off him from time to time. He usually had thoughtful, interesting insights to share. But the idea of teaming up with anyone other than Rat filled his stomach with noxious acid. Despite what had passed between them, Erasmo couldn't see anyone taking Rat's place.

And if Rat never stopped with his bullshit, then he'd rather just be alone.

"I don't have any other cases right now," Erasmo said, "but I'll let you know if something interesting comes along."

Andy gave a large smile at this, baring his tiny teeth. "Great! Oh, I brought these for you." He held out the greasy bag. "Some *conchas* from Panifico. Know you have a lot going on with your grandmother and figured you could use some breakfast."

Erasmo stared at the bag a moment before gently taking it, embarrassed at how moved he was by the gesture. A surge of guilt spread through him at the lie he'd just told Andy.

"Thanks, man. I appreciate it."

"No sweat." Andy turned to leave, carefully descending the porch stairs. "And try to get some sleep!" he yelled over his shoulder. "You look exhausted!"

Erasmo walked back inside and set the bag on the kitchen table. He then headed to his room and settled into bed, desperate for oblivion. But as he lay there, his skull throbbed, deep and unrelenting. Not to mention his arm still ached terribly from the fall in Ms. Jenkins's basement. He'd fully intended to come home and get some rest to clear the fog swirling in his head. But now the prospect of spending all day under the covers was just too damn depressing.

He grabbed his phone from the nightstand and checked his email. Best to keep busy. He'd decided to take as many cases as possible while on winter break. It was the only way he knew to keep the hordes of restless, hungering thoughts at bay. Not to mention he needed the money. Luckily, eight new emails had come in since last he'd checked, and several actually seemed promising.

> *To Whom It May Concern,*
>   *I understand your agency specializes in cleansing houses of spirits. I am in desperate need of someone with your talents. While I haven't visually observed anything abnormal in my house, I have physically felt a presence. What I mean to say is, the last few mornings, I've woken up with deep, savage bites covering my stomach.*

Erasmo reflexively placed his hand to his belly, feeling the scar tissue underneath his thin T-shirt.

> *I have attached photos of the wounds. Please contact me once you've had a chance to review them.*
>   *Patrick D.*

Against his better judgment, Erasmo opened the attachments, sucking in a shocked breath at the images on his screen. Each bite was massive and deep, the man's stomach a grotesque canvas of black-and-purple flesh. Most disturbing, though, were the teeth-marks. Their shape in and of itself wasn't the problem. As far as he could tell, they looked exactly like indentations human teeth would leave. The problem was their size. Whatever left these marks had a mouth at least twice the size of a normal human being.

Erasmo quickly closed the photos, not wanting to see any more. He mentally categorized the case as a maybe, depending on the rest of the emails. He opened the next one, hoping for something a bit less gruesome.

hey, word on the street is you guys take care of problems with ghosts and shit, that you can get rid of them perma- nent. me and my boys need that kind of help. we have a situation at our place of business. some people have died on the property, totally by accident, and now we're having some problems. give me a shout when you're ready to come down and take care of this for us. plenty of cash if the job gets done with no bullshit.
Marky

These types of messages always set Erasmo on edge. The kind where he couldn't quite figure out whether they were mocking him or genuinely asking for help. It was this parsing of fact and fiction, of making out the thin, blurred line between fantasy and reality, that often proved the most difficult for him.

Erasmo opened the next email and skimmed through the message. At first, it seemed like a lot of others he often received. Until the end.

Mr. Cruz,
I have an unusual problem I hope you'll be able to help with.
Time is working against me, so if possible, please respond immediately. I'd prefer to tell you all of the details in person. But to give you an idea of the situation, I'll at least share this one piece of information with you.
Some time ago, when I was only a teenager, I believe that I might've accidentally sold my soul to the devil. And now I'm terrified that payment has come due.
Bradley Erickson

Erasmo read the email a few more times, mulling the words over, considering their implications. His gut told him that

Bradley Erickson was just massively confused and had seen one too many movies. But there was also a persistent voice in the back of his head whispering the obvious but delectable question. *Why on earth does this man believe he sold his soul to the Devil?*

Erasmo read the message again, a tingle of nervous excitement growing in his belly. Sure, the guy was almost certainly delusional. But there was also a chance, however remote, that Bradley Erickson had an interesting story to tell. Screw it. There was only one way to find out.

CHAPTER 4

UNLESS HE WAS dealing with a possible haunting, Erasmo hated meeting clients at their houses. It was just too damn dangerous. The people who wanted to hire him sometimes ended up being a little unhinged, so he preferred doing business in public settings where he could weed out the crazies. You never knew when someone would react badly to being told that there wasn't *actually* a deformed imp living in their attic. For this meet, he'd asked Bradley to meet him at the Quarry to talk things over.

Erasmo's battered Civic groaned in protest as he turned from Basse Road into the entrance of the shopping center. He parked by the Corner Bakery, wanting to go for a stroll and stretch his legs for a bit.

The Alamo Quarry Market was built on the remains of an old cement factory that had operated for decades. He sometimes liked to walk around and imagine how the site must've looked back in its heyday of production. There were still four smokestacks from the original structure. They loomed over the market, their bases incorporated into the Whole Earth Provision Company, rising from its storefront. They could be seen from miles away, the four towering structures a reminder that the past wasn't so easily built over and forgotten. He eyed them warily as he passed through their shadows, imagining how terrible it would be to find himself stuck on top of one, teetering on its edge, inches from plummeting to a grotesque and meaningless death.

He shook this thought away and walked toward the bench in front of James Avery where they'd agreed to meet. When Erasmo arrived at the bench, he settled in and glanced around but saw only carefree shoppers enjoying the cool weather, eager to spend their money on overpriced Christmas presents. He envied this, though, as he had no money of his own to spend. And worse, no one to buy anything for.

Nervous energy spread through his gut, a usual occurrence when meeting a potential client for the first time. After distracting himself for a while by people-watching and taking in the market's Christmas decor, he checked his phone, which told him it was two minutes past noon. Punctuality must not be this guy's thing. Either that or he wasn't showing.

This wouldn't be the least bit out of the ordinary. The majority of people who contacted him usually ended up backing out. He never held it against them though. It was a strange business he'd come to find himself in, and knew these poor souls must be in dire straits to resort to contacting a paranormal investigator of all things. Surely, many of them must've questioned if what they were experiencing was even genuinely supernatural.

In truth, Erasmo had spent a lot of time lately pondering what exactly he himself believed. He'd been involved in so many extraordinary incidents, from his experience at the Ghost Tracks to all the craziness a few months prior. But it was hard for him to see these events clearly now. With each passing day, he questioned what he thought he'd seen. The events were hazy, as if viewing them through an opaque lens. But despite this, there were two things he was still certain of.

The supernatural *did* exist. He'd experienced enough, seen enough, to be absolutely sure. Erasmo was so certain that it felt like this knowledge was carved deep into his bones. Second, *actual* supernatural happenings were exceedingly rare, and those who thought they were experiencing one were usually mistaken.

Erasmo checked the time again and scanned the crowd, but no one approached him. Damn. This guy probably wasn't coming.

He suspected that prospective clients were often talked out of meeting him by concerned friends and family. Or perhaps they'd simply realized that what had gone bump in the night and scared them so was just a starved rat trapped in the wall, which was how these things usually went. Of course, there was also the possibility that whatever had gone bump in the night had risen up and savaged them. Who's to know?

He was just about to chalk this guy up as a no-show when a man in his midthirties, wearing a tailored, expensive-looking suit, approached the bench. Several female shoppers stopped to admire him, following his every motion. It wasn't hard to see why. Bradley Erickson cut a striking figure.

The man finally reached the bench and peered down at Erasmo quizzically, as if his presence might be some kind of joke. This happened more often than not.

"I know I'm on the young side," Erasmo said as he stood and extended his hand, "but I promise I can help with whatever troubles you're having."

"Well," Bradley said uneasily, not making eye contact, "that's the thing, Mr. Cruz. I'm not sure what my troubles even are." He looked Erasmo over again, then shrugged in a *what the hell* gesture before extending his hand. "Bradley Erickson."

His hand was buttery soft, but it pulsed with power.

"Erasmo."

"Let's sit for a bit," Bradley said, "and I'll tell you my story."

They settled onto the metal bench, each exhaling a shaky sigh. Bradley smelled of cologne that reminded him of a mild spring day.

He smells expensive is what he smells like, Erasmo thought, glad to know this guy wouldn't stiff him at least.

"I'm sure you hear this all the time," Bradley said, the muscles under his square jaw tensed, "but I'm not really sure where to start."

"Just tell it, however feels right to you."

Bradley nodded, coming to a decision.

"I guess I shouldn't start with what's happening now, but rather with something that happened eighteen years ago." Bradley sighed and glanced at the sky, as if searching for comfort in the leisurely cumulus clouds meandering above them. "You ever been in love?" he asked.

"I thought I was once," Erasmo answered, his stomach clenching. "Not too long ago actually."

Bradley glanced at him and nodded, sympathy encroaching into his eyes.

"I fell in love for the first time eighteen years ago. Her name was Gemma. And man, I had it bad. I was an absolute nobody in high school. So when she asked for my number one day, someone like her, I couldn't believe it."

Erasmo attempted to hide his surprise, but it emerged anyway. The idea that the man garnering stares at that very moment could've ever been considered a nobody was incomprehensible to him.

"Soon Gemma and I started hanging out after school. I can't even begin to explain to you how mindlessly happy I was. But then one day, she mentioned a few of her friends were getting together and having some kind of a gathering. And she wanted me to come along.

"I tried to get more details, but she was being so vague about the whole thing. I finally gave up, knowing damn well I'd go with her either way. I'd have done anything to please her, you know?"

Erasmo nodded. "I do," he said, his voice barely a whisper.

"When the day finally came, she said the gathering started at midnight, on some land her friend owned out in New Braunfels. It was a bit of a drive, but we eventually found the place. There was this big steel gate guarding the entrance to the property though. After a while, this man finally appeared to let us in. And that's when I got scared for the first time."

Bradley now paused, as if unsure how to continue.

"Was there something wrong with him?" Erasmo asked.

"No. At least, not exactly. It's what he wore that bothered me." Bradley stopped again, glancing at a passerby before continuing. "He was dressed in robes, with a hood hiding his face."

"Were the robes red?" Erasmo asked.

"No," Bradley answered, surprised. "But . . ."

"There was someone else there wearing red robes."

"Yeah, exactly," he said, shaking his head. "Someone I saw later that night. Anyway, this guy in the black robes opened the gate and we drove in. After a few minutes, we came to this huge bonfire with a bunch of people dancing around the flames. Honestly, it looked like a normal weekend party out in the woods."

"But it wasn't," Erasmo said.

"No," Bradley said softly. "It wasn't."

"What, then?"

"I hung out for a while with some of Gemma's friends. They definitely knew more than I did. One of them, a small runt of a guy, kept insisting to me that my life was about to change. It was about then everyone gathered in front of a wooden plat-form nearby. That's when it started."

"The ceremony?" Erasmo asked.

"Yeah," Bradley said, pursing his lips before he continued. "Four men in black robes walked out onto the stage, their faces hidden, just like the person at the gate. Each one scattered to a different corner. That's when this crazed guy wearing crimson robes came out. He was tall, a little hunched over, a jagged scar on his cheek. Around forty-five maybe. But he wasn't hiding his face with a hood like the rest of them. No. This guy looked out at the crowd, with these wild blue eyes. He said something like, 'Welcome . . . we are the Children of M,' and raised his arms skyward. And then everyone knelt."

The Children of M. Erasmo had never heard of this group before. But it was easy to guess what came next.

"And then the man with the scar began to chant," Erasmo said.

"Yeah, exactly. I was a little freaked out for sure, but I went along with it. I just figured these people were into some weird playacting stuff, like how those nerds dress up for *Dungeons and Dragons*. There were other parts of the ceremony, but I'll skip to the end. The guy in the crimson robe asked if we wanted our wildest dreams to come true, if we wanted to have everything we'd ever desired. Everyone shrieked *YES! YES!* at the top of their lungs, like goddamn maniacs. He said we just had to do one simple thing, which was to promise a gift to Him, and then all of our deepest desires would come true."

"But he never mentioned what that gift would be," Erasmo said.

"That's right," Bradley said, breathing heavier now. "Then he looked in my direction and motioned for me to go up onstage. It was the last thing I wanted to do, but Gemma prac-tically shoved me up there, hissing at me to go. When I finally went up, he made me kneel in front of him and asked if I was ready to make a pact that would ensure my happiness in this life and protect my soul in the next."

"And you said yes," Erasmo said.

"What else was I supposed to do, say no to some weirdo playing dress-up? That would've ruined my chances with Gemma. She obviously wanted me to play along. So I said . . . yeah . . . sure . . . I agree to the deal. Then he gave me this huge, creepy smile, and said something like, 'What you desire shall be yours, and what He desires shall be His."

"And then?" Erasmo asked.

"And then he did the exact same thing to a few other people and disappeared shortly after."

"What about Gemma?" Erasmo asked. "Did she . . . ?"

"Gemma," Bradley said, his brow furrowed at the memory, "never talked to me again after that night."

"Okay," Erasmo said. "Anything else I should know?"

"Yeah," he answered. "The most important thing of all. What the man in the crimson robes said came true."

"What do you mean?" Erasmo asked.

"I mean," Bradley said, "that after that night . . . I got everything I ever wanted."

CHAPTER 5

"I'M NOT SURE how to explain it to you," Bradley continued, "but after the ceremony, everything changed."

"How, specifically?" Erasmo asked, now genuinely intrigued.

"Well, I was overweight and unpopular at the time, not to mention my grades were terrible. But a few days after the ceremony, I decided to join the track team, even though I'd never *once* given thought to that before. Soon the weight melted off, and all of my grades improved, too. I started getting invited to parties every weekend. People were gravitating to me, even some who used to bully me. The complete turnaround was insane."

"And you believed all of this was because of the ceremony?"

"That thought," Bradley said, "never even crossed my mind." His jaw tightened. "Until a few days ago." He shook his head, as if disgusted with his own stupidity.

"At the time, I just thought I'd made some good decisions, and luck was finally smiling down on me. Life continued to get even better from there. Went on to college, met my beautiful wife, earned a degree in finance, now I have a great career at USAA, and just recently had a son. As close to a perfect existence as you can get."

Despite himself, Erasmo felt a pang of jealousy deep in his gut, as he always did when crossing paths with someone who'd lived a charmed life. How did the fates choose? How did they decide which souls to pluck out of the raging river of shit and misery everyone else flailed in and sprinkle luminous magic on them? He hated when these thoughts crept in. Wondering about the vagaries of circumstance and good fortune was enough to drive a person mad.

"But then a few nights ago, something terrible happened. My wife has been out of the country on a business trip, so it's just been me and the baby. I was asleep in bed when I began to hear whispers. Chants almost. I thought it was just a dream, but the chants kept getting louder and louder."

"What were they saying?" Erasmo asked.

"They kept repeating the same phrase in this horrible droning voice," Bradley said. *"Tempus est . . . Tempus est . . ."*

The way Bradley intoned the words, channeling the cadence of the chant, sent a chill through Erasmo's bones.

"I finally realized I wasn't dreaming," Bradley said. "It was all real. I shot out of bed and frantically looked around the room. That's when I saw them. There were four . . . one in each corner, lurking in the shadows." He took a hard swallow. "Figures in flowing black robes."

Bradley paused and shook his head, as if even now he didn't quite believe it.

"I jumped off the bed and sprinted out of the room," he continued. "My only thought was to protect my son, Eric. I ran to his crib and looked him over. He seemed perfectly fine. I was just about to call the police, but . . . then I thought about how crazy the whole thing would sound. So instead I grabbed my Smith & Wesson from the study and went back to the bedroom. Sure enough, there wasn't a trace of anyone. By the time morning rolled around, I'd managed to convince myself the whole thing had been some kind of hallucination."

Tears now welled in Bradley's narrow eyes, and he paused to wipe them away before they'd had a chance to fully exist.

"Until last night. Eric's crying woke me up around 3:00 a.m. He was screaming bloody murder, which isn't normal for him. I sprinted to his room, and that's when I saw it. There was something on his face, but I couldn't make out exactly what at first. I turned the light on and saw two words written on his forehead . . . *TEMPUS EST.*"

"Jesus," Erasmo said out loud, even though he hadn't meant to.

Tempus Est.

It's time.

"That's not all," Bradley said, plump tears now sliding down his sculpted cheeks. "The words. They were written in blood."

The two of them sat in silence as Erasmo waited for Bradley to compose himself. An old man wearing a baby-blue guayabera glanced over at the odd scene of a stylish businessman crying to a teenager dressed in jeans and a hoodie, but he kept shuffling along.

After a few moments, Bradley seemed in control of himself, and Erasmo decided to test the waters.

"So," he started, "you're worried that the ceremony you attended eighteen years ago was actually real, and the gift you owe Him is now coming due. Is that it?"

Bradley brought his head forward in a slow, stiff nod.

This was not at all what Erasmo had been expecting, but these first meetings rarely were. More often than not, the folks who contacted him were just looking to have their houses cleansed, or had questions about strange events they were experiencing. There'd been some exceptions of course. But this . . . this was a different sort of beast. He wasn't quite sure what to make of it.

What he did know was that Bradley hadn't sold his soul to the Devil at some random party eighteen years ago. Erasmo believed that communicating with a demon was possible, but this was the rarest supernatural occurrence of all. And it certainly hadn't been performed by some backwoods charlatan.

"It's called a Black Mass," Erasmo finally said. "Or at least, this group's approximation of one."

"What?" Bradley asked.

"The ceremony you attended. It's called a Black Mass, which is an inversion of a Catholic Mass. They're usually conducted by—and I use this term very loosely—Satanists."

"Oh," Bradley said. "Why do you say loosely?"

"Because there are very few actual practicing Satanists. I mean, there is the Satanic Temple, but most of its followers don't even believe in a literal Satan, or anything supernatural for that matter. But real, worshiping the Devil and making offerings to Him type of Satanists? No . . . those are few and far between. More of a construct of fiction than anything else."

"But the ceremony," Bradley said. "Everyone there fully believed in this man's power. And all of my dreams came true. Just like he promised they would."

"There's a simple explanation for that," Erasmo said. "I think it's fairly obvious that you made your *own* dreams come true."

"I don't know . . ." Bradley said. "Doesn't it seem like a huge coincidence that my life changed so drastically right after the ceremony?"

"There could be lots of reasons for that," Erasmo said. "Maybe the old man's talk about obtaining all of your deepest desires subconsciously motivated you."

"I guess," Bradley said, but he hardly seemed convinced.

"Look, like I mentioned before, there aren't many real Satanists. But do you know what there *are* a lot of? Bored and needy people who like to play dress-up in the hopes of impress-ing or scaring their friends. Sure, they might have an actual interest in the subject, but they pretend to know way more than they actually do. Anyone can read some chants from a book. But I guarantee you one thing about these people."

"What?" Bradley asked.

"Not one of them," Erasmo said, "has the power to truly communicate with a demon."

Bradley's eyes flickered back and forth at an alarming rate as he mulled this over.

"Okay," he finally said. "Let's say it was all bullshit, just some fringe weirdos in the woods entertaining each other. And let's say I imagined those hooded figures in my room. Then what about this?"

Bradley swiped his phone a few times and then showed it to Erasmo. A red-faced baby, its tiny mouth peeled back in a terrific scream, stared back at him. He read the bloody words dripping from the child's forehead and shuddered.

Well, that's a good goddamn question.

This didn't make a lot of sense. Of course, neither did the idea of a demon wanting a child in the first place. Although, he was by no means an expert in demonology. Rat had studied the topic far more than he ever had. The idea of fallen angels tempting people with sin had just never fully resonated with him. Probably because in order to truly believe in demons, you'd have to fully believe in God. And his thoughts on this particular matter were unsettled.

Erasmo had constantly prayed to God when he was a child, begging Him to send the parents he'd never known. He'd spent countless wasted days staring out his front window, waiting for two people who would never arrive. Erasmo eventually stopped praying, but had recently become so desperate that he tried again, pleading for Him to help his grandmother. Of course, her health grew worse shortly afterward.

Despite his ambivalence on the general topic of demonology, though, Erasmo had read enough books to gain an understanding of the basics.

Just for argument's sake he considered which particular demons would even want a child. None immediately came to mind. Although, he now realized he'd been thinking of strictly Christian demons.

Erasmo broadened his scope and remembered a creature he'd read about in the Testament of Solomon: Obizuth. She was a demon with wild hair and no limbs who detested newborns. Obizuth visited women in childbirth and strangled their children. For infants she didn't kill outright, Obizuth blinded and deafened them, or twisted their bodies and limbs until they were unusable.

But as far as Erasmo knew, she'd never had children brought to her, nor had she engaged in any dealmaking. And Obizuth didn't want to possess children, only to maim and murder them. He made a mental note to research which demons were known for desiring children, if any, just to sate his own curiosity.

Bradley closed the photo of his screaming child, which was quickly replaced by the phone's wallpaper. It displayed a picture of him and his wife, the baby in between them, all three dressed in white and beaming out at the world in perfect bliss.

"Look," Erasmo said, "I don't think I can help you."

"What?" Bradley asked, his sculpted eyebrows narrowed. "Why not?"

Erasmo tried to tell himself that the resistance building in his bones was due to how time-intensive this case would be. His grandmother remained priority number one, and nothing could get in the way of that.

But was that really the truth? Or was it because his heart ached deeply at seeing the picture of Bradley's perfect, intact family? Given his own history and his grandmother's current condition, perhaps this wasn't the best time to be so close to something he'd never truly had, and most certainly never would.

That was ridiculous though. Certainly he could be around a functional, loving family for a few days without falling apart. Couldn't he?

But then there was the subject matter to consider. Demonology was tough. He'd had a difficult possession case with a child not too long ago, and horrific scars on his stomach to serve as a reminder of how badly it had gone.

"I need a little bit of time," he said, "to think this over. Can I give you a call later?"

Bradley rose from the bench.

"I hope your ad wasn't bullshit and that you're actually able to help me." Bradley turned and walked away, quickly disappearing into the early afternoon crowd, leaving Erasmo to wonder just what the hell he might be getting himself into.

CHAPTER 6

ERASMO ENTERED THE curandera's shop, inhaling the herbal-tinged fragrances wafting around him. His eyes wandered over the narrow aisles, but she was nowhere to be seen. A single strand of sad Christmas lights lined the front counter, blinking at odd intervals.

Three children, siblings from the looks of them, intently studied the broad selection of Mexican candies against the back wall. The two boys each grabbed a few packages of Pulparindos, while their younger sister held a handful of Pica Fresas in her chubby little hand. All three walked over to the wheezing refrigerator and eagerly grabbed an ice-cold Big Red.

"Alma!" the older boy yelled as they shoved everything onto the counter.

The curandera emerged from the back and glanced at Erasmo, her eyes appraising him longer than usual. She quickly rang up the children and sent them on their way before turning her full attention to him.

"You need help," she said.

"I do."

"Come on back," she said, gesturing to the door behind her.

Erasmo walked behind the counter and through the door, entering the curandera's dimly lit store . . . her *real* store, as he thought of it.

She glanced back at him, a strange expression on her delicate face. "I don't think you've ever visited as much as you have in the last few months."

Erasmo glanced down at the floor, embarrassed, not sure how to respond. Had he really been coming by that much more often?

She walked over to the rear wall, which was covered from floor to ceiling with old plywood shelves, each overflowing with bottles, and jars, and herbs, and plants, and assorted items he didn't recognize. She stood on her tiptoes and reached for the top shelf, her short stature making this task difficult. Alma finally managed to snatch the small green bottle she'd been reaching for and turned to hand it to him.

"This might help with—"

"Oh, I'm fine," Erasmo said, confused. "I'm just here for some advice on a situation."

"I see . . ." she said, the slightest grimace forming on her small features. "What kind of situation?"

As Erasmo recounted Bradley's story, Alma took a seat in her ancient wicker rocking chair and lit a long, curved pipe with intricate carvings on its sides. She said nothing as he spoke, instead puffing silently as she occasionally arched an eyebrow. When the story was finished, he looked at the curandera expectantly, hoping for a reaction, but none came.

"So," he said, breaking the awkward pause. "I came here to ask if you've ever been involved in anything like—"

"Stay as far away from this man as possible," she said. "He is cursed, and if you're not careful, you will be, too, even more than you already are." Alma began to say something else but stopped herself.

"He clearly needs help though," Erasmo said. "Even if it's just to—"

"This man is beyond help. And to answer your question, yes. I was involved with something like this. Many years ago. And it did not end well for anyone involved."

"Okay. I understand. But . . ."

"But a part of you wants to help him anyway."

"If there's even a small chance the baby is in danger, shouldn't I . . ."

"It doesn't matter what anyone else would do, Erasmo. All that matters is what *you* can live with. So that's really the only question. Can you live with walking away from what this man is asking you to do?"

Could he? Bradley was a virtual stranger. He should be able to say no without any qualms whatsoever. But on the other hand, what had running away from ugly, uncomfortable situations ever gotten him?

Cold logic told Erasmo that Bradley would be fine either way. Of course Bradley hadn't made a pact with a demonic entity eighteen years ago. Some cult wannabe loser out in the woods wouldn't be able to manage something like that.

But Bradley had been *so* damned scared. Whatever he'd seen had certainly pushed him to the edge. And the baby. He couldn't stop thinking about the screaming, red-faced baby with blood scrawled on his forehead. Erasmo sensed that if he walked away now, he'd end up feeling like he abandoned this child.

And that he couldn't live with.

"I think I have to try and help," he finally said.

"If that's the case," Alma said after a long, disapproving sigh, "then I'll simply say this: trust no one, as we are all under the spell of one devil or another."

The faint whisper of shuffling feet floated into the room. Erasmo turned, surprised to see a young woman standing in the doorway. Her straight, jet-black hair gleamed, even in the room's dim light. She peered at him, eyes narrowed in either curiosity or deep suspicion.

"Vero," Alma said, "come here and meet Erasmo."

The young woman walked over, her gait measured but bristling with strength.

"This is Erasmo Cruz," Alma told her. "He showed up at my doorstep a few years ago, wanting to learn about mal de ojo." She flashed him a rare smile. "I still remember how nervous you were. This is Vero, my niece from Arcelia. She's visiting for a while, staying in the garage out back. She's fulfilling her responsibility to learn the skills our family has passed down for generations."

Vero frowned as an awkward silence settled over them. She finally broke it at his expense.

"Are we just going to pretend that it's normal," she said, peering at him with uncertainty, "to show up at a complete stranger's house and ask about the evil eye?"

A wave of heat enveloped Erasmo's face, sweat immediately soaking his forehead. Alma glared at her niece, jaw clenched. But Erasmo wasn't mad at Vero for asking the question. He studied her small, alert eyes for a moment and saw no malice in them. Only curiosity.

"I know that's a little strange," he said. "But I'd heard some neighbors talking about your aunt, about her expertise, and I had some questions for her. About things I couldn't find answers to online or in a book. And she's been nice enough to help me out in the years since." Erasmo glanced down, embarrassed, although he wasn't even sure why. "Anyway, I guess I better get going."

Alma grabbed his shoulder before he turned away. "Don't forget this." She forced the small green bottle into his palm and closed his fingers around it.

Erasmo turned and walked out to the front of the store, almost stumbling over a new group of children. The silent, entranced youths paid no attention to him as they fervently hunted the aisles for what their hearts most desired.

After stepping out into the parking lot, he immediately called Bradley, who answered on the first ring.

"If you still want to hire me," Erasmo said, "I'll take you on. You should know, though, the first thing I'm going to do is find out who that strange guy onstage was."

"How are you possibly going to do that?"

"I'm going to start by tracking down Gemma."

"Gemma?" Bradley said, biting down on her name. "And then what?"

"And then," Erasmo said, "I'm going to find out why the hell she dragged you down to that shit show in the first place."

"Well, in that case," Bradley said after a long pause, "you're hired."

CHAPTER 7

GEMMA HAYES WAS harder to find than Erasmo antici-
pated. After their call, he'd gone by Bradley's house to collect
more information. Bradley recounted everything he remembered about her, which unfortunately wasn't much. He also
showed Erasmo Gemma's yearbook photo. The smirking face
staring back at him exuded the slightest hint of danger and
impulsiveness. Dirty blond hair fell to her shoulders in thick,
lustrous waves. He could see why teen boys would've been
interested. According to Bradley, she'd moved away after graduation, and no one had heard from her since.

It didn't take long to discover that Gemma was a complete
ghost on social media. Of course, she could be married now
and listed under a completely different name. Erasmo was
perusing Facebook, studying the faces of what felt like every
single Gemma in Texas, when a better idea struck him. He
picked up his phone and searched his contacts, not remembering if he'd saved her number. But to his relief, the name he was
looking for appeared on the screen.

Ashley Ventrella.

Erasmo stared at the name, hesitant to make the call. She'd
definitely been a bit of a strange one. A few months back, they'd

received an email from her, asking for help with strange noises in her apartment. He'd gone out with Rat to investigate but hadn't found a damn thing. Ashley, though, had mostly seemed interested in peppering them with questions.

"So . . . what really went down at the Ghost Tracks?"

"Were you scared when that psycho kidnapped you this past summer?"

"What's the weirdest case you've had? Bet you've seen some crazy stuff, huh?"

They'd answered her questions but had to finally insist it was time to go. As she was looking through her wallet to pay them, Ashley mentioned she'd just graduated from Incarnate Word and had landed a job as an adjuster.

"I handle property claims, so if you ever have any questions about certain houses, there are databases I can access. I assume it would be helpful to know if there'd been a previous suicide at a house you're cleansing, stuff like that."

Erasmo had been a little taken aback at her casual morbidity, before deciding it was probably a feature and not a bug. But it was what she'd said next that now echoed in his ears.

"And I have access to LexisNexis, too, if you ever need to track down anyone."

He continued to stare at the phone, uncertain. He'd never asked anyone for help with a case before. Except for Rat, of course.

Screw it, he thought as he pressed the Call button. She'd offered, and he needed the help.

"Hello?" her voice said, somehow managing an interesting cadence with just the one word.

"Hi, Ashley. It's Erasmo."

"Hey!" she said. "That's so crazy. I was just wondering how you and your friend were doing. What was his name? Rat?"

"Yeah, that's right."

"So," she said, now sounding confused. "What's up?"

"Well, I hate to ask, but you'd mentioned that if I ever needed help finding some—"

"Yes!" she blurted out. "I can help you."

Erasmo breathed a sigh of relief. He'd half expected her to say . . . *Sorry, I can't. I could get fired for that.* But apparently, Ashley didn't give a damn about her employer.

"Screw 'em," she whispered into the phone, as if reading his thoughts. "May as well put these big-brother, fascist databases to good use for once. Send over what you've got and I'll text you what I find later."

While he waited, Erasmo ran a search on the Children of M, the name the old man had used for his group. Not a single hit. He tried different variations, but there was nothing to be found online.

True to Ashley's word, she messaged him only a few hours later.

> *Found her. She's in Floresville, just under a different last name. Gemma Stone. Not married though. Based on her previous addresses, it looks like she's moved around a lot. No vehicle registered to her. Poked around online using this new name. Looks like she works at some antiques store called Finders Keepers. No current home address on file, though. Let me know if you need anything else. Good luck!*

Floresville. How the hell did Gemma end up there? He'd only been once, when his grandmother insisted a few years back that they go to the Peanut Festival held there every October. It was a pretty small town. The kind of place someone young with a bright future would want to leave, not run to.

Of course, it was also the kind of place someone might go to hide.

He checked his watch. Almost 5:00 p.m. It was a forty-minute drive to Floresville, so there was still enough time to make it there and get back early enough to spend some time with his grandmother. Erasmo grabbed his keys and walked out into the faded light of the dying afternoon sun.

The place was a pack rat's dream. Its sheer volume of random items overwhelmed Erasmo's field of vision. There were curios crammed onto shelves, leaning against walls, and even more in stacks on the floor. Despite housing so many odd items, though, there was a definite sense of orderliness to the place.

In the less than two minutes he'd wandered around, Erasmo had seen: a fabricated metal shark hanging from the ceiling, a selection of blue-handled samurai swords, a rusted cheese grater used to display costume jewelry, three ancient bowling pins, and a glass with E.T. on it pointing to the sky. He was looking over an old tank of a typewriter, which had a sign on it that read, *PLEASE DO NOT TOUCH!!*, when a shrill voice rang out.

"Gemma! Got a customer out here!"

After a few moments, shuffling footsteps approached from the back of the store. He began to hide behind a battered armoire but then cursed himself. A chance to talk to Gemma was the whole reason he was even here. As the figure got closer, he pretended to study a glass jar filled with rusted keys.

"Something in particular you're looking for?" a hoarse voice said.

Erasmo turned and immediately saw this was indeed the person he was here to see. But she also wasn't. The woman standing in front of him no longer had the youthful vibrancy of the smirking teen in the yearbook photo. But the dilution of her vigor wasn't just the product of usual aging. Gemma looked at least ten years older than she should have, and appeared shrunken, as if she'd been hollowed out on the inside. Her skin was pallid, and limp hair fell to each ashen cheekbone, her once golden hair now faded and streaked with gray.

"I . . ." he started, but now wasn't quite sure how to ask why she'd done something extraordinarily strange eighteen years ago.

"Sir?"

"My name is Erasmo Cruz," he finally managed. "I'm actually here to speak with you, Gemma. There are a few questions I'd like to ask. About Bradley Erickson."

She flinched at the sound of his name, and what little color her skin had now drained from it. Her head jerked around the store with surprising quickness, as if she were scanning for an impending threat only she could see.

"I . . . don't remember anything from back then," she said, staring at the floor, a pronounced tremble in her voice. "You have to leave. Right now. I'll get into trouble."

"Please," he said. "It will just take a minute."

"I can't," she said, turning to walk away.

"Look, if you answer just *one* question, I'll leave here and never return. If not, then I'll keep coming back here every day until you do."

Gemma froze mid-stride, her delicate shoulders twitching, as if receiving a steady stream of electric shocks.

"*One* question," she said, turning back around but still not looking at him, her pale face turned to the side. "One."

"Okay," he said. "I'm not going to ask why you dragged Bradley to the ceremony. I'm just going to assume you were told to recruit people to attend. So, my question then is simply this. Who was the man in the crimson robe . . . the one with the scar on his face?"

Gemma's jaw clenched. Erasmo could practically hear her teeth grinding. She whispered something underneath her breath he couldn't make out.

"What was that?"

"You don't," she said, louder this time, "want to know him."

"I need a name, or I'm going to keep coming back."

After a few moments of silence, Gemma finally gave in. "Derrick," she said, her frail body slumping, "Derrick Vassell."

"Thanks," he said, surprised and relieved that his threat actually worked. "I won't bother you again."

"Wait," she whispered.

Gemma's delicate features trembled as she finally faced Erasmo and looked him in the eye, her hazel irises dull and lifeless.

"I understand that you're trying to help your friend, but you should know something."

"And what's that?"

"If the Collection has begun," she said, the corner of her mouth twitching violently, "then it's too late for him."

CHAPTER 8

AS ERASMO SAT in the parking lot of Finders Keepers, typing Derrick Vassell's name into his phone, an incoming call lit up the screen. He stared at the name a moment, confused.

Alma.

His gut writhed, as if filled with a mass of squirming eels. Alma *never* called. In fact, he couldn't remember a single phone conversation they'd ever had. His first instinct was to ignore it, but curiosity got the better of him.

"I need a favor," the curandera said when he answered, dispensing with any pleasantries. "There's a strange woman calling every ten minutes. She claims to have been cursed . . . something about a bad illness. I'm busy treating a sick child, so Vero is going to handle this for me. I told the woman any meeting would have to be in public, and she chose Hemisfair Park. Since Vero is still new to all this and I can't be there, I'd like for you to go with her."

Damn. This was the last thing he needed. He'd barely seen his grandmother today, and the guilt of it was gnawing at him. What if there'd been a change in her condition while he was away? And now he had solid information on Bradley's case to follow up on, too.

"It's not great timing," Erasmo said. "Can it wait until tomorrow?"

The cold, drawn-out silence on the other end answered his question.

"I'll get there as soon as I can."

When Erasmo pulled up to the curandera's shop, Vero waited for him outside, hands shoved deep into the black utility jacket enveloping her. She studied the Civic for a moment before finally striding over, flinging the door open, and plopping down into the passenger seat.

"Just for the record," Vero said, "I don't need a babysitter for this. Especially one who's practically the same age I am."

Erasmo decided not to engage, mainly because no good response came to mind. Instead, he steered the Civic out of the parking lot and headed downtown.

"Do we know what exactly is wrong with this person?" he asked.

"No," Vero said, rolling her eyes. "But we don't really need to, do we? It's probably just a wart that needs removing. Or a bad skin rash. Or if we're *really* lucky, we'll get to hear a long, dramatic story about how an enemy from work gave her ojo."

"Oh," Erasmo said, surprised. "I thought you'd be more excited to handle your first client."

"Well," she said, playing with one of her jacket's many pockets, "it's definitely better than being stuck in the garage, bored out of my mind."

"How can you possibly be bored?" Erasmo asked. "You're here studying with your aunt, learning amazing techniques—"

"That are all a bunch of antiquated foolishness," Vero said. "What, you think I *wanted* to come all the way over here and learn about a bunch of nonsensical mumbo jumbo?"

"But then why—"

"Family bullshit, that's why. You know how many times I was told growing up that I needed to carry on the legacy . . . that what we do is an essential part of our community, blah frickin' blah. You know what I want to tell them? I want to tell them that maybe it was important a hundred years ago, but nowadays there's a med-clinic on every corner for whatever ails you."

"Then why don't you just tell your family that instead of wasting their time?" He was more than a little aggravated at her complete dismissal of Alma's work.

"I decided a long time ago," she said, squinting out at the bruised purple sky, "that I'd rather carry resentment in my heart than risk breaking theirs."

Erasmo considered this, disturbed by the complete alienness of what she described. A surge of uncomfortable heat spread through him as he turned over how much Vero hated having these expectations placed on her, how much she abhorred her suffocating boundaries. It took him a few moments to realize this uncomfortable heat was jealousy.

He tried to imagine what it would be like to have firm hands guiding him, placing him on a safe, predetermined path, but he just could not conjure the feeling. So many times over the past year, when he was about to meet with complete strangers, or walk into dangerous situations, the same thought had floated through his head: *someone should really stop me from doing this.*

Was that why he continuously flirted with danger in the first place? In the hopes that someone would step in and save him? What a pathetic way to beg for attention. Or perhaps he courted trouble because deep down, he truly wished that some grievous harm would befall him.

It didn't matter. No matter how reckless he was, no one was ever going to stop him. He was free to do whatever he wanted, however he wanted to do it. And no one gave the slightest damn. He understood Vero chafing at her family's history and overbearing expectations, but part of him wanted to tell her how good she actually had it.

How beautiful it would be to have a family to disappoint, he thought.

"Enough about me," Vero said. "What's your story, true believer? My aunt hasn't said much about why you're . . . the way you are."

"First of all," he said, "I'm not a true believer. But I am a believer. There's a difference. I know for certain the supernatural exists. But I also think true paranormal experiences are pretty damn rare."

"Hmmm . . . a skeptical believer," Vero said. "Fairly odd, but I'll allow it. But that still doesn't explain how you know about all this stuff."

"Oh, I was raised by a coven of witches," he said. "Learned all about ghosts, and demons, and black magic from them. Your aunt didn't mention that?"

"Oh . . ." she said, nodding her head. "You got jokes. Didn't realize I was dealing with a funny guy here."

Vero stared at him as he took the exit for Commerce, left eyebrow raised, still clearly expecting an answer to her question. What the hell did she care what his story was? But then, to his great surprise, he blurted out a sentence he rarely said to anyone.

"My parents were both junkies," he said. "My dad OD'd underneath a house when I was a kid. And my mom ran off

with one of her boyfriends after she had me. The only people
I ever really had were my grandparents, but my grandfather
passed away a few years back. Just me and my grandma now."

Vero's eyebrow dropped from its high perch. Whatever
she'd been expecting to hear, it wasn't this. He was immediately
embarrassed at divulging this sacred information to a practical
stranger.

"I'm sorry," she said, barely above a whisper. And then to
his surprise, "Do you hate your parents?"

Erasmo marveled at the surgical precision of her question.
He had wrestled with this very thought almost every day of his
life, vacillating between indifference toward two people he'd
never met, and white-hot rage at what they'd done to him.

"Depends on the day," he said. "The one thing I know for
sure I hate about them, with one hundred percent certainty,
was their goddamn weakness. Every time I imagine them with
a needle in their arm, eyes rolled back, craving that shit, my
stomach turns. I hate that they were so stupid and weak to even
start doing it. I hate that they lived their lives a slave to finding
the next hit. And I hate that they were too selfish to get clean
for their son."

"I'm sorry if that question was too . . ."

Erasmo wondered for a moment why she was apologiz-
ing, but then felt the tears slipping down his face. He wiped at
them, even more embarrassed now. Jesus. A willing audience of
one was all it took to spill his guts. How pathetic.

"As for the agency stuff," he said, "I've had an interest in the
paranormal since I was a kid. Read every book on the subject I
could get my hands on. And then—"

"And then that incident at the Ghost Tracks happened,"
Vero said.

"So . . . your aunt did tell you a few things."

"Just a few. I'd love to hear your version though. My aunt was pretty vague about it."

"That," he said, "is a story for another time. Besides, we're here."

Erasmo pulled the Civic into a mostly empty parking lot on Alamo Street. They exited the car and crossed Cesar Chavez, passing Dough Pizzeria on their right. Erasmo was always amazed people paid over twenty dollars at that place for such a tiny pizza.

They entered the park and surveyed the area. Not many people were around, given it was a weeknight and the weather was chilly by San Antonio standards.

The Tower of the Americas rose high above them, looming over the city, its windows dark and impenetrable. He remembered his history teacher mentioning it was the largest observation tower in Texas. Its six-hundred-foot-high concrete shaft ended in a round rotating structure, which contained an observation deck and a high-end restaurant.

Erasmo imagined the lucky diners up there now, eating expensive steaks and enjoying the view of the downtown Christmas lights, oblivious to the mundane happenings underneath them.

After venturing farther into the park, they soon found who they were looking for.

A rail-thin woman in her late fifties stood by one of the benches, in the middle of a huge coughing fit. The wet retching sounds she produced reached them, even though they were still a distance away.

"Great," Vero said. "This should be a hoot. Maybe you should handle this. Since you're the expert and all."

"Nice try," he said. "Let's get on with it."

As they approached, the gaunt woman stopped coughing and squinted at them, her face morphing from discomfort to disgust.

"What the hell? You're just a couple of punks! I wanted Alma!"

"She's unavailable," Vero said in a cool, even voice. "But I promise we can help. And if we can't, Alma will take care of whatever the problem is tomorrow when she's free."

"I don't have until tomorrow. I need help now!" Another coughing fit wracked the woman's body. She glared at them when it finally stopped, but then sighed and threw up her hands in reluctant acceptance.

"Fine," she said, smoothing out her black wrinkled house-dress, which had been faded by too many washes. "But you better know what the hell you're doing."

"I'm Erasmo, and this is Vero."

The woman frowned, as if even their names aggravated her. "My name is Renata."

"Maybe we can start with what exactly is wrong with you," Vero said.

"What's wrong," Renata said, "is that I've been cursed."

"You've been cursed?" Vero asked, eyes narrowing.

"Yes," Renata said. "And one of the worst kinds imaginable."

"Is that so?" Vero asked. Erasmo could sense how badly she wanted to roll her eyes. "What are your symptoms?"

"I have many, but there's really only one thing you need to know." Her face tightened, as if it pained her to say the words. "I'm rotting from the inside."

The three of them stood in silence, underneath the clear dark sky and glowing crescent moon, each unsure what to say next.

"You have an intestinal issue?" Vero asked. "Or is your body—"

"No, you foolish girl. Listen to what I'm telling you. My flesh is literally rotting inside of me."

"If that's true," Vero said, "then you should go to a doctor immediately."

"Oh should I?" Renata said. "Last I checked, doctors don't know a *damn* thing about breaking curses. See? This is why I wanted Alma in the first place. I heard she knows how to handle problems like this."

"What makes you so sure that you're rotting on the inside?" Erasmo asked.

"It would be easier to show you than tell you," Renata said. She walked up to Erasmo, her gait slow and deliberate, until they were uncomfortably close. She smelled like raw meat that had been left out in the sun too long.

Renata stood on her tiptoes, loosened her jaw, and then stretched her mouth open as wide as she could. Erasmo took a step backward, but not before he caught a glimpse of something odd in her mouth.

The tiniest hint of movement.

Erasmo stepped forward and peered in. Renata's jaw trembled from the strain of holding it open so wide. Her tongue lay perfectly still, and there was nothing moving anywhere inside her mouth. Damn. He could've sworn that—

Another flicker of motion. But this time, Erasmo saw what had caused it. He took a reflexive step backward and lost his balance, tumbling to the ground. He lay there for a few moments, now unsure of himself.

It couldn't have been.

Renata's mouth remained open, inviting him to take another look. He rose to his feet and stepped toward her, again peering down her throat.

And this time there was no doubt. Erasmo continued to watch in disbelief as fat, pink maggots writhed their way up Renata's throat, their wet bodies glistening in the pale evening light.

CHAPTER 9

"JESUS," HE WHISPERED, pulling away. Vero then walked over to Renata and studied the inside of her mouth, a dour expression on her face. She stood silently, tilting her head at different angles for a better view. After seeing enough to satisfy her, she retreated next to Erasmo.

Renata erupted into another coughing fit, and this time he saw several maggots fly from her mouth, one landing on his right shoe. It wriggled a few times before he jerked his leg. It fell off and disappeared into the grass, leaving a slight red stain on his shoe.

"What do you think now?" Renata asked as she wiped her mouth with the back of her hand, almost pleased at their shock.

"How long have you been like this?" Erasmo asked.

"I started to feel sick about a week ago. But I've only been coughing up these hijos de putas for a few days. Once it started, I went to several curanderos around town. They all told me the same three things. First, none of them wanted any part of this. Second, they said Alma was the best, and I should talk to her."

Renata paused and grimaced, as if unsure whether to continue.

"What's the third thing?" Vero asked.

"They all said that only one person in town knows this type of black magic, a brujo named Hector Valles. And that he must've been the person who placed the curse on me."

"So you think some mysterious brujo cursed you?" Vero asked. "Assuming for a moment this person even exists, why would he do such a thing?"

"An enemy of mine hired him to do it, obviously," Renata said.

"You have enemies that hate you *so* much they want your guts to rot out?" Vero asked.

"When you get to my age, you'll find it's impossible to get through life without pissing off a lot of people." After another brief but violent coughing fit, Renata added, "They told me this brujo only does business after sunset, at the Devil's Den. Are you familiar with it?"

"Sure," Erasmo said. "Over behind Ingram." He'd heard of the place, but never had reason to go down there himself. The Devil's Den was a large swath of land where people used to go off-roading and throw unsupervised parties, among other questionable activities. The city purchased the area years ago, though, and had since added some hiking and biking trails.

"Apparently there's an abandoned structure out in the woods where this brujo can be found. He comes and goes though. We'd have to get lucky."

"We?" Erasmo asked.

"Yes. I wanted Alma to go down there with me and demand he remove the curse. I'm sure he'd listen to someone like her. And if he doesn't, Alma can put a curse on him until he helps me. I heard she knows plenty."

"You heard wrong," Vero said. "Alma is a curandera, a healer. She uses nature and spiritual forces to alleviate suffering. But inflicting a curse on someone using dark witchcraft . . . that's pure brujería. She'd have no part of something like that."

"I don't care what the hell you call it," Renata said. "It doesn't matter anyway. She's not here, and now I'm stuck with you two. But this obviously can't wait, so you're going down there with me to talk to this son of a bitch."

"What do you think?" Vero asked, glancing at him sideways.

"I think," he said, "that the customer is always right."

Renata followed as they headed down I-10, her old pickup occasionally swerving well outside her lane before veering back. Vero remained quiet most of the ride, pensive, not speaking until after they'd merged onto 410.

"This is a waste of time," she finally said.

"You think so?"

"What I think," Vero said, the highway lights casting oblong shadows on her face, "is that this old woman needs to get herself to a doctor."

"But what about the maggots crawling up her throat?" he asked. "Clearly this isn't a typical medical condition."

"Just because it's unusual doesn't mean it's not easily explainable. Maybe she has a wound in her mouth, and a fly got in while she was sleeping and laid eggs. Maybe she ate some old meat that had maggots in it and she vomited them out. Hell, maybe she's faking the whole thing and planted some in her mouth just to fool us."

"Why on earth would she possibly do that?"

"Because she's screwed up in the head like everyone else. Probably just wants some attention or sympathy or something. Wants us to make a big deal about her 'condition.' What . . . you think this brujo really placed a spell turning her insides to rotting meat? Give me a goddamn break."

"Hey, I don't disagree with you," Erasmo said. "I'm sure there's probably a simple explanation. I just like to leave myself open to the possibility, however slight, that it could be more than that."

"Knock yourself out," Vero said. "I'll stay here in the real world while you live in fantasyland."

Erasmo decided to ignore this, and they again drove in silence. As they passed Ingram Park Mall on their right, flutters erupted in his belly. Devil's Den was close by.

"Have you ever even heard of this Hector Valles guy?" Vero asked.

"No. Although brujería is not usually what I deal with, so I definitely have blind spots on the subject. Wonder if he'll even be here."

"Guess we're about to find out," Vero said as he pulled into the empty parking lot that led to the trails.

They exited the car and walked over to Renata, who leaned unsteadily on her truck.

"I found directions online where to find the abandoned structure," she said, "so just follow me. And if he's actually here, you better make him take the curse off me, or I'm not paying you a goddamn dime."

"Let's just head down there and see what we find," Vero said.

They quickly located the trailhead and started down the path, soon arriving at a rust-colored bridge that stretched over a waterless creek bed. As they crossed, Erasmo glanced down to his right, his stomach uneasy at the steep drop. The channel was lined with lush trees, but its bed was filled with rocks and large formations of stone, covered with cans and bottles and other assorted trash.

"I remember before the city constructed this trail," Renata said as they finished crossing the bridge. "Kids would come down here and drink and do drugs and act like animals." She paused before adding, "I'm sure they still do."

As they walked farther in, and the woods around them thickened, Erasmo had to agree with her. The clusters of trees surrounding them were filled with desolation and darkness, perfect for slipping away and committing acts of destruction or self-destruction, whichever way your particular illness leaned.

A sign for one of the hiking paths approached on their left. He stopped and looked, a bit taken aback at what it read.

Treachery.

What an odd name for a hiking trail.

"Not that way," Renata said. "Shouldn't be much farther though."

"Why do they call this place the Devil's Den?" Vero asked as they pressed on.

"Because this place has always been trouble," Renata said. "Not just because of the kids, either. There've been rumors of devil worshipers out here for as long as I can remember. Not to mention those two murders back in the nineties."

After a few minutes, another sign came into view on their left. Erasmo shone his light on it and read the single word.

Limbo.

Another odd name. Several seconds of confusion gave way to a flicker of recognition, then understanding.

Dante. Each path was named after one of his nine circles of Hell. Whoever had constructed these trails had a wicked sense of humor.

"This is it," Renata said. "He should be somewhere down that path."

Erasmo peered down the trail and saw nothing but life-less dark. He almost suggested they go back, that it wasn't worth fumbling around blindly in the woods for a person who probably wasn't even there. But they'd come this far. May as well see it through.

They proceeded down the rocky trail, which was level at first but then grew increasingly steep. He held Renata's wiry arm, guiding her down. When the path leveled off, Erasmo saw hints of a large structure on their right, barely visible through the trees. They approached closer and there was no doubt: They'd reached the heart of Devil's Den.

The abandoned husk loomed over them, held up by rectangle concrete pillars covered in graffiti. Erasmo stared at the large structure they supported, its broad, rectangular shape offering no clues as to what it might have once been used for.

He turned his attention back to the shadowy concrete pillars. Anything could be hiding behind them.

"Hello?" Erasmo said, his voice shakier than he would've liked. "Is anyone there?"

A slight rustle of branches and leaves was the only response.

"Doesn't seem like the brujo is here," Vero said.

"Let's just wait a few minutes," Renata said. "Maybe he'll come."

Erasmo walked underneath the large structure and examined a few of the broad, rectangular pillars. Every inch of them was covered in colorful spray paint, too many words and images and figures for him to make out anything coherent. Several caught his attention though. A rudimentary Eye of Providence, a perfectly rendered infinity symbol, the inexplicable words *NEEDLE ONLY* in large black letters.

It was then a figure stepped out of the shadows, lanky and graceful. He wore a dark leather coat that hung to his knees, and a black cowboy hat sat on his head, long bleached hair spilling from beneath it.

"Well, what do we have here," the man said as he approached. The many rings and necklaces and bracelets he wore clinked as he walked. Most had various symbols and markings on them. Some Erasmo recognized, like a triquetra and the Eye of Horus, and others he'd never seen before. "Paying customers, I hope."

He was younger than Erasmo initially thought. Midtwenties at most, his features smooth and round, black stubble covering a weak chin. His outfit and accessories and black eyeliner seemed like an affectation, as if he were trying his damndest to appear mysterious and well-versed in dark teachings. But to Erasmo, he looked as if he were just playing dress-up, hoping to scam poor unsuspecting fools out of their money.

The man raised his hands in the air with a flourish, like a cut-rate magician.

"Feliz Navidad," he said through a crooked grin. "Hector Valles, at your service."

Erasmo was unimpressed, but Renata wouldn't be happy unless they at least tried. May as well get on with it.

"We were told," Erasmo said, "that the person who does business here knows how to cast certain spells. Knows how to inflict harm, if necessary."

Hector's grin disappeared as he studied the three of them closer, lingering on Vero. "You were told correctly. If the price is right." He then turned his attention to Erasmo. "And if I find your situation sufficiently interesting."

"I told you," Renata screeched from behind them. "He knows the black magic!"

Erasmo gestured to her. "This is Renata. She says she's suffering from a curse. Has anyone come here, asking you to harm her?"

Hector looked her over, a subtle smirk appearing on his thin lips.

"That woman there? No, I haven't been asked to hurt her. Is this why you came here tonight? To accuse me?"

"You're lying!" Renata screamed. "It *had* to be you. They said no one else in town knows this curse!"

"And what curse is that?" Hector asked, now appearing genuinely interested.

As if on cue, Renata erupted in a coughing fit. Hector studied the ground, somehow aware of what she'd expelled from her throat despite the darkness. A look of confusion settled over him. After a moment, he nodded to himself, as if realizing something.

"That's an ugly piece of work, no doubt. Whoever managed to do this is delving into practices they shouldn't. But I did *not* place this curse on you, and don't appreciate the accusation. Now do yourself a favor and leave. We have no business to conduct here."

"Please!" Renata screamed. "It's getting worse. You have to take it off me!"

"There's nothing I can do for you. Only the person who placed it can remove it."

"¡Chinga tu madre!" Renata yelled.

"Sorry, but you're beginning to bore me," Hector said, and snapped his fingers, a sharp pop echoing around them.

Renata gasped and slowly raised her hands to her face.

"Dios mío," she said. "What did you do to me?"

"What's wrong?" Erasmo asked.

"Everything is blurry," she said, true fear in her voice. "I'm having trouble seeing."

"It's probably from all the coughing and yelling," Erasmo said. "Maybe your eyes just need a minute to refocus. Let me take a look."

Renata turned to face him, her face cloaked in shadows. Erasmo approached and shone his phone's light on her eyes. He almost dropped it as he stared in disbelief, barely stifling the scream on his lips.

"What is it," Renata asked. "Why are you looking at me like that?"

Erasmo found himself unable to tell her the truth: he stared because her frightened, bulging eyes were now filled with dark-red blood, every vein engorged and ready to burst.

He whirled around, searching the shadows, but Hector was nowhere to be found. In those few seconds, he'd slipped into the darkness and disappeared. Had he done this to Renata's eyes? Had he punished her for accusing—

"Everything's okay," Vero said, studying Renata. "You've just burst some blood vessels in your eyes from coughing and screaming so much."

"It was him!" she screeched. "He did this!"

"We should get you to a clinic," Erasmo said. "You need to get looked at—"

"No! They won't be able to help me. Just take me home and I'll wait for Alma. You two are completely useless!"

Erasmo considered trying to persuade her, but it seemed pointless. They couldn't force her to see a doctor. He slowly led Renata back to the main path and the Civic, where she collapsed into the back seat and curled into a shivering silhouette.

She gave them her address through soft sobs, and the ride to her house was silent but mercifully quick. He soon pulled up to a modest but well-maintained single-story house, the color of an overripe avocado.

"I can get inside by myself," Renata said, opening the car door and stepping out onto the sidewalk. She immediately wobbled, almost falling.

Erasmo was alarmed at how unsteady she looked. "Let me help you—"

"No!" she screamed louder than necessary. "Just make sure Alma gets here as soon as possible." She lurched up the cracked concrete walkway to her house, alternating between violent coughing and spitting out wet mouthfuls, soon disappearing inside.

"Do you really think it's just burst blood vessels?" he asked Vero as they pulled away from the curb.

"Of course," she said. "It happened right when she was screaming her face off. What, you think that wannabe scam artist somehow screwed up her eyes because she annoyed him?"

It did sound ridiculous when she said it out loud. But still, the exact timing . . . the way Hector had disappeared . . . so odd. "She said her vision was blurry, though. That usually doesn't happen from burst blood vessels."

"Who the hell knows," Vero said. "She's an old lady who clearly has massive health issues. Do you know how many people *exactly* like her come by my aunt's on a daily basis? People in crappy health who blame their bodies' decline on curses or mal de ojo instead of old age or their terrible habits? Hopefully she comes to her senses and goes to the hospital soon. Either way, I'll tell my aunt to go by as soon as she can."

Vero had a point. Something was clearly wrong with Renata, but the culprit was probably some strange condition they weren't familiar with. That certainly seemed more likely than an odd guy in the woods placing a curse on her.

They rode in silence the rest of the way to the curandera's. As Erasmo drove away after dropping Vero off, he was at a complete loss as to why Alma asked him to come along. Vero had handled everything with ease, as if it were second nature. In fact, this trip had made one thing abundantly clear.

Vero was a complete natural at this.

CHAPTER 10

AS ERASMO DROVE home, he studied the stars peeking through a thin layer of clouds. They seemed faint and dull, almost listless. His phone buzzed. He was mildly surprised to see Andy's name on the screen, but answered anyway.

"Hey, man. Do you happen to be out? I could use a little help."

He debated how to answer. If he said yes, then his research on Derrick Vassell would be delayed even further. But Andy sounded a bit out of sorts, and this worried him.

"Yeah, I'm out. Is everything okay?"

"Sure, just need your expertise for a few minutes. Know this is a little weird, but I'm at the Siesta Motel on Fredericksburg Road. Room 107. I'll be waiting for you."

He hung up before Erasmo could respond.

The Siesta Motel was an absolute fleabag. Maybe Andy was doing some research there for his book. He already regretted saying yes, but at least the place was close by.

A few minutes later, he pulled into the motel parking lot. Several figures lurked in the shadows, only the glowing tips of their cigarettes visible. Research or not, what on earth was Andy doing at a shithole like this? He slid into the parking space closest to room 107, jogged to the door, and hurriedly knocked. Thankfully Andy answered immediately, his face paler than usual.

Erasmo stepped inside and glanced around with apprehension. The room was exactly as he'd expected. Yellowed walls, dingy curtains, dim lighting to obscure the room's nightly abuse. The air was dense with the smell of cigarettes, cheap alcohol, and stale sweat.

"There's not much to see in here," Andy said, "but do you mind looking around for a bit?" Erasmo waited for further explanation, but his friend just stood there, eyes nervously darting around the room.

This was getting odder by the minute. He walked to the other side of the lumpy, uneven bed and then to the cramped bathroom. Nothing seemed out of the ordinary for a cheap motel like this one.

"Is there anything in particular I'm looking for?" he asked.

"Not really," Andy said, his voice a bit strained. "Do you, uh . . . you see anything? Or sense anything unusual?"

Erasmo's stomach dropped. Was that what Andy's visit this morning had been for? Laying groundwork to ask for this favor? He turned from the bathroom, back to his friend.

"Andy, what are we doing here?"

"Nothing. I—"

"Whatever it is, you can tell me. It's okay. I promise."

Andy took a hard swallow and wiped at his forehead. Erasmo hadn't noticed until now how drenched in sweat Andy was. His friend then released a long sigh and slumped down, as if in the beginning stages of melting.

"Okay. I'll tell you because you're my friend and I trust you. But this is really hard for me to say. My mom . . . twelve years ago, she was found in this room. Strangled." Andy's breath hitched, but he continued. "My dad always hints that she was a . . . that she was here making money. But I know that's not true. My mom wouldn't have done that."

Plump tears now slid down Andy's cheeks, which now burned red, and he absently wiped at them. "Anyway, I really miss her, you know? Especially this time of year. So I come here once in a while and rent this room. To feel close to her, I guess."

A pained expression flitted across Andy's face. "I invited you here because I thought . . . maybe you'd be able to sense something, sense *her* maybe. You know, because of what happened to you at the Tracks."

Everything then became clear to Erasmo. Andy's obsession with haunted hotels, his desire to learn as much as he could about the supernatural, even their own relationship. Is this why Andy had befriended them in the first place?

"It doesn't work that way, man. You know that. I can't sense anything different than you or anyone else. What happened at the Tracks was a very particular experience."

"Oh. Okay. Sorry, I was just hoping . . . I don't know." Andy's jaw clenched, muscles flexing underneath his layers of flesh. "It was a dumb idea, I guess."

"Wish I could help you," he said, placing his hand on Andy's shoulder. "I really do."

Andy nodded wordlessly. "I appreciate you coming at least," he finally said, gesturing to the door. "I'm sure you're busy though."

Erasmo was uneasy about leaving him like this, but Andy now seemed eager to be alone. And this, he could understand.

"Let me know if you need anything," Erasmo said as he left.

"Will do," Andy said as he stared out the doorway at him, a strained smile on his face. "Will do."

When Erasmo arrived home, he retreated to his bedroom, eager to finally do some research on Derrick Vassell. This time, he didn't need Ashley's help to find who he was looking for. A simple internet search brought the information right up. No trace of a home address, but apparently he was the owner of a business called the Soul Center. Erasmo surprised himself by erupting in laughter. It had been a while since he'd found anything even slightly amusing and the laugh felt good, sour as it was. Was this a joke? Could this really be its name? The words on his screen stared back at him and insisted it was.

The listed address was just outside of downtown, on McCullough. He checked the clock to see it was a little past 9:00 p.m. He could head over to the Soul Center right now. They'd probably be closed for the day, but that might be better. He could poke around a bit without attracting attention, look through the windows maybe.

While Erasmo contemplated whether he should go or not, he ran a quick search on demonology. While he was somewhat familiar with the topic, he was by no means an expert and wanted to brush up before speaking with Vassell. There was so much he didn't know, as an article about pre-Christian demons made clear.

The article said that ancient Greeks referred to gods and supernatural beings as *daimon*. Erasmo was surprised to read that Greek philosophers generally perceived daimons as *good*.

He kept reading, fascinated. When translating the Hebrew Bible into Greek, the old scribes used *daimon* as a catchall for several different concepts, including pagan gods and diseases. What they did not use *daimon* to mean, though, was angel.

The articles noted several pre-Christian texts in which angels did have a connection with demon-like creatures. In the Book of Enoch, a being called a giant was produced when angels and human women mated. Erasmo read this passage again. He'd never heard of humans and angels reproducing before. When those giants died, their souls transformed into "evil spirits."

It wasn't until the Gospels of Matthew, Mark, and Luke in the New Testament, though, that demons and evil spirits were equated.

This was interesting but not much help in finding out what kind of demons might want children. He ran a different search, and this time an article on demons within different religions and cultures caught his eye.

Christian demons were the ones Erasmo was most familiar with. He perused the creatures who corresponded to the seven deadly sins: Lucifer (pride), Beelzebub (gluttony), Satan (wrath), Leviathan (envy), Mammon (greed), Belphegor (sloth), and Asmodeus (lust). All terrible behaviors, to be sure. But if he could annihilate one demon, it would most certainly be Mammon. Perhaps if there was a little less greed in the world, his grandmother's life wouldn't be in the hands of student doctors who always looked too exhausted to function.

In Judaism, the creature Lilith was an important part of Jewish demonology. According to this article, Lilith coupled with fallen angels such as Lucifer and Samael. But another detail about her interested Erasmo more. Apparently Lilith had a fondness for attacking infants and mothers in childbirth. Erasmo noted the similarity to Obizuth and wondered if there was a connection.

In Hinduism, there's the Dakini. Hindu texts describe them as a female race of demons who eat human flesh and devour the essence of humans. As they believe this essence is in the liver, head, and heart, these are the body parts Dakini most often feast on.

The article then turned to Japanese demons, who often appear in folklore instead of religion. Erasmo found this intriguing, perhaps due to his affinity for urban legends. As he skimmed through, the Japanese creature that most interested him was the Yamauba.

These types of demons were thought to be old women who'd once been human but had now turned into monsters. They lived deep in the woods and had a hunger for human flesh. The Yamauba offered to take in pregnant women, intending to eat the baby when it was born. They also explored surrounding towns, searching for children who were home alone.

Well, that's certainly a demon who might steal a baby.

Continuing with the folklore aspect, the article discussed a demon in the Philippines called Manananggal, which means to separate. This female demon can transform into a creature with large wings. As their wings emerge, their bottom halves drop away from their bodies. Erasmo imagined their upper halves flying around, intestines and other innards dangling beneath them. The Manananggal were said to hunt all kinds of prey, including pregnant women. As legend tells it, their tongue pierces the woman's stomach and sucks out the baby's heart.

The number of demons said to inflict harm on children unnerved Erasmo. Oddly, this particular sick behavior seemed to be shared across a wide variety of religions and cultures.

He shuddered and closed his laptop, still unsure of whether to head down to the Soul Center.

Screw it, he finally thought. Erasmo grabbed his keys and headed for the door.

A suffocating shroud of guilt settled over him as he remembered his intention to go back to the hospital and spend time with his grandmother. Visiting hours were over by now. Erasmo cursed himself underneath his breath, then again a little louder. He'd just have to make it up to her tomorrow.

When he pulled up to the listed address, Erasmo was struck by how nondescript the place was. The building was a small standalone with a tiny parking lot in front. But for supposedly housing a place of business, its exterior was damn secretive about what went on inside of its walls.

The front of the building was painted a drab brown and had no windows at all. There were also no signs, lights, or any other indication the building was even in use. Only a slight glimmer from the dented silver metal door broke up the depressing monotony. Erasmo parked in an empty lot across the street and trotted over to take a closer look.

He tried the front door, yanking on the rusted handle, but it was locked of course. He placed his ear to the cool metal, but heard nothing—

Wait. Maybe there *was* some kind of noise. He closed his eyes and focused only on the sound. Yes. There was a low humming on the other side, vibrating through the door. No. Not humming. It was more like. . .

A chant.

What the hell is going on in there? Erasmo thought.

He walked over to the side of the building, but it was just as devoid of life as the front. This left only one place to check. He crept along the dingy, mold-covered side wall to the rear, not sure what he was even hoping to find. After turning the corner, though, he was nervously excited to see a back door, made of thick, imposing metal.

And it was cracked open, just a tiny bit.

Up until now, it had seemed Derrick Vassell was damn intent on keeping everyone out. It made no sense for this door to be ajar. Maybe one of his people had just forgotten to lock it.

Or maybe, he thought, *they left the door open on purpose, hoping a dumbass like you would walk in and find out the hard way what they're doing in there.*

Erasmo slowly approached the door, half expecting it to swing open at any moment. He put his ear up to the tiny sliver of space between the door and the frame, and his heart shuddered at what he heard.

It hadn't been his imagination. There were a multitude of voices inside, chanting in unison.

But what exactly they were saying he couldn't make out. The words themselves were too muffled to hear, and the rhythms sounded neither Gregorian nor Byzantine. He listened closer, but already knew full well what needed to be done. He swallowed hard, placed his hand on the door's cool metal handle, and pulled.

When Erasmo stepped inside the cramped, unlit hallway, the chants immediately grew louder, but he still couldn't place them. As he shuffled forward, feeling his way along the dark corridor, he finally saw there were two doors at the end of the hallway, one on each side. A pale blue glow emanated from the one on the right.

Soon he stood in front of this door, sweat covering his body. The door was made of pitted, opaque glass, so what lay behind it was nebulous and blurred. But one fact was clear: There were people behind this door. Lots of them. And each one appeared to be on their knees.

Except for one figure, standing regally in the middle of all those bodies, like a conquering god.

Erasmo gripped the doorknob, and despite what Rat had done, desperately wished his friend was here now. He was *supposed* to be here with him, goddamn it. Tears threatened, as well as genuine panic, but a fragile sense of calm finally prevailed.

He took a shallow breath, turned the knob, and slowly pushed the door open.

Several things surprised Erasmo all at once. The first was that, instead of the sinister figures he'd half expected to see, there were a variety of drab, middle-aged men and women glaring up at him, a mixture of curiosity and annoyance etched on their faces. Most of them were clearly still dressed in their work attire: disheveled suits, wrinkled shirts and blouses, and loosened ties hanging off their limp, doughy bodies.

The second surprise was that they weren't chanting the demonic incantations he'd been braced for. In fact, they appeared to be doing something so benign that its innocuousness startled him. These tired, melancholy-looking men and women were simply on their knees . . . *humming* while they meditated. He continued to stare at their aggravated faces, unable to reconcile his initial suspicions with the sad scene playing out in front of him.

"Can I help you, young man?" a smooth, commanding voice said.

Erasmo turned his attention to the only other person in the room who was standing. This older gentleman was tall, gaunt and slightly hunched over. The man's blue eyes—wild some might say, but to Erasmo they were just shy of crazed—appraised him. A long, jagged scar blazed down his right cheek. The same one Bradley had described.

Derrick Vassell.

Except he wasn't wearing a crimson robe like eighteen years ago. No. Instead, he wore a rumpled blue oxford, brown corduroy pants, and scuffed loafers. Not exactly the wardrobe of a demonic mastermind. The prospect of this man having any useful answers seemed dim at best, but it was too late to back out now.

"Hi, Mr. Vassell," he said, walking over and extending his hand. "Erasmo Cruz."

The old man stiffened at the sound of his own name, but only for a moment.

"Please, call me Derrick," he said, a broad smile spreading over his thin, cracked lips.

"Is there a place we can talk?" Erasmo asked.

Vassell tilted his head and studied him, as if trying to decipher an annoying puzzle.

"Certainly," he finally said without much enthusiasm. "Follow me. Everyone, keep humming your internal melody and remain in your plane of existence. If you sense that you are about to emerge back into this world, remember what I taught you about mastering the gravity of your true self. I'll be right back."

Vassell walked out the door, heading directly into the small room on the other side of the hallway. A lopsided wooden desk sat in one corner, and a worn-out cot in the other. Unruly stacks of paperwork covered every inch of the desk. The old man walked behind it and gracefully lowered himself onto a metal folding chair that squeaked badly.

"So," he said, spindly fingers laced together, "I must say this is quite a surprise. Don't get many people walking in here. Especially since we make a habit of keeping the doors locked. This gathering is strictly invitation only."

"Sorry," Erasmo said, "the back door was open."

"Is that so?" he said, bushy eyebrows raised. "Must have been an oversight."

Get on with it, Erasmo thought, sensing Vassell's growing agitation.

"The reason I'm here," Erasmo said, "is that I've been hired to look into an incident that happened some years ago. An incident I believe you were involved in—"

"Hold on a minute," Vassell said, looking bemused. "I have a hard time believing that a young pup like you was hired to look into *anything*."

"I have some experience and expertise in the subject matter."

"Oh, do you now? And what subject matter is that?"

"Mr. Vassell," Erasmo said, ignoring the question, "it's my understanding that you conduct ceremonies, during which you offer participants good fortune in exchange for—"

A piercing cackle erupted from the old man, his thin lips stretched so far back that the corners of his mouth almost reached his ears.

"Oh, my dear, Mr. Cruz," he finally said. "Is that really why you're here? To ask about unfortunate incidents from almost two decades ago?"

"I spoke to Gemma Hayes. She was very clear that you were the person to talk to about—"

"About what, Mr. Cruz? Some regrettable indiscretions in my younger years?"

"Bradley Erickson said that—"

"Who?" Vassell asked, flinching slightly before a disdainful scowl spread over his face.

"The person who hired me. He was at one of the ceremonies you conducted in New Braunfels. Gemma invited him. He would've been seventeen at the time."

Vassell shrugged his slight shoulders and raised his eyebrows. "I am sorry, Mr. Cruz, but there were quite a few ceremonies back then. We brought a lot of folks onto that stage." He waited a moment before adding, "To my great shame, of course."

Erasmo had expected Vassell to say something like this. It was still disappointing, though, to track him down and get no useful information at all. Wouldn't hurt to press him a bit at least. "So those ceremonies you conducted . . . none of it was . . ."

"What . . . real? Mr. Cruz, this may come as a shock to you, but I don't, in fact, have the power to make deals on behalf of Satan. And let me also add that I'm now a very different person than I was back then. I've changed . . . turned my life into something completely different than the confused mess it once was. Instead of pretending to be dark and hateful just to bask in some desperately needed attention, I now spend my time in the humble service of others. All those folks across the hall, whose ruminations you rudely interrupted, are suffering from one type of severe crisis or another. I teach them meditation, and self-love, and how to find their stasis with the universe. After many lost years, I've finally found my place, and it's right here in this building, helping those who need it most."

Erasmo couldn't think of a single response to anything Vassell had just said. Of course he couldn't make Faustian deals on the Devil's behalf. He was just a man. And an unimpressive one at that. Not to mention that Vassell certainly seemed sincere in his efforts to help the sad-looking group of folks across the hall. The way they'd looked at him . . . with reverence, almost . . . he must be providing the guidance they obviously craved.

Vassell rose from his chair with the vigor of a much younger man and gestured his slender fingers toward the hallway.

"I trust you can find your way out, Mr. Cruz."

Erasmo turned and left the room, a wave of heat spreading through his chest. He trotted through the cramped hallway, eager to be out of the humid, suffocating building. There was some indefinable quality about Vassell that unnerved him. Despite his general unsavoriness, though, Vassell had made some compelling points. Why would a man whom Bradley met one time eighteen years ago be involved in anything happening currently? It strained credulity, to be sure. But there was something off-putting about the guy, and that just couldn't be dismissed.

Erasmo exhaled a long sigh when he finally reached the Civic, slumping down inside it in relief. He replayed their conversation in his head several times, hoping to pick up on something he might've missed. It was so damn hard to think straight, though. His head throbbed with no mercy, as if a hammer were pounding the top of his skull, cracking it into jagged shards. And he was *so* goddamn hungry. He couldn't remember the last time he'd eaten. The cravings were so intense now that he could barely hold a thought in his head.

Erasmo rested his burning face against the blissfully cool steering wheel, willing his headache and hunger pangs to go away. There was so much more to do tonight . . . he didn't have time to feel like garbage. Maybe closing his eyes would help. Just for a few minutes.

The relief that settled over him as he gave in was intense and immediate. Before Erasmo could even attempt to fight it off, darkness crept in around him. He fell away, tumbling backward, floating in a vast expanse of endless time and infinite space, whispering a desperate prayer that he wouldn't be lost forever.

When Erasmo woke, he still felt dazed and hazy, his tongue dry as a bone. But he could now at least function. The dashboard clock told him only an hour had passed. It wasn't too late to go by Bradley's and tell him how the meeting with Vassell had gone. He started the Civic, which groaned a few times before reluctantly coming to life, and pulled out onto the desolate road.

During the drive, Erasmo found himself unable to take his eyes off the thick, amorphous clouds sliding across the night sky. They were different this evening, seeming to change from moment to moment into multitudes of fantastical shapes . . . animals, landscapes, galaxies, even strange, emaciated beings. Erasmo was just about to exit the highway, eyes still flitting from the road to the sky, when his phone buzzed. He was surprised to see it was Bradley.

"Hey," he said, "I'm actually just about to get to your—"

Bradley attempted to speak, but his whispers were panicked and unintelligible.

"I can't hear you," Erasmo said.

More noise, like static, erupted from the phone.

"I still don't know what you're saying, man."

Bradley spoke again, but this time his words, while still whispered, were crystal clear.

"Please hurry," he said, voice shaking.

"Why?" Erasmo asked. "What's happening?"

"There's something in my house," Bradley said, "and it has my baby."

CHAPTER 11

Erasmo frantically scanned Bradley's front yard as he brought the Civic to a screeching halt. There were no obvious signs of a break-in. He jumped out and sprinted toward the house, his shoes sinking into the lawn's plush and immaculately sculpted grass. As he ran, floodlights erupted from the roof, covering him in a harsh blue light. After reaching the front door, an imposing slab of oak, his heart sank when he saw it was ever so slightly ajar. He pushed against the heavy door and it silently swung open.

Erasmo slipped his phone out and dialed 9-1-1, fingers trembling. "There's been a break-in," he whispered. "Intruders might be inside." He then quickly gave the address and hung up.

After stepping into the foyer, he peered around the corner. A spacious living area lay in front of him, decorated with pristine white furniture the same shade as baby powder. A massive Christmas tree sat in the corner, mounds of perfectly wrapped presents lying underneath it. He tiptoed through this room, unsure if he should rush upstairs or investigate down here. Erasmo stifled the urge to call out to Bradley, in case there actually was someone else in the house. He listened closely for any unusual sounds and soon became alarmed at what he didn't hear.

No sounds of a baby, crying or otherwise.

Erasmo exited the living area and stepped into the kitchen. He couldn't help but note it was at least five times the size of his grandmother's. There was so much stainless steel, it seemed as if even the walls were made of it. He tiptoed along and found himself in a massive family area.

A spiraling white staircase rose from the middle of the room into the upper reaches of the house. Bradley and the baby had to be up there somewhere. He began walking toward the staircase when a gentle creak whispered through the room. Erasmo jerked his head in every direction but saw no movement. It was only when another soft groan floated in the air that he realized his mistake. The sound hadn't come from down here.

It had come from above.

Erasmo glanced up and saw a flicker of movement at the top of the stairs. His heart roared in his chest, but each of his limbs remained frozen and useless. A cry then reverberated through the house, breaking his paralysis.

This particular scream was heart-chilling, but not because it seethed with urgency and shock and outright terror. No. It froze Erasmo's heart for another reason.

This shriek had clearly come from a baby.

Erasmo sprinted up the stairs, his worn-out Adidas thudding loudly on each step. Whoever was up there would surely hear him coming. He was almost at the landing when he saw the back of a figure who was most definitely not Bradley. Whoever it was looked unnaturally large, and by the hunch of its shoulders, it appeared to be cradling something in its arms.

As Erasmo jumped off the last stair, he took in the full scene and lost the ability to breathe. The massive figure was dressed in a flowing black robe, complete with a large hood.

Based on the uneven way the fabric lay, the hood looked as though it covered a grotesque, misshapen head.

A glimmer of movement on the floor caught Erasmo's attention. He was horrified to see it was Bradley. His client lay unconscious, splayed in front of the robed figure, his limbs jerking in uneven rhythms.

The baby continued to wail, each scream increasing in urgency, as if he somehow understood just how precarious his situation was. Erasmo stood perfectly still, unsure of what to do next. But then the massive hooded shape turned around.

When Erasmo saw the figure in its entirety, he began to weep. He had no idea if his tears were out of terror or surprise, or validation that there were beings from planes of existence beyond this one, but the reasons were unimportant. What now stood in front of him was all that mattered.

The demon glared at Erasmo, wisps of smoke rising from the corners of its fierce, onyx eyes. Erasmo understood now why its head had appeared misshapen under the robe. Two horns rose from the demon's forehead, both jagged and broken, their razor-sharp points pressing unevenly against the robe's hood.

But his eyes locked on the demon's large, protruding jaw, which took up a majority of the creature's face. Its writhing lips slowly parted, revealing massive teeth, each one dripping with thick mucus.

Erasmo watched in horror as a shimmering strand of the liquid slowly dripped from the demon's lower jaw, stretching for what seemed like an eternity, until it gently landed on the face of the screaming infant in its arms.

The creature stared at Erasmo, its breathing deep and ravenous, like a hunger-crazed animal assessing its prey. A thick scarlet tongue, split down the middle, unfurled from deep within its throat and stretched out toward him, as if it desired nothing more than to lick his sweaty flesh.

Erasmo took a fitful step backward, then another, before realizing his mistake. He'd been standing too close to the edge of the stairs, and now felt his left foot come down on nothing. The sickening feeling of his balance giving way erupted in his belly. He saw a brief flash of ceiling right before the back of his head cracked against one of the steps. Erasmo tumbled down the stairs, each part of his body absorbing punishment, helpless to stop his descent.

He was almost to the bottom when his head struck yet another stair, bringing a sudden wave of darkness over him. But before he lost consciousness, one last image seared itself into Erasmo's brain. The hulking demon looked down on him, the creature's face betraying a hint of pleasure as its long, forked tongue took just the slightest taste of the red-faced baby screaming in its arms.

CHAPTER 12

ERASMO WOKE TO the sound of his name being spoken. He normally hated hearing his name uttered out loud. The syllables were like nails on a goddamn chalkboard. But as this person whispered it, the tone was somehow familiar and comforting. The back of his head throbbed manically, and his right arm ached down to the bone. He opened his eyes to a surreal flurry of activity: investigators walking around carrying bags of evidence; paramedics treating a pale and sweaty Bradley; a photographer aiming his camera around the room taking photos. Multiple fervent conversations assaulted his ears all at once. The only figure who remained static was the one looming above him, still calling his name.

Erasmo turned his eyes to this person, and when he saw who it was slowly closed them, a sharp twinge in his heart.

"Detective Torres," he said, his voice pathetically weak.

"You all right?" she asked. "The paramedics are going to look you over next—"

"I'm fine," he said, forcing his eyes back open. "The baby . . ."

"Missing," Torres said. "Mr. Erickson told us there was an intruder in the house and that he got attacked from behind.

Never saw who did it. We still have a ton of questions obviously. And you can only imagine my surprise when I showed up to find *you* here."

"It's a long story," he said, gingerly getting up from the floor.

"I've got plenty of time."

"Come outside with me. Don't want your coworkers thinking any less of you."

They navigated the tumultuous scene and made their way out to the front yard. The temperature had dropped, and Erasmo shivered uncontrollably as he recounted the story for Torres. He left nothing out, and her stoic expression betrayed no hint as to what she thought at hearing such a batshit story. When he finished, she stopped writing in her notepad and appraised him in silence for what seemed like a very long time.

"Look," she said, "just because you and I have a history doesn't mean I can accept this—"

"I know," he said. "And I'm not asking you to. Just recounting what I saw. Or what I thought I saw, anyway. Honestly, now that I'm out here shivering my ass off and a little more coherent, none of it even seems real to me. Haven't been feeling so hot lately. Maybe that's got something to do with what I thought I saw in there."

"I'm glad you mentioned that," she said. "You look terrible. I'm going to have the paramedics—"

"I'll live," he said. "Anyway, that's all I can tell you about what happened."

"Back to Bradley for a minute," she said. "Are you really entertaining this insane story he told you? And just so we're clear, he's a suspect in the baby's disappearance."

"What? Why?"

"The two of them were here alone together and now the baby is nowhere to be found. That makes him, unofficially, prime suspect number one. Look, there's a *child* missing. This is as serious as it gets. The FBI is going to get involved at some point soon. If you've got anything else to tell me, now would be the time."

"Bradley," Erasmo said, after a moment to mull it over, "seemed believable to me. He was truly scared, completely rattled at finding those words written on his baby. It was the kind of fear that's hard to fake."

But, he considered, was it really *that* hard to pretend to be frightened? Erasmo had certainly been fooled before. But it just didn't make any sense for him to lie. Why would Bradley have come to him in the first place, if not to try and stop this *very* thing from happening? As if reading his mind, Torres offered a possibility.

"He could have been trying to use you," she said.

"Use me? How?"

"Who knows," she said. "Maybe as some kind of pawn in a game we can't make out just yet. I've seen some horrible things in my years on the force, Erasmo. Sometimes, men don't want to be fathers or husbands anymore, and they try to absolve themselves of their responsibilities by committing truly evil acts. And they usually drag innocents into their half-assed plans to get away with it."

"Maybe you're right," he said, unable to completely dismiss this possibility. "I'll give it some thought. If I think of anything that would be helpful, I'll let you know."

Just then, a stocky man with a walrus-like mustache approached and whispered into her ear. Torres's jaw clenched and she nodded.

"I have to go," she said. "The statement you've given me will do for now. We might have some follow-up questions depending on what we find, but I'm going to tell these guys that you have a concussion and it can wait until morning."

"Okay," he said. "Look, if anyone else asks, all I'm going to say is that Bradley hired me to investigate some threats, he called tonight in a panic, and when I arrived, he was unconscious. Then while I was looking around, a hooded assailant caused me to fall down the stairs. All of which is true."

"Well," she said, releasing a long sigh, "that matches up to what you already told me, so I wouldn't have a problem with that statement."

He nodded and turned to leave, but Torres reached out and grabbed his shoulder, her grip powerful but tinged with tenderness.

"I . . ." she said, struggling to find the words. "I thought things were going to be different. That we'd keep in touch. You know, after everything we went through. But I stopped hearing from you, and all my calls went unreturned."

"Sorry," he said, not turning around. "Just hit a rough patch, that's all."

"I'm here if you need anything," she said, her grip tightening. "I mean that."

Torres let go of his shoulder, and he walked across the street toward his car.

"Hey!" she called out behind him. "Where's Rat? Why isn't he here? Is he all right?"

Erasmo ignored these questions, allowing them to float in the night air unanswered, and felt blessed relief when they were carried away by the arrival of a brisk, cleansing breeze.

CHAPTER 13

WHEN ERASMO STUMBLED into his house, exhausted by the day's bizarre happenings, he wanted nothing more than to drift away into the ether.

But an object in his room called to him, the only item he owned that was worth a damn. He pulled out a rumpled box from underneath his bed and reached in, immediately feeling better once he held the familiar shape in his hands. He studied the battered cover, fearful of the day it would fall apart. The book's design was simple, a maroon background with the title centered at the top in a plain, gold font: *A Practical Guide to the Supernatural and Paranormal: The Writings of John F. Dubois.*

This was one of the few items his father had left behind. Erasmo had no idea if the man had even read the book. For all he knew, it was just forgotten clutter left in his closet. But the fact that it was once in his father's possession was enough to imbue it with an almost mystical significance. He'd read the damn thing countless times growing up, no doubt fueling his interest in the topic. Erasmo opened the musty book and perused the first page.

Introduction

When faced with unspeakable tragedy, it is human nature to search for answers. I have endured such tragedy, and after much suffering, my search for answers begins now. Some might say that what I am embarking on is pure madness, but they have not endured the loss that I have.

I am keeping this journal in order to fill it with my findings and investigations. My dear daughter Emma may be gone from this earth physically, but I will not stop until I have found a way to communicate with her spirit, wherever it may be. I will travel to the ends of the earth and pay any price, if it means learning of a ceremony, or a deity, or even a malevolent demon that would allow me to hear Emma's sweet voice one more time.

If anyone finds this journal, it most likely means that I am dead. If I have filled these pages with useful information, I would be eternally grateful if you shared it with the world. Conversely, if there are dangerous practices in these pages, please burn this entire book until only ashes remain.

Respectfully,
John F. Dubois

Erasmo had never been able to find any information about the book online though, despite extensive searching. To add to the mystery, its copyright page, as well as a few other random pages, was missing.

He remembered Dubois had written a chapter about seeking deals with demons. Given what he'd seen tonight—or thought he'd seen—it wouldn't hurt to revisit what Dubois had said about it. Erasmo skimmed through the pages until he found the entry.

<u>On the Dangers of Faustian Bargains</u>

Every person has at least one desire that they would give anything for, even their very soul. Some wishes are common and unimaginative: money, romance, power. But others seek to bend the very rules of nature, or perhaps break them entirely. And what is to be done when one's obsession exceeds their worldly grasp? They seek the otherworldly, of course.

Most know the story of Faust's pact with the Devil. But in truth, the same deal can be made with lesser demons. For example, Gerbert of Aurillac was rumored to have entered into a pact with the female demon Meridiana, who helped him ascend to the papal throne. Of course, it was also rumored that the Devil killed this same Pope, and gave his eyeballs to demons to play with.

This serves to illustrate an important aspect of making a deal with the Devil: the price it extracts. Whatever item or status is sought, one rule always applies: the more one asks, the higher the price.

While some may gladly give up their own soul, I've learned through my research that the Devil may want something else entirely. The exact nature of the cost is different for everyone, but know this: the price is whatever makes one suffer the most.

Another warning. There is no reneging on an agreement once it is struck. While some, like Brigadier General Jonathan Moulton, have attempted to trick the great beast, such a plan almost always ends badly.

So if you must enter such a deal, enter it with the full knowledge that you will lose a part of your humanity, and endless suffering awaits.

For some, this is a fair trade. I myself would have gladly made such a bargain if it meant seeing my Emma again. I attempted endlessly to summon the Devil, or any demon willing to enter in an arrangement with me. I used numerous methods, and even inflicted bloodshed to gather the required materials. And still, even with all my attempts, only once was I successful in summoning an inhabitant of hell.

Curiously, it was the one time I'd made few preparations. On the anniversary of Emma's death, I'd gone to spend the night in the woods, as my disposition made me unfit to be around others. I indulged in too much wine and screamed into the black void of the night sky. I begged for Him to appear, spewing flecks of blood from my raw throat. I offered everything to Him if only he'd let me see Emma again.

It was then I heard a rustle behind me, slow and wet. A snarling voice entered my head.

"You have nothing of value to offer," it said. "If you call for me again, I will steal your daughter's soul and burn her forever."

The screams in my throat died. In truth, His threat made me terrified to breathe, much less make the slightest bit of sound. I stood there, afraid to turn around for what felt like hours. When I finally moved, I found there was nothing else with me in the forest, and collapsed onto the ground.

Which leads to my last piece of advice: if you plan to make a deal with the Devil, make damn sure you have something that He wants.

Erasmo closed the book and laid it on his crooked nightstand. While it was all very interesting, none of what Dubois had written pertained to Bradley's situation. At least, not that he could tell anyway.

He was desperate for sleep, but his mind was racing too much for him to drift off. Maybe a friendly voice would help steady his nerves. He grabbed his phone and reflexively pulled up Rat's number without even thinking. Erasmo grimaced, staring down at the name.

Get your shit together.

He scrolled through his phone, searching for names that weren't there. Rat was really his only friend at school. The rest of the students regarded him as the weirdo who'd been involved in that strange incident at the Ghost Tracks. Last month, some of his classmates had found out about the Craigslist ad, which made his already questionable reputation even worse. Most of the students let him be for the most part. Although, lately, some had taken to calling him Ghost Boy as they passed in the hallway.

Sometimes he considered reaching out to his friendlier classmates, see if they wanted to hang out. But then he ran through the conversations in his head, ones which would surely happen.

Hey, where are your parents? Oh, sorry to hear that. What did your dad die of? So your mom just ran off? It's just you and your grandmother, then? Hey, how did you get that scar on your forehead? And that ugly one on your stomach?

He could try to explain, maybe massage the answers until they didn't sound quite so bizarre. But the thought of having to deal with those questions burned a hole in his gut. And even if he did answer them, the truth would just make these people uncomfortable. They'd never understand. Not really. Just like he'd never be able to understand their lives.

He stopped scrolling when he got to Mario's name. Maybe his cousin would be up for a chat. It was past midnight, but Mario was usually up until all hours. They'd been fairly close when they were children, but their bond had faded over time.

In truth, he felt like an outsider around most of his extended family. They were cordial to him, sure. But also wary, as if his father's habits were contagious. Or maybe they just thought his interests were odd and potentially harmful. Which, to be fair, wasn't untrue. But Mario had always been the friendliest of his cousins, so it was worth a try at least.

He answered on the second ring, a Bad Bunny song blaring in the background.

"Hey, cuz. Everything okay?" A burst of drunken laughter almost drowned out the words.

"Yeah. Just checking in. Seeing how you're doing."

"Oh, thank God. I thought you were calling with bad news. Hey, I'm at a party right now. Can't really talk. I only picked up because I thought it was about Grandma."

The call ended before Erasmo could even apologize for bothering him.

A bone-shaking chill wracked his body. When it finished coursing through him, he continued scrolling.

Andy. Maybe Andy could talk if his shift at the hotel hadn't started yet. Besides, it'd be good to check on him after that incident at the motel. He answered on the first ring.

"Hey, man," Andy said, sounding more than a bit surprised. "Everything okay?"

"Yeah, everything's good," he responded, but now realized he had no idea what to talk about. "Just thought it'd be nice to chat."

"Oh . . . okay. I'm getting ready for work. These damn split shifts are killing me. Hey, thanks again for coming out earlier. I know it was—"

"Andy!" a voice screamed in the background, followed by a TV being turned up full blast.

"Sorry," Andy said, almost whispering now. "My dad's drinking tonight. I thought he passed out, but I guess he got a second wind."

"Hey," the same voice slurred. "Where the hell did you hide my Stoli?"

"You finished it, Dad. Remember?" Andy was clearly holding the phone against his body to muffle the sound, but Erasmo still heard enough to make everything out.

"Stop lying to me, you piece of shit!" the hoarse voice said.

Frantic rustling for a few moments, until Erasmo heard a car door shut and the sputtering hum of an engine.

"Sorry about that," Andy said. "Do you need to go?"

In truth, he did want to leave this awkward, unpleasant conversation, and was sorry he'd even called. But the sadness in Andy's voice, his resignation that Erasmo no longer found him worth talking to, made this impossible. So instead he blurted out a question he'd had no intention of asking.

"Have you ever seen a demon?"

"A demon? Like . . . a real one? No, of course not." Andy remained silent for a few moments, clearly turning the question over in his head. "Oh my God," he said, sounding both excited and horrified. "Are you saying you saw one? How on earth did you manage to—"

"No," Erasmo said. "That's not it. I was just curious. Been doing some research on them lately."

"Oh," Andy said after a long sigh. Erasmo imagined him slouched in disappointment. "Was there something specific you were looking to find out?"

Erasmo almost said no, but Andy was a good resource. Wouldn't hurt to ask.

"Are you aware of any demons who want children? Who demands them in return for a granted wish?"

Andy remained silent for a few moments as he considered this. "None comes to mind, but that doesn't mean much. I've always been skeptical about the number of demons that have historically been documented."

"What do you mean?"

"I just don't think those are the only demons in existence," Andy said. "I have a hard time believing that a few books written centuries ago somehow managed to identify and categorize every demon that's ever lived. What if some have never presented themselves to us? Or what if others defy our ability to observe them? For example, I'm sure there are some demons who can drive us mad with just a glance. Whoever encountered a creature like that would be in no shape to document their experience."

Erasmo had never considered this before, but what Andy said was hard to disagree with.

"What about the grimoires though? You don't think they're at least partially accurate?"

"Sure, to an extent," Andy said. "But they certainly have their flaws. Did you know there are lots of words in *The Sworn Book of Honorius* that are unpronounceable, just complete gibberish? Who knows what these words might mean, or what they're trying to tell us. All this information that's been floating around for centuries is clearly inexact and incomplete. So yeah, I think there are plenty of creatures that slip in and out of our existence who we don't know the slightest thing about."

Andy again made some compelling points. But this didn't get Erasmo any closer to figuring out which specific demons, known or unknown, might be interested in taking children.

"I don't mean to pry," Andy said, "but this sudden interest in demons that make bargains wouldn't have anything to do with your grandmother, would it?"

"No," Erasmo said, harsher than he intended. "Of course not."

"Sorry," Andy said. "Didn't mean to overstep. Just trying to look out for you."

"I know. It's just been a rough night. I'll catch up with you later, all right?"

Erasmo disconnected the call and lay down, finally ready to tumble into oblivion. But just as he was about to surrender to the rapidly encroaching darkness, his phone vibrated. He stared at the name with trepidation, not wanting to answer but knowing there wasn't a choice.

"It's Torres," she said, her voice tight, as if speaking through gritted teeth. "Look, we found something. There were rags in Bradley's closet. Bloody ones. He's been placed under arrest."

Her words were like a punch to his stomach, leaving Erasmo both unable to breathe and urgently needing to vomit.

"This thing is at a whole other level now. Look, I'm getting some grief over here for letting you leave the scene. Make sure you show up at the station at 8:30 a.m. sharp to go over your statement again. Don't make me look like an ass."

Before he could answer, the line went dead. Erasmo closed his eyes, desperately trying to find the darkness that had slipped over him so easily just moments ago, but it was useless. Sleep would not come, only questions that refused to let go, like blood-gorged ticks clasping their eager mouths on to tender flesh.

Could Bradley really have done something to his own child? That just didn't seem likely. And yet, there were those rags in the closet to consider. Sure, the blood on them could be completely unrelated, but it certainly didn't look great.

Of course, he was also dancing around the issue of what had happened on the stairs and what it might mean. But could he even be sure of what he'd seen, especially given his history? Not to mention, he'd been scared shitless at the time. Could he be *absolutely* sure of what he'd seen? Of course not.

But that didn't mean he was going to discount it entirely.

Erasmo sat up and threw off the thin blanket he'd been clinging to. It was doing a shitty job of keeping him warm anyway. He wasn't going to get any sleep, and it was useless to pretend otherwise. A child was missing, one he'd been hired to help keep safe, and he was going to turn over every goddamn stone to figure this thing out.

If what he saw was real, then his course of action was clear.

Erasmo reached under his bed and pulled out the gym bag he kept stocked with supplies. He then navigated through the uneven stacks of books on the floor, grabbing a handful of texts necessary for the ritual.

He held his gym bag and books close to his chest in a death grip, contemplating what he was about to do. No need to over-think it. His plan was simple.

Erasmo was going to attempt to summon this demon, and demand it give the child back.

Of course, he had no idea which exact demon this even was. He could try a general evocation though, and hope his recent proximity to the creature helped to summon it. The odds were surely slim, but he had to at least try. Erasmo yanked open his lopsided back door and stepped out into the cool night air.

He stumbled out of the garage an hour later, dazed, shivering, and soaked with sweat. Erasmo had conducted the ceremony as best he understood it, but nothing at all had appeared. Not even the slightest gleam of dark energy shimmering in the air. Of course, there were many texts on the subject of how to sum-mon various entities, and they often conflicted with each other. This being the first time he'd attempted the ritual in earnest, he just couldn't be sure what had gone wrong. Or, for that matter, if it were even truly possible. What he needed was to talk with someone who'd actually performed the ritual successfully.

In fact, what he *really* needed was to speak to someone who had communed with this particular demon before.

Erasmo checked his phone. Almost 1:00 a.m. He could wait until morning, but wasn't inclined to waste any more time now that this idea had taken hold. He shuffled to the driveway where his Civic sat, its dull gray metal barely visible in the weak moonlight. A whisper in the night air told him this was a bad idea. But Bradley's child was missing. Something had to be done. He got into his car, gripping the steering wheel so hard his fingers felt like permanent deformed claws that would never straighten again.

Erasmo turned the engine over, its strained hum almost comforting. He backed out of the driveway, fingers still strangling the wheel. One way or another, he was going to get answers tonight, and he didn't give a damn what he had to do to get them.

CHAPTER 14

ERASMO PULLED INTO the barren parking lot of the Soul Center and cut the engine. It seemed like he'd just left, but the dashboard clock told him that had been over four hours ago. He knew perfectly well Vassell might not be here. But there'd been no home address for him online, and that cot in his office had been worn to shit. There was good reason to think Vassell might still be inside.

He crept along the side of the building, hidden in the shadows, making his way toward the back entrance. Even if the old man was here, would he have any useful information to give? It was hard to say. Whatever the case, in the hours since Erasmo had been here, a quiet, persistent thought had steadily morphed into a firm belief.

Vassell had been lying about something.

It was in the way he'd flinched at the sound of Bradley's name, and how eager he'd been for Erasmo to leave. The old man had done a masterful job telling his story for sure, but there was something suspect about the way he'd so easily explained away his questionable past.

Erasmo reached the back door and tugged on its handle. The hulking slab of metal didn't budge an inch. Damn. He knew he probably wouldn't get lucky twice, but it was still a disappointment. He glanced around, and his eyes quickly settled on the next best option. A small window sat above the door, reflecting just a hint of pale moonlight. He studied its dimensions, worried the window was too narrow to squeeze through. His thin frame gave him a chance, though, and there weren't really any other options.

He scanned the area behind the building, which wasn't much bigger than an alleyway, looking for anything he could use to boost himself up. Nothing caught his eye. A concrete wall about five feet high separated the property from its neighbor behind it. Erasmo's shoes scuffed against the lot's rough asphalt as he walked beside the wall, hoping for a discarded crate, a trash can, anything. He was just about to give up when a different sound arose from underneath his feet, not of asphalt, but of a smoother surface. Erasmo knelt down, flashing his phone's light against the ground. He studied what he saw, confused.

He was kneeling on a manhole cover.

What the hell was this doing back here? Seemed like a damn strange place for one. He ran his fingers over the metal and found it oddly smooth. There should've been markings from the city, the Texas star logo, identification numbers . . . something. Erasmo was about to stand up when he noticed some writing on the cover's bottom left. The words were so faint, they'd go unnoticed unless someone was looking closely. The short phrase was written in Latin.

Flectere si nequeo superos, Acheronta movebo

Interesting. Too bad he didn't have the slightest idea what it meant. He knew a little Latin from his study of Catholic exorcism rites, but didn't recognize this particular phrase. He ran a search of the sentence on his phone. The first hit was a translation from a scholar named Robert Fagles. Erasmo read the sentence, and his skin prickled.

If I cannot sway heaven, I'll wake the powers of hell!

Damn. What did that even mean though? Could be that Vassell had the phrase carved on the manhole cover as a subtle ode to his past. Could be that it wasn't even him and someone else entirely had inscribed it. Could be lots of things. But what he knew for sure was that this one phrase made him even more confident he needed to talk to Vassell.

Erasmo studied the manhole cover again. Was it possible they used this opening as a way to get in and out of the building? As an exit in case of an emergency? This could be his way inside. He just had to get the cover open, and for once, luck was on his side.

He trotted back to the Civic and popped open the trunk. After feeling around in the dark, his hand finally curled around the crowbar's cool metal. Erasmo liked to bring it along on his investigations, just in case there was trouble. He was too traumatized from a previous experience to ever want to see a baseball bat used as a weapon again. And he couldn't afford a gun, so this was the next best option. Up until now, though, he'd never had to use it.

Erasmo walked back to the manhole cover, found a slight indentation on the side, and slid the tip of the crowbar in. He shoved down as hard as he could, but the damn thing wouldn't budge. He tried again, his injured right arm throbbing from the strain, but still no movement. Damn. Moving heavy objects had never been his strong suit. Erasmo glanced around, as if there might magically be an answer staring him in the face.

And then, amazingly, there was.

Two large, quivering eyes peered at him from the other side of the short concrete wall. Erasmo, startled at the realization he was being watched, dropped the crowbar and stepped backward.

"You shouldn't be messing with that stuff," a gruff voice said. The rest of the man's face slowly rose from behind the wall, revealing a bulbous nose and a black, unruly beard.

"I . . . I'm just trying to . . ."

"It doesn't matter what you're trying to do, son," the man said. "What's down there isn't for you."

The shock of seeing this towering, bulky man now lessening a bit, Erasmo found his voice.

"How are you so sure?" he asked. "Do you know what's down there?"

"No," the man said, "I've never been down that particular hole myself. Others, but not that one. What I can tell you, though, is that I sleep huddled against this wall every night. And sometimes I hear sounds coming from that side of the wall. Disturbing sounds. On nights like those, I get the hell out of here and find somewhere else to sleep. So believe me when I tell you, down there is not somewhere you want to be."

"I have my reasons," Erasmo said.

"If there's one thing my disappointment of a life has taught me," the man said, "it's that the reasons we think we *have* to do certain things are almost always complete bullshit."

"Look," Erasmo said, uneasy at this stranger's interest in his situation, "I understand you think this is a bad idea, but I need to get this cover open. I'll give you ten dollars just to push down on this crowbar. I'm going to find a way to get down there, whether you help me or not."

The man sighed, his disappointment exceedingly clear.

"We all have our path to follow," he said. "If you believe yours leads you down that dark hole, then who the hell am I to say otherwise?"

After placing his meaty hands on top of the wall, the man effortlessly pulled himself up and over. A filthy plaid shirt hung from his sizable frame, and stained gray sweatpants much too small for his girth clung to his legs.

Erasmo watched as the man walked straight to the crowbar, picked it up, and slid it under the manhole cover. He was just about to walk over and help, when the man shoved down on the crowbar and unleashed a feral grunt. The cover rose just enough for the man to violently jerk the crowbar, shifting the cover off to the side with a loud *clang*. He turned and walked back to Erasmo, a blank expression on his broad face, as if he'd done nothing more than open a jar of peanut butter.

"Here you go," he said, handing the crowbar back to Erasmo.

"Thanks," Erasmo replied, embarrassed, feeling acute shame at having another man do his work for him. He reached into his pocket and dug around.

"Keep your money," the man said. "I did it for my own reasons." He turned away and walked over to the wall, pulling himself up and over with the same ease as before. "I'm finding somewhere else to sleep tonight, far away from here," the man said in his gruff voice, the words floating over the wall. "I hope you find what you're looking for."

Erasmo turned and stared at the open hole in the ground. It was dark as hell down there. Making out anything in that pitch-blackness was going to be a problem. He unlocked his phone and turned on the flashlight app. The light it gave off wasn't as strong as he would've liked, but it would have to do.

He walked to the edge of the hole and peered down. All he could clearly see was the top of an iron ladder that plunged into darkness. His throat tightened at the sight, but he knew what needed to be done. Erasmo tucked his phone away, placed his foot on the ladder's first rung, and began descending.

At first, he could at least glance up and see the manhole's outline. But after lowering himself farther, even this minor comfort faded from view. It was only when he found himself immersed in absolute darkness that cold, wispy strands of fear curled through his chest and tickled his heart. Despite this, he kept lowering himself, the only sounds around him the unnerving clang of the ladder and his heavy, arrhythmic breaths.

Finally, after what seemed like a long time but was surely no more than a few minutes, his left foot touched down on damp concrete. He stepped off the ladder, reached into his pocket, and pulled out his phone, turning on the flashlight app.

Erasmo immediately realized it was going to be almost useless. The beam of light emanating from his hand was completely devoured by the darkness, like a pure soul struggling to exist in a mad, cruel world.

Given that he could only see a few feet ahead at best, Erasmo shuffled down the tunnel cautiously. He felt around, soon realizing he could touch both walls without even stretching his arms out all the way. As far as he knew, these tunnels weren't supposed to be quite so narrow. He flashed the weak light in every direction, desperately looking for a ladder that might lead up to the Soul Center. One had to be around here somewhere.

Erasmo pressed on, his breathing becoming erratic as panic slowly dripped into his veins. It seemed like he'd already walked *more* than far enough. He should've been under the building by now. Damn. He must've somehow overshot it. Or was being immersed in absolute darkness playing tricks with his perception of time and distance?

Maybe he'd just been wrong and the manhole cover didn't have a damn thing to do with either Vassell or the Soul Center. But the inscription . . . it had to mean something, didn't it? He was seriously considering just turning back when the wall to his right abruptly stopped, leaving a gap before the wall continued a few feet away.

It was the opening to a different tunnel.

He eyed the narrow passage, unsure whether to enter. Screw it. He was already down here and certainly didn't plan on coming back. May as well check it out.

Erasmo stepped into the new tunnel with trepidation and found it even smaller than the first one. As he shuffled along, an internal debate raged: What would he do if yet another tunnel appeared? The risk of getting lost down here was becoming increasingly real. But then he aimed his phone to the right, and what appeared out of the darkness rendered that train of thought irrelevant.

A ladder.

He could hardly believe it. But did the ladder go up to the Soul Center, or was his head going to pop up in the middle of a downtown street?

Only one way to find out.

Erasmo placed his hand on a rung and was just about to start climbing, when he heard a faint whisper behind him. He let go of the ladder, whirling around. And what he saw shocked him.

There was an opening in the wall behind him. But this one wasn't like the other tunnels down here. Its edges were rough and asymmetrical, as if it had been hacked into existence with blunt instruments. And this tunnel was even narrower, just wide enough for a single person. The reason Erasmo's breath left his body, though, wasn't the opening itself.

No. His lungs were shut tight because deep inside of the passage, a faint, warm glow flickered against the uneven walls.

How could this be possible? He hadn't seen any other sources of light down here. And even stranger, this light didn't appear to be of the stable and harsh variety that came from a bulb or fluorescent lamp. It was warm and natural, fluctuating in uneven waves.

This light could only come from fire.

Erasmo's first instinct was to run, to flee this oppressive darkness, away from whatever lay inside that tunnel.

But then what . . . spend the next several days curled in bed, chastising himself for being a goddamn coward? Tell Bradley that he'd had a chance to find some information that might help locate his son, but he'd been too scared to even try?

No. He had to go see. It might be nothing. A trick of the light, maybe. Or perhaps a sewage worker inspecting an overnight problem. Could be lots of things. But either way, he had to know. Erasmo gripped his phone with its weak light, held it out as far as he could, and stepped into the cramped passageway.

CHAPTER 15

HE IMMEDIATELY HAD trouble breathing, as if steel wire had been wrapped around his throat. Erasmo had never thought of himself as claustrophobic, but maybe this was just something he hadn't discovered about himself yet. Hell of a time to find out. The jagged walls pressed in on him, wanting to squeeze the already shallow breath from his lungs.

Erasmo pressed forward as sweat poured from him, stinging his eyes. The fire's glow was definitely getting closer, but he was too disoriented to accurately gauge how much longer until he reached it. His head throbbed in a thick, pulsing rhythm, still aching from his fall down the stairs. And his arm was tender to the touch now. Maybe he should have let the paramedics—

A faint sound echoed through the tunnel. At least, he thought so. The sound of his uneven, labored breaths made it difficult to tell for sure. He stopped and strained to listen. Nothing. Perhaps he'd imagined it.

But just as he was about to take another step, the sound rang out again. And this time, Erasmo knew what he'd heard. His stomach muscles convulsed. Now he did continue forward, steeling himself for whatever he was about to witness.

More light now filled the tunnel, and the sound vibrating through its walls grew louder. After a few more steps, he saw why. There was an opening approaching on his right, about ten feet away. The light he'd been chasing glowed from inside.

Erasmo slipped the phone into his pocket, heart jackhammering as he crept closer to the opening. After reaching it, he stood frozen, unable to force himself to look inside.

He reminded himself again why he was doing this. A child needed help. A baby. If there was even the slightest possibility answers were in there, he had to look.

Besides, if he left now and abandoned this child, that would make him no better than his parents.

This thought spurred him forward. He clenched his teeth, took a breath, and peeked his head out just enough to glimpse inside. And what Erasmo saw was so much worse than he'd feared.

The area was large and dimly lit, torches scattered throughout. Their warm light faintly illuminated a mass of hooded figures, all wearing bizarre, grotesque masks. Each of them knelt in the middle of the room, forming three perfect squares side by side, chanting the wicked prayer to their master he'd heard in the tunnel. A winged, snarling demon loomed over them, its enraged eyes staring down at their subservient bodies.

The statue had been created in painstaking detail, every inch of it carved to bring its menace and savagery to life. But this was not a likeness of the demon he'd seen at Bradley's. In fact, Erasmo did not recognize this muscled, furious creature at all, or its majestic black wings. None of this made any sense. The worshipers continued to chant in the demon's honor, a Latin prayer that sounded vaguely familiar but which he couldn't quite place.

Every kneeling figure wore an identical black robe, except for one worshiper at the very front who was clearly leading the prayer. This figure wore a crimson robe and now slowly rose from his knees. Erasmo froze, realizing this was the only person in the entire room not wearing a mask, and he immediately recognized him.

Vassell.

The old man stood in front of the statue, raised his arms with a flourish, and slowly brought them down. The worshipers heeded his command and the chants ended on a long, dissonant note.

"Bring forth the sacrifice to our master," Vassell said, reaching inside his robes and producing a thin aged book.

Immediately, a figure materialized from the shadows. This person wore a boar's mask with a thick upturned snout and miniscule black eyes. He carried an actual young pig in his arms, pink and squirming. Vassell opened the book and read from it.

"Worship unto me, and receive an eternity of everlasting pleasure. Youth shall be our lifeblood, Youth shall light our way."

Vassell lowered the book. "You are owed young blood, Master," he said. "Accept this offering through me."

The person in the boar's mask produced a curved knife from his robe, and with no hesitation, slit the young pig's throat. The poor animal squealed, confused and terrified. Vassell cupped his hands underneath the piglet's neck, collected the blood gushing from it, and placed the glistening liquid to his lips, grinning wildly as he poured it down his throat.

"For you, my Master, from the Children of M," Vassell said, arms raised upward while thick streams of blood dripped down his pallid face. "May this blood flow from my lips to your lips, from my throat to your throat." He then knelt in front of the statue, head bowed.

Erasmo dry-heaved as he watched this unfold, desperately trying to stay silent. Even though he'd been braced for something bizarre, this was still a grotesque shock.

But there was yet another surprise. A sudden flicker of movement from behind the statue caught his attention. A new figure emerged from its shadow and slowly took his place in front of the still-kneeling Vassell. This person's robe was neither red nor a simple, plain black. Instead, a rich, deep onyx cloth flowed down his body, covered with intricately embroidered symbols stitched in bright crimson. The brilliance of the thread made the symbols appear to glow red in the dim light. Erasmo strained to see, but this person's hood obscured his face, and it was impossible to tell if he wore a mask like the rest.

"It is unfortunate that all we have for our master tonight is blood from a filthy animal," this new figure said. There was an odd quality to his voice, but Erasmo was too far away to make out why exactly it sounded strange. "Soon we will have a proper tribute for Him. Very soon."

"Yes, Vorax," the kneeling faithful said in a deep, droning monotone.

"Now," he said, "we will proceed with the reason for our gathering tonight. The welcoming of our newest member."

Two figures emerged from a shadowy area near the back of the room. One was black-robed like the others and masked, a fly with massive red eyes, a jutting proboscis, and long, yellowed human teeth. But the other figure, a stout middle-aged man, who the Fly gently guided to the front of the room, wore only a tattered brown robe and a thick blindfold. When they reached the front, the Fly gestured for the brown-robed man to lie down at the foot of the statue. He complied with eagerness.

"Take your positions," Vorax said.

The Fly stood over the brown-robed man and then strad-dled him, leaning in close so they were face-to-face. The Fly took off the man's blindfold, and then his own mask.

"Open your mouth," Vorax said, "and prepare to receive His Promise."

The brown-robed man on the bottom did so, stretching his mouth into a gaping maw, lips trembling in anticipation. The person who had once been the Fly but was now a bald fifty-year-old with fogged glasses, opened his mouth wide as well and began to tremble. His body's spasms were subtle at first, but soon his limbs jerked and convulsed. He then leaned directly over the brown-robed man's face, as if they were going to kiss with their stretched-open mouths.

Erasmo watched with dread and confusion. This ritual wasn't one he was at all familiar with. Vassell again read from the book.

"Accept His Promise," Vassell said, *"which has been blessed by Him, swallowed by your new brother, and is now infused with His essence. By accepting His Gift, you will now be His, and He will be yours. Forever."*

The thought of leaving while they were preoccupied crossed Erasmo's mind, but before he could, the convulsing man's body suddenly became still. A crazed grin spread over his face, eyes alight with excitement and pleasure.

A thick torrent of vomit then erupted from his throat, directly into the waiting mouth below. But the glistening, vis-cous liquid that flew from his mouth wasn't vomit exactly. It appeared smooth in texture, and its color uniform through-out: a deep, rich maroon. Erasmo watched in horror as the brown-robed man gulped this liquid greedily, his Adam's apple bobbing up and down at a furious rate. It was when Erasmo saw this fluid dripping down the side of this man's cheeks, pooling around his neck, that he understood what the substance was.

Blood.

Erasmo dry-heaved again, barely able to keep the bubbling juices in his gut down. He'd never heard of a cult initiation like this. For that matter, the creature they worshiped didn't look familiar, either. Perhaps they'd invented the ceremony, and the deity, themselves.

One thing was clear though: these people were dangerous. He had to get the hell out of here. Now.

Erasmo was just about to turn and sneak away, when a gentle chime echoed in the tunnel. He glanced around, trying to figure out what the sound was, where it came from. It wasn't until he heard the chime again when its source became clear.

His phone was ringing.

Erasmo fumbled with it, trying to silence the call. It took several excruciating moments to finally mute it. He whipped his head around, glancing back inside the room, desperately hoping they somehow hadn't heard.

But what he saw was a roomful of madmen staring back at him.

He now beheld the full assortment of masks they wore, each one macabre and hideous. A demented rabbit with blood-stained teeth and crazed, red-rimmed eyes. A humanoid bird with mournful eyes, its dingy yellow beak long and thick. A leering monkey, its left eye socket a gaping, gory wound. Even the pair on the floor turned their faces to stare at him, long strands of blood-vomit hanging from their mouths.

But what drew Erasmo's attention was their leader, Vorax, who stood regally in front of their master's towering statue, the crimson symbols on his robe alight. Erasmo could now see this person did indeed wear a mask: a horse's skull, with filthy black hair falling around its elongated, yellow bone. It took Erasmo several seconds to realize, with complete and utter horror, that this monstrosity stared in his direction, and pointed a bony finger directly at him.

He stood frozen, unable to make himself believe any of this was actually happening. Erasmo knew he should turn and flee from this insanity, but a part of him insisted it all must be an elaborate hallucination. Perhaps he was still lying unconscious at the foot of Bradley's staircase. Or for that matter, he could still be asleep in Ms. Jenkins's basement, dreaming all this bizarre lunacy. How could he truly be underneath the city, with these deranged cultists staring back at him? It was too insane to be real.

But then several of the masked figures charged toward him, and the icy fear suddenly flooding his veins was *very* real. He tried to move but found himself paralyzed, unsure of what to do, where to go.

It was then that two hands, bristling with strength, clamped down on his shoulders and violently jerked him away from the opening. Erasmo turned to whoever had done this and found himself face-to-face with one of *them*. This figure wore a goat's mask, yellow eyes glowing in the dim light, a bloody pentagram etched on its forehead.

Erasmo whimpered, now at the complete and utter mercy of these masked butchers. The Goat grabbed his shirt, pulled him close, and looked down on him, its fur tickling his skin. But instead of the Goat dragging him into the room full of crazed worshipers, it glared down at him and grunted just one word.

"Run."

CHAPTER 16

ERASMO HESITATED, STILL too much in shock to fully register what was happening. The Goat acted for him though, turning and dragging Erasmo down the tunnel. This snapped him out of his paralysis, and he now struggled to keep up.

They soon emerged into the main tunnel. The Goat pointed to the ladder Erasmo had been about to climb before the light drew his attention.

"Go," the figure said, fierce brown eyes twitching behind the mask. "Now."

This time, Erasmo wasted no time following directions. He sprinted to the ladder and immediately began to climb. He was only a few rungs up before remembering that he had absolutely no idea where this ladder even led to. The urge to look back at his rescuer was too powerful to resist, but when he did, saw that the Goat had vanished.

Erasmo continued to climb, hands slick with sweat. He tried to push away everything he'd just seen, of what it might mean, and focus on getting aboveground. But this proved impossible.

Vassell had lied to him, obviously. He was just as entangled in this cult—or whatever the hell it was—as he was years ago.

And those other worshipers down there with him, were they the same sad sacks he'd seen at the Soul Center earlier? Not to mention that Vassell apparently wasn't even the leader of this group.

But two other questions burned brightest of all. Who had been underneath that goat mask, and why had they helped him get away?

The higher he ascended, the more difficult the climb became. Lactic acid scorched his muscles, causing each limb to tremble wildly. Jesus. This was pathetic. He needed to give serious thought to starting a workout regimen.

Erasmo glanced up, hoping to see a sign the surface was near. But only darkness hovered above, deep and swirling. He continued on, the black miasma surrounding him thick and oppressive, as if he were at the bottom of a lifeless ocean. Erasmo felt as if he were drowning, arms outstretched, reaching for light, searching for salvation that was just out of reach.

Nothing to do but press on. On top of everything else, he was starving. He'd have to get something inside him the first chance he got. A few minutes later, desperation and panic now building, he allowed himself to glance up again. And this time his hope was rewarded.

A delicate sliver of curved light hovered above him.

Erasmo climbed faster, trying to ignore the molten fire tearing through his muscles. The sliver quickly grew larger, until he recognized what it was. A manhole opening sat above him, its cover partially moved aside, creating the crescent shape of the light.

He'd been in such a rush to reach the surface, it never even occurred to him a manhole cover would block his way out. But now here it was, already moved aside. Had it been the Goat who'd done this, knowing he wouldn't be able to open it by himself? Or was it always open, so their members would have an easy way in and out?

Erasmo reached up to shove the cover aside a few more inches but stopped himself. He'd been assuming the Goat was helping him, but perhaps this was some kind of a trap. Maybe there was a roomful of masked cult members up there right now, eagerly waiting to slice his guts open in honor of the bloodthirsty demon they served.

He pushed this thought away. Going back down the ladder wasn't even a remote possibility. They were probably swarming through the tunnels right now, searching for him. There was nowhere to go but up.

Erasmo shoved the cover with every ounce of strength he had left. It moved only a few inches, but now there was enough clearance for him to comfortably slide through. He placed his hands on the rim of the opening and pulled himself up and out, immediately whipping his head around in every direction.

Only to see that he was standing in the middle of an empty alley.

His limbs shuddered in relief. He staggered to one of the brick buildings that lined the alley and leaned against its mold-infested back wall. Unable to stay upright, Erasmo slid down, every ounce of energy drained. He closed his eyes, only wanting to rest for a few moments. But when he opened them again, Erasmo was alarmed to realize he wasn't quite certain exactly how much time had passed. Shit. It was dangerous to be out here in the middle of the night. He had to get home.

With any luck, his car wouldn't be too far away. Once he saw where the alley led, it wouldn't be hard to find—

A soft clicking sound rose from behind him. Erasmo stopped cold. Whatever it was continued to tap delicately against the asphalt. It sounded organic . . . like fingernails, maybe. Or hooves. He stood still, listening, but the sound stopped and failed to reappear.

It was nothing. Just his nerves. He was about to take a step forward when another noise drifted through the night air. But this wasn't the sound of subtle clicks and taps. No.

This was a harsh, violent growl. Deep and inhuman.

Every instinct Erasmo possessed screamed at him to run, to flail madly through the alley until he was far away from whatever had produced that abhorrent sound. But he needed to see, needed to know if, in fact, there was anything even there. He slowly turned, heart thrashing in his chest, and recoiled at the answer.

This new demon, sickeningly gaunt, appraised him with curiosity, as if he'd never seen a being such as Erasmo before. The creature's face was barely a face at all. Instead, it was more a deformed humanoid skull with a thin layer of gray skin stretched over it.

The creature's cracked lips parted, displaying a mouthful of long and impossibly thin teeth, ending in points so sharp they were almost invisible. Unlike the demon at Bradley's, this one wore no robe, and its shriveled body horrified Erasmo. Pus-filled abscesses covered the creature's emaciated limbs. The grotesque sight made Erasmo's need to vomit urgent and unstoppable. Before he could even attempt to hold it back, a torrent of stinking bile erupted from his mouth onto the asphalt.

The atrophied demon raised a finger and pointed at him. This extended digit was as bony as the rest of its body and culminated in a long, needlelike tip. Erasmo watched as the finger trembled, and a single drop of thick, glistening liquid appeared at its razor-sharp end.

Blood.

Even through the fog of his rising panic, something about this creature struck Erasmo as oddly familiar. He tried to place it and thought he almost had for a moment, but the connection fluttered just out of mind's reach. Had he studied this demon, maybe?

Yes. Or one similar, at least. He'd spent a rainy afternoon last year with Rat researching Japanese folklore. There had been an entity they'd read about that had deeply disturbed him: gaki.

The hungry demon.

Artwork they'd found online depicted a creature consisting of skin and bones, barely there flesh covering a withered skeleton. Just like what stood in front of him now. Gaki were also eternally starving, as their hunger was never sated. Erasmo stared into the demon's eyes and saw only voracious and all-consuming desire.

But gaki also had distended stomachs, not the sunken gut this creature possessed. And their mouths were supposed to be tiny and useless, unlike this demon's large, salivating maw.

It was then the creature lunged at him, ravenous hunger in its dry, deep-socketed eyes. Erasmo turned and sprinted down the alley, the sound of his pounding shoes echoing around him. Surely he would leave the demon behind. Such a sickly looking creature wouldn't be able to run very fast. This was the last thought Erasmo had before the demon's coarse claw wrapped around his right ankle, pulling him down to the asphalt in a shrieking heap.

Erasmo twisted his body violently, managing to roll over.

The creature stood over him, warm, clumpy pus from one of its many abscesses dripping onto Erasmo's face. It then straddled him, studying his features, searching. The demon must've found what it was looking for, as it screeched in shrill triumph. It then raised both hands, splaying wide every needlelike finger.

Erasmo's eyes widened as the demon brought one of its finely pointed fingers in line with his left eyeball, slowly lowering it toward his pupil. A slight pinch formed on the side of his neck. Erasmo glanced over and saw that one of the demon's other fingers now pressed firmly against his carotid artery. This creature was going to penetrate him, to invade his body with its own putrid excretions, to take over his very existence, pathetic as it was.

And what could he do but shriek and beg the universe to intervene? He'd done nothing to deserve this. Nothing. And yet here he was, at the mercy of this creature, unable to conjure even the slightest bit of resistance. The tip of the demon's finger now made contact with the center of his eye, its spongy surface already dangerously close to giving way. Erasmo shrieked. The pinch on the side of his neck also grew in severity. Soon the weak flesh covering his artery parted, allowing entrance to this creature.

Erasmo continued to scream prayers to the night sky but understood the pointlessness of it. The universe never conspired in his favor. If anything, it actively sought to beat him down at every given opportunity. Expecting the universe to intervene now, as this withered demon penetrated him, would be ludicrous.

But then, miraculously, it did.

A noise rang out from behind them. The creature turned, its eyes searching the dark. Erasmo crawled backward, just a few inches, but enough to relieve the pressure on his neck and eyeball. He glanced at the area behind the demon. A young man lurched and stumbled down the alleyway, blind to his surroundings. The creature appraised this derelict hungrily, its eyes widening, as if in recognition.

Erasmo tried to scream at this person, to warn him of the danger, but his throat only produced a raspy wheeze. He tried again, but the young man remained oblivious to the creature hungering for him.

Maybe he could distract the demon, lure it away. Erasmo scrambled to his feet and flailed down the alley, too frightened to glance over his shoulder and see if it gave chase. But then the creature grunted ravenously behind him, close enough to tickle his left ear, and his question was answered. Erasmo ran even faster, lungs burning, off-balance and dangerously close to toppling over. The end of the alley approached and he screamed in hope, desperate to reach it, as if there were some invisible barrier that would prevent the demon from leaving.

He finally emerged onto the street, too out of sorts to tell which one, and kept running madly through the cold night. A few moments later, he spotted his car parked only a block away and almost wept. When Erasmo finally reached the Civic, he was unable to breathe, and his legs were just moments from giving way. He collapsed into the car and quickly scanned the area around him. To his astonishment and deep relief, there was no trace of the creature. Not one.

But all of this *couldn't* just be a coincidence. A demon had appeared to him, had wanted to pierce his flesh, immediately after stumbling across Vassell and his followers. He'd been so very wrong. This group did have the power to summon monsters. He'd now seen it with his own eyes, and had felt its sickly flesh against his own.

It was clear. They must've summoned this creature and sent it after him because he'd discovered their group. Which meant he still wasn't safe. That thing could manifest again at any moment. He needed help, and there was only one person he could turn to for something like this. Once again, he'd have to retrace his steps tonight. Erasmo exhaled a long sigh, started the Civic, and slid out onto the dark, lifeless road.

CHAPTER 17

ERASMO PULLED INTO the store's empty parking lot, now having second thoughts. She'd be asleep, of course, and would probably be aggravated with him for coming by so late. But he also knew how intrigued the curandera might be. Besides, his gut told him this couldn't wait until morning.

He exited the Civic and headed to the back of Alma's store. In addition to running her business here, she also lived out of it, her bed tucked into a corner surrounded by a collection of kunzite crystals. He'd once asked her what the appeal was of working and living in the same place.

The same reason people keep a gun on their nightstand, she'd said, gesturing to her roomful of talismans and medicines and stones and religious symbols. *If anything ever comes for me, I'll be ready for it.*

At the time, he'd thought she was being overly dramatic. Now he wasn't so sure.

Erasmo approached the back door, as the entrance up front was closed for the day. He was just about to knock when a noise arose from inside. His phone told him it was 3:10 a.m. He'd never known Alma to be much of a night owl.

He placed his ear to the door, its cool metal a soothing balm against his burning skin. And what he heard was unmistakable. Voices.

It was impossible to tell whose and how many, but there were definitely people talking in there, excitedly from the sound of it. He turned to leave, filled with disappointment. Maybe she'd had a friend over for a late-night visit. She wasn't unattractive after all; she was sure to have many suitors. But then what . . . go home and lay in bed, unable to sleep, fearful of the creature manifesting again?

No. He needed her. Erasmo raised his hand and gently knocked on the door. Immediately, the voices stopped. No. Not stopped. They'd morphed into harsh whispers, as if in argument. After a few moments, there was only silence. Then footsteps approached the door.

"We're closed," the curandera said, steel in her voice.

"Even for me?" he asked.

Dead silence on the other side. Was she really not going to open the door for him? His limbs trembled at this outright rejection. He felt himself teetering on the edge, dangerously close to falling backward into a bottomless black vortex, its cold vastness eager to suck him in.

But finally, a loud *thunk* broke the silence as the dead bolt retracted, and he managed to regain his mental balance. The curandera stood in the doorway, wearing a wrinkled black housedress. She didn't step aside to allow him in.

"It's late," she said. "It must be bad."

"It is. Am I interrupting something?"

"No," she said without hesitation. "I was just watching TV. Getting ready for bed though. What is it I can help you with?"

Erasmo quietly seethed that she didn't invite him inside, but he wasn't in a position to press the issue. So, standing at her door, under the mild light of the moon, he told her the entire story. Everything poured out of him, from the moment he stepped into the Soul Center to when he'd emerged from the alley, sprinting away from that emaciated creature.

The curandera stood in the doorway and regarded him with an expression that was either outright fascination or abject pity. Her perpetually tranquil face had always been difficult for him to read.

"Erasmo," she finally said, "you come to me in the middle of the night, looking haggard, stinking of vomit, with this elaborate story. What is it you're asking me for help with exactly?"

He stood in front of the curandera, unable to find any words. The urge to come over here and seek help had been so powerful, but now, no specific question came to mind.

"Studying those horrific creatures," she continued, "is more your specialty than mine."

"I . . ." he started, still at a loss. "I guess I wanted to ask if you knew what I should do."

"What you should do?" she repeated.

"Yes," he said, "about this creature they've sent after me. About any of this really."

She started to speak, paused for a moment, and then said, "Well, I think what you need above all else is a cleansing ritual."

A cleansing ritual. *Yes.* He should've thought of that before. It made perfect sense. The demon had latched on to his essence, which needed to be cleansed. Then that thing wouldn't be able to find him.

"I know just the one," he said. "The Lesser Banishing Ritual of the Pentagram. It's basic but should work. I'm embarrassed I didn't think of that myself. Sorry for coming by so late." He turned to leave, eager to conduct the ceremony before the demon had a chance to return.

"Erasmo," she called out, a strained tone to her voice. "I'm sorry for not asking earlier, but how is your grandmother doing?"

He stood perfectly still, not wanting to talk about this. Especially after everything he'd been through tonight.

"I tried everything within my power to help her," she said. "You know that, right? There's nothing else to be done."

"You could still try to—"

"No. That's dark magic. The darkest. And we don't go near it. You know that, Erasmo. It's like I told you before. Resorting to unnatural means only leads to an unnatural end."

"It wouldn't hurt to at least try—"

"Look, I've devoted my life to healing. When someone comes to me, I do my best to extend their time here. Sometimes it's for years, and others just for minutes. But every life is finite, no matter what we do. And sometimes . . ." Alma grimaced, the words clearly uncomfortable on her lips.

"Sometimes what?"

"Sometimes . . . the end is all that's left."

A sudden urge overcame him to scream at her, to beg her to stop talking. He somehow managed to bite the words down, and they crumbled to bitter ashes in his mouth.

"And once this is clear," she continued, "you have to accept that loss is coming and deal with it head-on. Because if you don't, then you might—"

"I really need to get started on this cleansing ritual," he said, turning away from her.

"Wait," she said, a hint of panic in her voice. "Erasmo, I think you should—"

"Thanks, again," he said, and walked back to his car, unable to remove his eyes from the curved moon hanging in an otherwise empty sky.

Erasmo walked into the lobby of the Emily Morgan Hotel, desperately hoping Andy was working the front desk and not stuck in the back office. Relief washed over him when he saw his friend half-asleep behind the counter.

As Erasmo approached the desk, he felt the building's immense power thrumming around him. The lobby's bland, corporate stylings and tasteful Christmas decorations did little to mask its history as one of the most haunted hotels in the world. It was like trying to put a cardigan on a gargoyle. The building's true essence still burst through, dangerous and unrestrained.

"Hey," Erasmo whispered when he reached the desk. "I need a room."

Andy started awake, almost toppling off his chair.

"Christ, man," he said, wiping at his bleary eyes. "You scared the shit out of me."

"Sorry."

Andy shook his head and sighed. "It's these damn graveyard hours they've got me working. Was trying to get some research done when I dozed off." He gestured to a book on the desk, *When Darkness Falls: Tales of San Antonio Ghosts and Hauntings.*

"Did you know the Grey Moss Inn is haunted by its first owner, Mary Howell?" Andy checked for available rooms as he talked, his thick fingers typing furiously. "Apparently she starts causing problems if the Inn isn't being run properly."

"Didn't know that," Erasmo said, a bit embarrassed at this lack of knowledge.

"Yeah. She breaks dishes and sends silverware flying across the room when she's pissed." Andy hit the Enter key with a flourish. "Okay, I got something for you," he said. "But"—his eyebrows arched high—"are you going to tell me what this is about?"

Erasmo actually very much wanted to bring Andy in on this, to spill everything and ask for his perspective. But the thought of rehashing the whole story again made him nauseous.

"I can't right now. But tell you what. If anything happens while I'm up there, I'll call you right away. Keep an eye on your phone."

This must've satisfied Andy, as he eagerly handed over the key card.

"Don't screw me on this," he said, glancing around to make sure no one was looking. "Just an hour. Two max. Not like last time, okay?"

"Sure thing," Erasmo said, taking the key card, "and thanks."

Erasmo had been in the room twenty minutes, lying in bed while attempting to calm his thoughts enough to begin. The ceremony required a clear and precise mind, but disturbing images from the last few hours continued to seep through his mental defenses.

Maybe doing some research would help ease his nerves. Besides, it certainly wouldn't hurt to learn more about what he faced. Erasmo pulled the laptop from his backpack and ran a search on the history of demon worship. Most of the results pertained to the Devil specifically, but maybe there was some information here that would shed some light on Vassell's group.

As far as he could tell, the idea of devil worship began during the Inquisition. Inquisitors were unleashed on whoever was believed to practice witchcraft and former Christians who'd given up their faith.

In 1484, Pope Innocent VIII redefined witchcraft to mean actual devil worship. Just two years later, *Malleus Maleficarum* was published. This book became a kind of guide for the brutal actions taken against whichever poor souls identified as witches or Satanists.

These articles also said that devil worship was thought to include gatherings of thirteen people, parodying Christ and his twelve apostles, and the conducting of a Black Mass. This Mass might include the Lord's Prayer said backward, the sacrifice of a baby, or sexual fornication.

Erasmo read this line again, a spasm convulsing through his gut.

The sacrifice of a baby.

He continued on, reading that the first real evidence of a devil-worshiping group came in the court of French king Louis XIV. A fortune teller conducted Black Masses to help members of the court, promising that their wishes would come true. Unfortunately for her, she was later convicted of witchcraft and executed.

Erasmo skipped ahead to information a little more recent. Sometime in the late 1950s, Anton LaVey, a former carnival worker, taught classes in the occult. A core group of his students went on to form the Church of Satan. They conducted elaborate rituals, using costumes and music in their ceremonies.

Vassell's group wore robes and detailed, hideous masks, Erasmo considered. And chanted that odd, dissonant hymn during their ceremony. Perhaps they were affiliated with the Church of Satan somehow.

After perusing a few more articles, most of which were unhelpful, he closed his laptop. From what he could gather, many experts claiming to understand the inner workings of Satanism had never actually met a Satanist, or attended a satanic gathering. Their "research" was simply a mix of old texts and pure fiction.

Then how, Erasmo wondered, was anyone to know what truly went on within these groups?

He debated whether his mind was clear enough to start the ritual. Screw it. His psyche wasn't going to stop showing him glimpses of those horrific masks, or the person underneath the city gulping down blood-vomit, or of that skeletal abomination in the alley. May as well just get on with it and hope for the best.

He reached into his pocket and took out the switchblade, which he still thought of as his grandfather's even though the old man had been dead almost five years now. A dagger was normally used for this particular ceremony, but he thought the knife would work nicely, given his personal connection to it. Erasmo got off the bed and prepared himself for the first of the four sections.

The Lesser Banishing Ritual of the Pentagram was designed by the Hermetic Order of the Golden Dawn, a secret society that operated around the turn of the twentieth century. They were obsessed with the study and practice of all things occult and paranormal, eager to uncover their mysteries. The ritual he was about to perform was probably the group's greatest accomplishment.

The Order created it in the late nineteenth century, a mix of assorted religious influences. The ceremony had been used and adapted by all types of occult practitioners over the years. It was usually used to banish unwanted forces, including lingering entities. Just as importantly though, the ritual calmed the mind and cleared negative energies, allowing whoever conducted it to be centered in the metaphysical universe.

That is what Erasmo attempted to do now as he began the first portion of the ritual. He closed his eyes and visualized his body growing larger, taller, until the top of his head scraped the room's ceiling. His breath flowed in and out of his rapidly expanding metaphysical body. Erasmo now saw himself rising above San Antonio, until the downtown buildings were simply pebbles underneath his feet. Soon, each leg was immersed in a different ocean, the cold waters of the Pacific and Atlantic nipping at his heels. Now the Earth was underneath him, tiny, but still brimming with power.

The other planets of the solar system soon became grains of sand. He lifted his hands and they slipped through his fingers with ease. Finally, the entire galaxy was but a small light glowing at his feet. He glanced above his head to see what he already knew was there, an orb of pulsing light, a gift from the source.

Erasmo raised the knife, placing its tip in the center of the orb. He then brought it down, drawing a thin beam of light to the center of his forehead, which filled his head with a luminous brilliance.

ATAH.

Erasmo slid the point of the switchblade down his body until it pointed toward the ground. The light followed, leaving a shimmering trail over his body, down to his feet and beyond.

MALKUTH.

He brought the blade up to his right shoulder, the trail of light following.

VE-GEBURAH.

Now his left shoulder.

VE-GEDULAH.

Erasmo held his hands together in front of him, as if in prayer. He visualized within his chest a brilliant, golden glow.

LE-OLAHM, AMEN.

He stood perfectly still, feeling the power of the universe, of the divine light, of the extraordinary building his physical body was contained in. After a long exhale, he placed the knife to his lower left hip.

Time to draw the pentagrams.

Erasmo faced east and walked forward until he was almost to the wall. He brought the knife above his head, then outside his lower right hip, then to his left shoulder, right shoulder, and back to the starting point. He visualized the symbol in the air, each line alight in blue flame.

He inhaled, feeling the universe's energy flowing through him, and then thrust the dagger into the middle of the flaming blue pentagram, activating it.

YOD HEH VAV HEH.

Erasmo was about to turn south and continue the drawing of the banishing pentagrams when something so unexpected happened that he dropped the switchblade.

A burst of knocking erupted from the hallway.

Erasmo stared at the door, eyes wide in shock. No one knew he was here. Except for Andy, and they'd agreed he wouldn't come up unless called.

Another explosion of knocks, this time even louder.

Shit. Could it be Vassell . . . or one of his people? Maybe they'd been following him ever since he crawled out of that manhole.

He tiptoed toward the door, took a breath, and placed his eye to the peephole. When he saw who it was, Erasmo sucked in a lungful of air, stepped away from the door, and wondered in disbelief how on earth she could possibly have found him.

CHAPTER 18

ERASMO, STILL TRYING to process who was on the other side of that door, looked through the peephole again. He hadn't been seeing things. This made absolutely no sense.

He considered remaining perfectly still, ignoring the pounding at the door until she gave up and went on her way. But another round of frantic knocking disabused him of this notion. Clearly he was going to have to let her in. Everything would be fine though. It shouldn't take long to make an excuse and then get back to the ritual. Besides, wasn't there a small part of him that was curious, even excited at who was standing out there at this very moment?

Erasmo took a jittery breath, grabbed the knob, and slowly pulled the door open.

Vero stood in front of him, arms crossed, appearing displeased at being there, even though she was the one pounding on the door demanding entrance.

"Took you long enough," she said, brushing by him.

Vero stopped a few feet in and surveyed the room, gesturing to the switchblade.

"I interrupt your knife-fighting practice or something?"

Erasmo shut the door and walked over to the switchblade, picking it up as he stared at her in shock.

"What are you doing here?" he asked. "How did you even know I was—"

"Funny thing," Vero said as she plopped down on the bed. "I was sleeping . . . you know . . . as one does when it's an ungodly hour of the night. But then I was rudely awoken by some voices outside."

Damn. That's right. She was staying out in the garage.

"Heard most of your conversation. Have to say . . . that was quite the story you told my aunt."

"Sorry we woke you," he said, "but that still doesn't explain what you're doing—"

"Aside from possibly Renata," she said, exhaling an impatient sigh, "do you know the number of truly interesting things that have happened to me since I've been in this town?"

"Well, based on the expression on your face, I'm going to guess none."

"Oh, you're a smart one, Erasmo. No wonder my aunt likes you so much. But then the gods saw fit to smile down upon me. I woke up, listened to you tell that crazy-ass story, and watched you scamper off to conduct the vanishing dance of the decagram—"

"The Lesser Banishing Ritual of the Pentagram," he corrected, annoyed at the cavalier way she described something he thought of with reverence.

"Whatever," she said. "The point is, I wasn't going to miss out on the first truly interesting thing I'd stumbled across since I got here, so I followed you."

"You shouldn't be here," he said. "Your aunt will—"

"My aunt won't be expecting me at the store for at least a few hours," she said, her tone steely and defiant. "So . . . are you going to show me this ritual or what?"

Damn. Vero clearly had no intention of leaving. Alma would be pissed if she knew about this. But what the hell was he supposed to do?

"If you think it's all a bunch of crap," he asked, "then why do you even want to see this ritual?"

"Oh, I'm not really here for the ritual," Vero said, eyes blazing. "I'm here for the crazy."

He stared at her, unsure how to take this.

"I know some people run the other way when they see something batshit about to go down. Me personally? I can't get enough of it."

Erasmo wanted to protest, to explain that all of the night's happenings were serious and real and not batshit at all. But as he stood there, Vero's eyes locked on his, the words refused to coalesce in his mouth.

"C'mon," she said. "You have to admit that investigating whether a middle-aged man sold his soul to the Devil when he was a teenager is a little out there."

"I do admit," he said, "that this case is especially abnormal."

"Sorry," Vero said, "but I need to ask. Do you *really* think it's possible what he's claiming could be true?"

"I honestly don't know. Look, I'm not some delusional paranormal hard-liner who sees dark spirits lurking in every corner. Almost every case I've worked on has *not* ended up being paranormal or occult in nature. My default assumption is that anyone claiming to have had a supernatural experience is mistaken. But I do keep an open mind while I investigate, because the ones that *have* proved to be supernatural, well . . . those were pretty damn ugly."

"Okay, fair enough," she said. "But someone thinking their house is haunted is one thing. What this guy is claiming . . . I mean, come on . . ."

"Did you know," Erasmo asked, "that Robert Johnson recorded some of his songs right here in San Antonio? Room 414 at the Gunter, not too far from here actually."

"Robert Johnson, the blues guitarist who supposedly sold his soul to the Devil in exchange for otherworldly guitar-playing skills? You can't really believe that's what happened. Even forgetting the impossibility of it for a moment, who on earth would exchange eternal torture just so they could plink steel wires really well?"

"And you don't think that people have sold their souls for *far* less?" Erasmo asked. "Haven't you ever marveled at how some can do the seemingly impossible . . . at the feats of top athletes, and world-class musicians, and those assholes who generate unimaginable wealth? You think all those people were just born lucky, with the ability to do what .000001 percent of the population can only dream of? Maybe they were, but sometimes I wonder if it's more than just happenstance and winning the talent lottery."

Vero nodded her head. Not in agreement, it seemed to him, but at least in understanding.

"That's a long way of explaining why I try to keep an open mind," he said.

An awkward silence settled over them, until Vero finally hopped off the bed.

"Well, in that case," she said, "are we going to get to the bottom of this thing or what?"

"I'm not sure what you mean," Erasmo replied, even though he was pretty sure he did.

"Let's do this," she said. "I want to join you in the investigation, even if it's just for the next few hours. After all, you helped with mine. It's only fair."

"I don't know if that's a good—"

"C'mon. I won't slow you down." She held up her right hand in a familiar gesture. "Scout's honor."

"That's the Vulcan sign for live long and prosper."

"Whatever . . . close enough."

Erasmo started to object again but stopped himself. Arguing with her was pointless. Vero had followed him here, and would probably follow him again even if he said no. And if he was being completely honest, the idea did excite him a bit. Maybe even more than a bit. Vero thrummed with energy, with directness, with subtle power she wielded with ease. The exact opposite of how he currently felt. Would it be so bad to have her close, to siphon off some of her light for himself? Not to mention, she must've picked up a ton of useful knowledge from Alma, even if she didn't believe it all herself.

"Okay," he said. "But honestly, I don't even know what my next step is. I got through enough of the ritual to cleanse the negative energy around me. But now . . ."

"Well," Vero said, "I have a suggestion. You said Vassell was with those masked cult members, participating in that ritual. Are you absolutely sure it was him?"

"One hundred percent."

"Well, then he's obviously involved in all this and knows *exactly* what's happened to that baby."

"I already tried asking him about Bradley," Erasmo said, "but he shut me down. There's no way he'd be any more forthcoming now."

"That's because you asked nicely. This time we're going to try something different."

"What do you mean?" he asked, his palms suddenly sweaty.

Vero stared at him with a frightening intensity, the muscles underneath her jaw flexing wildly.

"Do you know where we can get a gun?"

CHAPTER 19

THE IDEA OF looking backward repulsed Erasmo. What was the point of lingering over the past, retracing where you'd been, what you'd lost? May as well slice your palm open with a rusty blade and sit under the moonlight, watching it bleed. Every day he woke up and told himself that proceeding forward, with a callous disregard for what had come before was the only way to survive.

He noted the irony of this as they pulled up to Bradley's. This was the second time he'd been to this house in one night, just like the Soul Center. Perhaps the universe was laughing at him as it forced him to revisit these places he'd rather never see again.

"Looks empty," Vero said. "Guess the cops have gone for the night."

"Seems like it," he agreed. "Since Bradley is in custody and his wife's out of town, we should have the place to ourselves. His wife is surely on her way back though."

"And you're positive there's a gun in there?" she asked, eyebrow raised.

"Yeah. Bradley said he grabbed a Smith & Wesson from his study when he heard noises in the baby's room."

"Well, in that case, let's do it, then," she said, jumping out of the Civic.

"Wait! We should—"

But it was too late. Vero jogged through Bradley's front yard, surveying the lavish neighborhood to make sure no one was milling around at this time of night. She headed straight for the massive wooden fence that surrounded the backyard, climbing over it with ease. Erasmo ran after her, out of breath when he finally reached the fence. He tried pulling himself up and over as she had, but he could barely get his feet off the ground.

"Christ," Vero muttered from the other side after his third attempt.

Her arm descended from above and Erasmo grabbed hold, momentarily enjoying her gentle strength as she pulled him up and over.

The lawn was so picturesque, Erasmo at first thought it must be fake, some kind of artificial turf painted a deep emerald. But the rich, earthy smell wafting from the ground told him otherwise. The yard was completely bare of any decorations or furnishings, except for one item. A large shed stood with double doors in the far corner, almost hidden in the shadows.

"We should be prepared in case he keeps his gun in a safe," Vero said. "Those little electronic ones aren't shit. You can usually bust them open pretty easily. Let's see if he keeps any tools in that shed."

Erasmo was about to ask how on earth she knew about breaking into gun safes, but Vero was already jogging away.

"It's unlocked," she said when he caught up to her, pulling the shed doors open with ease.

They entered and glanced around. Finally, some luck. Bradley did keep his tools here. Saws, hammers, wrenches, and more all hung neatly on the wall, an eager army waiting to be deployed. They looked pristine, as if none of them had seen even a single use. In fact, the entire shed was immaculate, as if it had just been assembled. The only sign of life was a stout refrigerator humming against the back wall.

Vero inspected the tools, pulling several hammers off their hooks.

"Perfect," she said as he approached, "We should be able to—"

BANG

They both jumped at the sudden sound. The quality of the light had changed, the shed somehow darker than before. It took Erasmo a moment to realize what had happened.

Someone had slammed the doors shut. Someone who was still outside. The sound of scraping metal floated in the air. Erasmo tried to open the doors, but they wouldn't budge. He shoved harder and then slammed his shoulder into them with the same result. Shit. Whoever was out there must've slipped something between the two door handles. Like a crowbar maybe, which was preventing the doors from opening. Fear wrapped its cold, mutilated fingers around his throat.

They were trapped.

He strained to hear what was happening outside, hoping to glean anything that might help them. But all he heard was a long, muffled sigh, and the sound of heavy footsteps walking away into the cool, still night.

CHAPTER 20

"ISN'T THERE ANYONE you can call to get us out of here?"

Erasmo peered down at his phone, again ashamed at the meager list of contacts he now scrolled through. A name gave him pause, and he stared at it for a few moments.

RAT.

He'd come running, no doubt. But there was no way Erasmo could call him. No goddamn way. He continued scrolling.

"If you don't get someone out here I'm going to have to call my aunt, and that will be a guaranteed disaster—"

"Wait. I know someone who'll come," he said, glancing down at the name. Erasmo fired off a text with a quick explanation and the address, afraid the insanity of the situation might result in a nonanswer. But he'd barely had time to slip his phone into his pocket when the response came.

On my way

"Just have to sit tight," he said.

"Somehow," Vero said after a few moments, "I didn't think my day would include being trapped in some rich guy's shed."

"Well," he said, flashing his light around the room, "you said you were looking for some crazy. Guess you found it."

Erasmo walked through the shed again, looking for anything unusual. This property had been the site of a kidnapping after all. Who knows where the perpetrators might have wandered into. But everything looked as it should: tools perfectly hung, organized shelves, and pristine floors. No drops of blood, no scraps of cloth, nothing to indicate anyone had even been in here recently.

He eyed the small refrigerator sitting under a window against the far wall. Seemed a bit odd to have one in here. Especially since the shed didn't appear to get much use. He approached it, a knot forming in his gut.

"Hope your friend gets here soon," Vero said, busy studying some of the tools. "It's cold as hell in here."

Erasmo reached for the handle, its metal cool and slick under his fingertips. He pulled the door open, a soft hiss escaping. His heart beat faster as he crouched down to peer inside. But as his eyes quickly scanned the small shelves, he was relieved to see the refrigerator was completely empty.

He closed the door and stood up, a little embarrassed. It was silly to think something ghastly might've been inside. His nerves were making him jump at shadows that weren't even there.

Erasmo peered out the shed's window, glancing up just in time to see the moon slip behind a smattering of clouds. He released a long sigh, and a thin layer of condensation formed on the glass. He began to turn to Vero, but something odd in the condensation caught his eye.

He studied the glass for a moment, surprised to see distinct lines. They formed a pattern, triangles maybe, but it was hard to tell for sure. Erasmo took a deep breath and blew on the entire window. A full image then formed on the glass, and he stopped breathing.

A perfectly drawn pentagram.

"Vero," he called, wanting to make sure that what he saw was really there.

She walked over and stared at the symbol, mouth hanging open.

"What the hell?" she asked. "This doesn't make any sense."

"Someone must've been in here recently," he said. "And drew this on the window with their finger."

"Why on earth would they do that?"

"That's a good question," he said. "To bless this property with their Master's symbol? To mark their territory? Maybe they drew it out of boredom while they waited."

"Waited for what?"

"While they waited to sneak into Bradley's room and scare him," he said. "Or while they waited to take the kid maybe."

"Goddamn lunatics," Vero said. She began pacing around the shed, hands clenching and unclenching. "So, here's another question I can't wrap my head around. Who the hell would even want to trap us in here?"

Erasmo had been wondering this very thing. So far though, he hadn't been able to think of a single person who'd even know they were in here, much less want to lock them in.

"I'm at a loss," Erasmo said, his mind continuing to grasp for an answer.

"Have you considered," Vero said, "Bradley's wife?"

"His wife?"

"Think about it," Vero said. "She just *happens* to be out of town while all of this is going down? Convenient."

"You think," he said, "that *she* arranged for her own child to be taken?"

"It's a thought," Vero said. "Maybe she's a part of this brainwashed cult. Maybe she got back a little early and saw us poking around, decided to hold us here for a bit while she figured out what to do."

"This is the baby's *mother* we're talking about. What kind of mom would abandon her child, would sacrifice him to . . . to . . . ?"

A sudden wave of dizziness overtook him. The room flipped over, rotating at a sickening speed as his legs buckled and he toppled to the floor.

"Erasmo!"

"I'm okay," he said, managing to slowly sit up. "Just haven't been feeling well lately."

Vero plopped down next to him. "Let's sit here and rest," she said. "It's been a crazy night for you."

Erasmo shook his head and this helped clear it a bit. He was still starving to death, which was probably the reason for his dizziness. When he placed his hand down, he felt Vero's warm, comforting hand underneath it.

"Sorry," he said, drawing away in embarrassment.

"It's okay," she said, guiding his hand back. "You can leave it."

His head swam again, but this time he wasn't sure if it was from fatigue and hunger or from being so close to Vero.

"Since we're stuck in here for a while," she said, "do you mind if I ask you a question?"

"Shoot."

"Do you ever have any doubts?"

"About what?"

"You know, all of this . . . the paranormal . . . the occult. Don't you ever wonder if none of it is real? If everything you've ever read is nothing more than meaningless words on a page?"

"It's like I told you before," he said. "I think most people who believe they're having a paranormal experience are just jumping at shadows. But that doesn't mean the supernatural isn't real. And it's more than just what I've studied. I've seen things . . . felt things."

"I'm sure that's true," Vero said. "But have you ever considered that what you saw and felt were nothing more than misfiring neurons? Or that your experiences were self-fulfilling . . . a result of what you expected, of what you needed? It's easy to fool yourself into seeing what you want, when you want to see something bad enough."

"I know all about that," he said after a long moment.

"Yeah?"

"Yeah. In the past, I've . . . blocked some stuff out. And believed some things had happened which really didn't. Defense mechanism, I guess. Still do my best to guard against it. But sometimes I have to check myself, make sure I'm certain of what's really going on."

"You'll have to tell me some of those stories sometime."

"You're quite the prober," Erasmo said. "Do you ask everyone to share their darkest moments with you?"

"Nah," she said, "only strange guys I'm trapped in a shed with."

Despite their current situation, the slightest of grins crept onto Erasmo's face. "So, what about you? I barely know anything about your life."

Vero stiffened next to him, and he immediately regretted asking.

"What," she said, "you want to hear some sob story so you can try to deduce the dark secrets of my psyche?"

"No, I was just curious. I didn't mean to—"

"Relax," she said, but now letting go of his hand. "Guess it's only fair that I share, too. It's just been awhile since I told it."

"Told what?"

Vero turned to face him, her eyes somehow managing to glisten in the dim light.

"My sob story, of course."

CHAPTER 21

"I WOULDN'T EVEN be in San Antonio if my father were still alive," she said. "He always stood up for me . . . for what I wanted. He would've told my mom and aunts to let *me* decide if I want to learn about all this nonsense. But he's not here to do that anymore.

"My father understood me in a fundamental way no one else did. Everyone was always trying to change me, to crack my core self into small pieces and rebuild it into something better. But not my dad. He just allowed me to be. And no matter how badly I messed up, I only ever saw understanding in his eyes, not disgust or disappointment. He was truly the most decent man I've ever known."

Erasmo's skin prickled as he listened to Vero praise her father, his inherent goodness. He couldn't help but think of his own, whose traits and qualities he knew practically nothing of. He imagined Vero's dad, dark-haired like her maybe, with compassionate eyes and a friendly face. He then imagined his father, slunk down in a corner, eyes rolled back, a needle sticking out of his infected arm. A sliver of vomit crept up Erasmo's throat, but he managed to swallow it back down.

"Don't get me wrong. I love my mother, but my dad and I had an unbreakable connection. Sometimes I'd lay awake at night, unable to sleep because I was so fearful of something happening, of him not coming home. And then one day, he didn't."

"Hey, you don't have to tell me if you don't—"

"It's okay," she said. "I want to." Vero exhaled a shaky breath and continued. "My father drove a taxi in Arcelia. Not much money in that, but it kept a roof over our heads. One day, two extremely drunk young men got into his taxi, wanting to go to the fair our town holds every year. During the drive, they discussed a hit that would soon be carried out on a young woman who'd crossed their boss. We later found out they were members of Los Ardillos, a violent drug gang based out of La Montaña. After my father dropped the two men off, he went straight to the police station to report what he'd heard."

"But aren't the police over there corrupt?"

"There are corrupt police everywhere, Erasmo. But yes, I agree, it wasn't a wise idea. But I understand why he did this. The officer he went to see was Oscar Portillo, his childhood friend. They were like . . ." Vero trailed off, as if the word burned her tongue.

"They were like brothers," she finally said. "The two of them grew up together, and my father would've trusted him with his life. And that's exactly what he did the moment he stepped into that station. He told Oscar what happened, gave him descriptions of those two men, and then went home and told my mother everything I just told you. My father was sure he'd made the right decision. He told my mom he wouldn't have been able to live with himself if he let that woman get murdered without even trying to stop it."

Vero slowly rose, as if it were wrong to say whatever came next while sitting on the floor. He immediately missed her presence, a dark void now next to him instead.

"They found his body on the side of the road in Palos Altos," she said, her voice measured but shaky. "It was crammed into an ice chest. Every limb had been hacked into pieces. They decapitated him, too, leaving his head displayed on top of the ice chest. But even that wasn't the worst part."

Vero shivered, her teeth momentarily chattering. Erasmo wanted to tell her to stop, that he didn't want to hear anymore. But it was too late for that.

"His face . . . his kind, beautiful face . . . had been peeled off. They left the flayed skin just lying there on the ground. When first responders found it, insects had already eaten away most of his cheeks. And during the autopsy, two of his fingers were found stuffed down his throat. A warning to anyone else who might say things they shouldn't."

Vero exhaled a shaky breath, but her face was pure stone.

"And now here I am in San Antonio, being forced to study something I hate but dreading going back to Arcelia because of what I lost there. All of it did teach me an important lesson, though."

"And what's that?"

"It taught me—"

The sound of footsteps sinking into plush grass approached.

"Your friend?" she whispered. "Or is it—"

"Are you in there?" a soft, trembling voice asked from outside.

"Yes!" Erasmo said. "We're here. Can you get us out?"

"I think so," the voice said. "There's a tire iron jammed inside the handles. Let me try to slide it out."

The same scraping noises he'd heard earlier spread through the room, along with a few occasional grunts. Erasmo worried the tire iron might be jammed in too tight, but then the double doors swung open, and a sweaty, familiar face peered in.

"Hey there," Ashley said, eyes blazing with excitement. "Need a hand?"

"That's quite a story," Ashley said, even though he'd only told her they'd gotten trapped while following a lead. He felt a pang of remorse at using her twice now, once to run the background report on Gemma, and now to come rescue them in the middle of the night.

"Really appreciate you coming," he said.

"No sweat. I mean, this is actually kind of awesome." Ashley peered at them, eyes wide. "So, what's next? Are you going to try and figure out who trapped you in here? I can help—"

"No, we've had enough for one night," he said. "Just going to head home now. But I'll let you know if anything comes up. Promise."

"Oh . . . okay," Ashley said, the wounded look on her pale, perfectly oval face hard to miss. "Guess I'll get home, then."

"Before you leave," Vero said, looking troubled, "I was a little curious about something."

"What's that?" Ashley asked.

"It's just . . ." Vero said. "I was wondering how you managed to get here so fast."

"So fast? I don't—"

"Erasmo *just* texted you, and yet somehow you're already here. It's almost like you were already nearby or something."

"Well, in fact," Ashley said, splotches of crimson rapidly spreading over her face, "I *was* nearby, seeing as how my apartment complex is just a few miles away." She turned and began marching through the yard, the force of her stomps creating indentations in the lawn. "If I'd known getting here so fast was going to be a problem," she said over her shoulder, "I would've taken my sweet time getting your asses out of that hole."

The two of them watched as Ashley exited through the gate, slamming it shut behind her. After a few moments of uncomfortable silence, Vero finally spoke.

"So," she said, "are we going to get this gun or what?"

CHAPTER 22

AS IT TURNED out, finding the gun wasn't a problem at all. They'd checked all the entry points and got lucky with a window on the right side of the house. It slid open easily, and within moments, they were bounding up the stairs to the study. After a quick search, they'd found a small gun safe tucked inside one of the desk drawers. As she'd promised, Vero managed to break it open, needing just a few well-placed blows with a hammer.

The two of them were silent on the drive to the Soul Center, neither one daring to speak of what they were about to do. Now sitting in the parking lot, Erasmo glared down at the gun, undeniably fearful of the energy pulsating from it. Until now, he'd never held one in his hands, and the sensation was different than he'd imagined it would be. A flurry of images showing him what the gun could do . . . of what *he* could do with its immense power, flashed through his head.

And those images frightened him.

"Remember," Vero said, "it's for show only. We're just going to use it to scare him into talking. Don't even *think* about pulling the trigger unless something goes horribly wrong."

He nodded, caressing the gun.

"So, having said that . . . grab the top and pull back."

Erasmo did as he was told but nothing happened.

"You're going to have to pull a lot harder than that," Vero said, slightly annoyed.

It took a few tries, but the top finally slid backward, a satisfying *click* his reward.

"Okay, there's a bullet in the chamber now and it's ready to fire. This gun has no safety, so if you pull the trigger, it will most definitely go bang. Be careful."

Erasmo nodded, his skin covered with a light sheen of cold sweat. "If something happens in there—"

If something happens in there, I've got this," Vero said, patting the hammer she'd used to break open the gun safe.

They took in a long, simultaneous breath, opened their doors, and stepped out into the empty parking lot.

"There's a window above the back door," he said as they went around the side. "I was going to use it to get in earlier, before I noticed the manhole cover."

When they reached the rear, Vero eyeballed the window. "I can squeeze through that," she said. "Give me a boost."

Erasmo placed his hands together and knelt down. She planted her left foot on his laced fingers and whispered, "Now."

He lifted as hard as he could and Vero ascended as if weightless. At first, he was surprised at how easy she'd been to lift, but then saw she was pulling herself up using a ledge below the window. She'd just needed a small boost to reach it.

Vero tried to shove the window up, but it wouldn't budge. With no hesitation, she then smoothly slid the hammer from her waistband and smashed the glass, shards of it raining down around him. She unlocked and opened it, then wriggled through the opening, disappearing from view. Seconds later, a loud *thunk* emanated from behind the door and it swung open, a grim-faced Vero behind it.

"Let's go," she said.

They crept down the narrow hallway, using the light from their phones to guide them. Erasmo had no idea if Vassell was actually here, asleep on that dingy cot, but they had to at least check. If the old man was nowhere to be found, then tomorrow would be a long day of staking out this shithole and waiting for him to show. But his gut told him Vassell might be around. After all, that son of a bitch had to sleep sometime.

They quickly approached the door to his office on their left. Not even the slightest bit of light seeped from the room. Either Vassell wasn't in there, or he was fast asleep, nestled in complete darkness. After reaching the door, they stopped in front of it and stared at each other, unsure what to do. Erasmo felt pleading in his eyes as he gazed at Vero, even though he wasn't quite sure what he was even pleading for.

Vero reached over and squeezed his shoulder, rigid determination on her face. He trembled, now energized, as if she'd somehow infused him with her own vast power simply by touching him. She nodded, eyes still locked on his, and he knew they could do this.

Erasmo grabbed the doorknob and turned, praying the spindle wouldn't make any noise. It didn't. He carefully pushed the door open, bracing for the squeak of a rusty hinge, but it opened smoothly and without a sound. He peered into the room and almost gasped at what he saw.

Vassell lay on the threadbare cot in the corner, eyes closed and lost in sleep.

He tiptoed in, completely unsure of what to do next. Deep regret at not thinking this through beforehand immediately struck him. Should he scream at Vassell to wake up, gun aimed at his head? Should he tie him down so the old man couldn't move? While his mind furiously tried to decide, his body seemed to make the decision for him.

Erasmo found himself glaring down at Vassell's weathered face, the barrel of the gun gently pressed against the old man's forehead. He felt disconnected from the action, as if it were someone else entirely performing it.

"Vassell."

The old man didn't move.

"Wake up," he said, now shoving the barrel against his forehead.

This time, Vassell's eyes flew open. The old man blinked a few times as he stared at Erasmo, clearly trying to process what was happening.

"Mr. Cruz," he finally said, calmly and without the slightest trace of panic. "I take it that our earlier meeting didn't end to your satisfaction."

"Which meeting, *asshole*?" Erasmo asked, a sudden surge of anger coursing through him. "The one where you lied about being involved in all this, or the one where I saw you pour pig's blood down your goddamn throat?"

The muscles under Vassell's face tensed. "I think," he said after a moment, "that I underestimated you, Mr. Cruz. And that's not a mistake I often make."

"I don't give a shit what you think. I want information. And if you don't give it to me right now, I'm going to put a bullet in you."

"I see," Vassell said, eyebrows raised. "If you don't mind me saying, Mr. Cruz, I think it's fairly obvious from the way you're holding it that you have little experience with pistols. I—"

"You're right," Erasmo said. "I don't. But I'm fairly sure that I know how to pull this back."

He placed his already trembling finger on the trigger, caressing it.

Vassell swallowed hard, his large Adam's apple undulating under his sweaty throat.

"I believe so, too," he said after a moment, his eyes locked on Erasmo's finger.

"Where's the baby?" Erasmo asked, again shoving the gun against the old man's forehead.

"I'm . . . sorry to say that he's gone," Vassell said. "And before you ask, there's absolutely no way to get him back."

"Bullshit," Erasmo said.

"I apologize, but it's true. Our Master has him now. I commend your tenacity, but believe me when I say you're at the end of the road. Our Master will never—"

"Summon him," Erasmo said.

"What?" Vassell asked, incredulous.

"Perform an evocation. Right now. And when he appears, you're going to ask him to return the child."

"Mr. Cruz . . . you don't know what you're asking. This isn't something to be taken lightly. He might kill all of us just for awakening him."

"Believe me when I tell you," he said, "that I don't care in the slightest if I die tonight."

Vassell studied Erasmo's face, as if now seeing him for the first time. "I do believe you mean that," he whispered, a hint of fear in his voice.

"You're going to summon this demon. Right goddamn now."

The old man nodded and slowly sat up. "All right, then. If you insist, Mr. Cruz. We need to go across the hall. That's where I conduct the ceremonies."

"Okay," Erasmo said, keeping the gun trained on him. "Don't do anything stupid."

The old man rose from his cot and for the first time noticed Vero in the doorway. She stood perfectly still, warily observing them, her fingers caressing the hammer's handle.

"Hello, young miss," Vassell said, each drawn out syllable infused with unmistakable hunger. "If I may say, you're far too enchanting to keep company with this poor, misguided youngster. I—"

"Don't talk to her," Erasmo said, again fingering the trigger.

Vassell nodded, hands raised as if in surrender, and led them across the hall to the other room. After they walked in, he motioned to the interlocking rubber mat on the floor.

"I need to remove this."

Erasmo nodded, and Vassell began pulling away pieces of the mat, soon revealing a drawing underneath. Despite everything that had happened tonight, despite the reason they were even here, Erasmo felt a tickle in his belly. Nerves? No. He knew better. Excitement.

Yes, he'd read the grimoires, along with other books that claimed to know the secrets of summoning demons and other damned beings. But reading and researching was not *doing*, as his failure in the garage had amply demonstrated.

But Vassell, for all of his lies, all of his manipulations, had done it. At least, it sure seemed that way. Bradley's life had changed considerably after the Black Mass Vassell had conducted. This fact in and of itself didn't prove anything, of course. But taking into account the demon he'd seen at Bradley's, what he'd seen of Vassell and his cult underneath the city, the monstrous creature in the alley . . . No, at this point, all the evidence supported that this old man possessed the rarest gift of all.

"How did you learn to summon him?" Erasmo blurted out. He was curious, of course, how such a vile person had managed such an extraordinary feat.

And the information might be useful later if—

He banished this thought as quickly as it had arisen.

"It's quite an interesting story," Vassell said, continuing to remove the mat. "I usually wouldn't be inclined to say. But given that you're pointing a gun at me, who am I to refuse?

"The ugly truth is that I'd gone through most of my life lonely and aimless. My mother could never stay out of jail, and my father had left long before to pursue something more interesting than raising me. Most of my childhood was spent bouncing around violent foster homes. As I got older, I found myself adrift, searching for something I couldn't even define." The old man turned to Erasmo and glared at him, his left eye twitching. "Certainly you can understand that, can't you?" Vassell turned back to putting the mat away.

"One day I'd found myself scrounging for scraps in an alley, with no one to turn to for help. As I forced myself to swallow a rotting apple, gagging on its putridness, I'd reached a low point and knew I needed some kind of guidance.

"But from where? I'd always had an aversion to religion. It had never seemed to actually help anyone around me and was clearly infested with fraudsters and con men. But I needed some kind of path forward, so I began to research various religions, hoping that one might sit right with me.

"I found the mainstream religions bland and banal, almost naïve and childish in their understanding of the universe. Texts and philosophies that might be considered 'fringe' by the uneducated drew my attention, and I buried myself in researching them. And once I descended that rabbit hole, there was no going back.

"An intriguing work, referenced in several books in a hushed manner but with great admiration, drew my attention. It supposedly held many secrets and divine knowledge of a sacred being. I became obsessed and spent countless hours scouring libraries, antique bookstores, and estate sales. Until finally, one glorious day, I found the text I'd been searching for. In truth, I had to resort to an obscene act of violence to obtain it, but this was in the service of a greater good. And when I finally read the sacred book, the words within set me free.

"In accordance with its teachings, I sought to spread His word, and so the Soul Center was born. It serves as a gentle way to ease recruits in over time before approaching them with His truth."

The old man removed the last piece of mat, revealing in full what Erasmo already knew was underneath: a summoning circle.

"And yes," Vassell said, "the book even taught me how to contact Him."

The circle was less intricate than he'd imagined. In fact, there wasn't much to it at all. Aside from the actual circle, its only other feature was two perfect triangles. One sat directly in the middle of the circle, and the other a few feet outside of it. His face must've betrayed the surprise and slight disappointment he felt.

"This isn't the movies, Mr. Cruz," Vassell said. "There is no benefit to adorning the circle with superfluous nonsense. The only thing that matters is love and absolute devotion."

"Love and devotion for what?" he asked.

"Well . . . for the creature you're summoning, of course."

Vassell walked over to a small desk in the corner and rummaged through one of its drawers. After a moment, he held up a razor blade. "Part of proving your love," he said, pulling the top of his nightshirt down while locking eyes with Erasmo.

He placed the blade against his chest, a fat drop of blood forming immediately. "You can't just stand there and light candles and wave incense around like an idiot," the old man said as he slid the blade across his wrinkled skin in smooth, practiced movements. Vassell maintained perfect eye contact, never flinching once as he carved deeply into his own skin.

"You must give a piece of yourself each time you summon your beloved. *That's* what it takes." Vassell slid the razor over his skin one last time, finishing with a dramatic flick of his wrist, as if he'd just concluded a magic trick.

Drops of blood flew from the edge of the razor, landing on the old man's pale face. When Vassell placed the blade down, Erasmo finally saw what he'd carved into his chest: a sigil. He studied the lines and clusters of circles and sharp angles, immediately recognizing which demon it belonged to.

"Now . . ." Vassell said, eyes flickering with eagerness. "Let's begin."

The old man entered the summoning circle, taking his place inside the triangle. He bowed his head for a few moments, and then in a booming voice unleashed a torrent of perfectly enunciated Latin phrases. Some were familiar to Erasmo, but others he didn't recognize at all. Then Vassell bellowed a chant that Erasmo did recognize in full.

"Dies irae, dies illa
Solvet Saeclum in favilla
Teste Satan cum sibylla.
Quantos tremor est futurus
Quando Vindex est venturus
Cuncta stricte discussurus.
Dies irae, dies illa!"

Erasmo tightened his grip on the gun and stroked the trigger. Maybe Vassell had made a mistake. Maybe—

"Sanctus Satanas, Sanctus
Dominus Diabolus Sabaoth.
Satanas—venire!
Satanas—venire!

Ave, Satanas, ave Satanas.
Tui sunt caeli,
Tua est terra,
Ave Satanas!"

Erasmo scrutinized Vassell as he continued the chant, his arms gesticulating wildly. Sweat poured from his now red face, fat drops hanging from his nose. Finally, after several minutes, the old man abruptly stopped mid-sentence. He appeared exhausted as he turned to Erasmo.

"It's not working," he said, out of breath. "This happens occasionally. It's possible that He's predisposed with other, more pressing matters. Or perhaps it's me. My focus may not have been sufficient. I'm not used to performing an invocation at gunpoint."

Erasmo stared at Vassell, trembling. A mental image of Bradley's child shrieking, desperate for the comfort of his mother, flashed through his head. A bone-melting fury spread inside of him. These people thought they could just play God with this child's life? That they could give it away as they pleased? The entitlement, the selfishness, both astounded and enraged him. His face blazed so hot that, for a moment, the world around him wavered. But his fury brought him back from the edge.

"I don't think there's much sense in continuing," the old man said, shrugging his slight shoulders.

"Okay," Erasmo said, nodding as if in agreement, now knowing what needed to be done.

He walked up to Vassell, placed the barrel of the gun against the old man's left hand, and pulled the trigger.

CHAPTER 23

"SON OF A bitch!" Vassell screamed, staring in wide-eyed disbelief at the bloody, ragged hole in his hand.

Erasmo stood there, ears ringing, incredulous he'd actually shot someone. It seemed impossible he'd do such a thing, but the old man's maimed hand proved otherwise. He tried to fight through the shock and get the answers they came for.

"Where's the baby?" Erasmo asked as his temples throbbed in a disorienting rhythm. He turned to Vero, who stood on the opposite side of the room, her face drained of color but her eyes blazing. He waited for her to tell him to stop, that he'd taken it too far. She didn't.

"I did what you asked!" Vassell screamed. "I tried as hard as I could!"

"Did you?" Erasmo asked, pointing to the symbol carved in Vassell's chest. "Then tell me . . . what demon does that sigil represent?"

Even in the excruciating pain he must have felt, the old man's eyes narrowed in surprise.

"I . . . this sigil belongs to my Master," he said. "A fearsome demon. He—"

"You're lying," Erasmo said. "That's Morax's sigil."

Vassell froze, surprised, and appeared unsure of what to say next. He blinked for a few moments, staring blankly at Erasmo. Then he finally spoke.

"Yes, you're right," he said. "It is indeed Morax's sigil. He is the demon who we worship. Morax is a powerful entity—"

"Morax teaches goddamn astronomy," Erasmo said. "*This* is the entity you claim took the child? *This* is the entity that you worship above all others and make blood sacrifices to?"

"Morax is not to be underestimated," Vassell said. "You don't comprehend his true nature."

"Is that so?" Erasmo said. "Tell me, then, what were those words you were chanting to summon him?"

"Those," Vassell said, "are ancient verses passed down—"

"Bullshit!" Erasmo said. "Those are generic, run-of-the-mill satanic chants that can be found online and won't summon a goddamn thing."

"That's not true. I—"

"You know what I think?" Erasmo said. "I think you put on a show, that you wanted me to believe you were actually trying, so we'd go away. I think that you made all of this look as authentic as possible, with the circle, and the blood, and the chanting, assuming I wouldn't know the difference. But I *do*, asshole."

Vassell's eyes narrowed into barely visible slits. "I see," he said after a long moment, his voice now tinged with both anger and confusion. "When you said you were an investigator, I assumed you were just an ambitious youngster who did nothing more than locate people. But you're obviously more than that. And it's clear you possess specialized knowledge. However, you truly *don't* understand what's going on here. A deal made with our Master extracts a great price and—"

"I understand," Erasmo said, "that unless you tell me the truth, I'm going to put a bullet through your other hand."

"Look there's no way that I—"

Another image of Bradley's screaming, terrified child flashed through Erasmo's head. He took a step forward and placed the gun's barrel against Vassell's uninjured hand.

"*STOP!*" the old man screamed. "I'll tell you what you want."

"Now!"

"Okay," Vassell said. "All right. At least let me wrap this up first." He slid off his nightshirt and gently wrapped it around his mangled hand. As he did so, drops of blood from his chest slid down his pasty white torso, coming to a sudden stop at his belly.

Erasmo was at first confused as to why the blood acted so strangely. But then he took a closer look at Vassell's body and understood. The old man's stomach was covered with thick, fibrous scar tissue. Erasmo wondered what accident might have befallen him, but then realized this hadn't been from an accident at all. The scar tissue formed a pattern. In fact, it wasn't just a pattern.

"That's a sigil," Erasmo said, gesturing to Vassell's maimed flesh. "But . . . it's not one I'm familiar with."

"That is because you obtain all your information from books."

Erasmo wanted to press him on this strange sigil, but there was no time.

"Just tell me where the baby is."

"Okay," Vassell said. "But before I tell you the truth, you have to promise me something."

"And what's that?"

"You have to promise," the old man said, "that after I explain what happened . . . you won't kill me."

Erasmo's stomach spasmed, threatening to eject the noxious bile simmering in his gut. He needed to hear the truth but was terrified of whatever Vassell was about to say. He felt a sudden urge to wrap his hands around the old man's throat, killing the nascent words in their womb before they had a chance to be born. He shook this impulse away and steeled himself.

"Okay," he said. "I promise."

Vassell grimaced before he spoke. Erasmo couldn't tell if his distress was from the wound in his hand or from the words he was seconds away from speaking.

"We needed money," the old man said softly.

"Money?" Erasmo asked. "I don't . . . what the hell are you talking about?"

"Our group . . . it needs money for various activities. To maintain properties that we own, to carry out different projects, and most importantly, to spread the word of our savior and recruit new members to worship Him."

"What the hell does that have to do with—"

"We took the baby," Vassell said, "so that Bradley would give us money for his safe return."

"That doesn't make any sense. How would—"

"It's simple, really," he said. "Several years ago, in dire need of funds, we came up with the idea of tracking down individuals who'd attended our masses. Specifically, those who had accepted the pact we offered. The plan was to find a few who had done very well in life, and then . . ."

"Then what?" Erasmo asked, stomach lurching. He knew what the old man's answer was going to be, but needed to hear it.

"Then," he said, "we fooled those idiots into thinking that *we* were responsible for their success." Vassell grinned, unable to help himself. "And that they owed us everything."

Immense pressure built under Erasmo's skull, and his legs threatened to dissipate underneath him. A scam. The whole thing had been nothing but a goddamn scam from the beginning. He should've known. But instead, he'd believed that what Bradley had said might actually be true. In fact, up until a few moments ago, he thought this pathetic old man might actually conjure a demon from Hell. Idiot.

"Bradley's not the first one," Vassell said. "We've done it before. Quite successfully."

"I still don't understand how you were going to get money from him."

"Well," the old man said, "I can tell you what was *supposed* to happen. Bradley was going to receive a call informing him there was a way to get his child back. If he wired fifty thousand dollars into the account number we provided, we would choose a different child as a tribute to our Master. After we got the money, we'd tell Bradley where to find the boy, and move on to the next person."

"Victim," Erasmo said. "You mean the next victim."

"They entered into the agreement willingly—"

"You said that's what was *supposed* to happen. What went wrong?"

"Isn't it obvious?" Vassell said. "You did."

Erasmo's breath left his body as if he'd been punched in the chest, and found himself unable to draw another one.

"Me?"

"You showed up at Bradley's and called the police, didn't you? It's not possible to ask a man sitting in jail for money. We thought about waiting for him to get out, but too much attention has been called to the situation already. The risk was too great. Our leader made the decision to move on."

"Move on . . . what the hell does that mean?" Erasmo asked, his chest still clenched tight.

"It's over," Vassell said. "Since we had no other use for the child, we summoned our Master and performed the sacred ritual."

"Ritual? I don't—"

"Mr. Cruz, I believe you understand perfectly well what I mean. Do you really need to hear me say it?"

"Yes," Erasmo said, his voice catching on the word.

Vassell nodded, a slight grin emerging on the corner of his mouth.

"Very well," he said, eyes twitching in his sockets. "Thanks to your unfortunate interference . . . we sacrificed the child to our Master an hour ago."

CHAPTER 24

ERASMO STUMBLED OUT into the parking lot, immediately unleashing a torrent of bile. The stink of his innards made him vomit again, even more forcefully this time. He remained bent over, hands on knees, and watched as his tears fell into the clumpy yellow mess below.

"Hey," Vero said from behind, sounding severely shaken but still in control of herself. "Try to pull yourself together. We need to get out of here. I should probably drive." She reached into his pocket and took the keys out.

Erasmo managed to lurch to the Civic and open the passenger door, falling inside just as his legs were about to give way. Vero slid into the driver's seat, and they sat in silence for a moment, the only sound Erasmo's ragged breaths.

"Vassell could be lying, you know," Vero finally said as she pulled out of the parking lot onto the empty road. "Maybe he just said whatever he thought would get rid of us."

This was true, of course. It was possible everything the old man said was a complete fabrication. All of it. The whole goddamn story was insane. But attempting to scam Bradley out of money, that part at least rang true. It was certainly in line with Vassell's general lack of decency.

But the rest of it . . . his churning gut told him something wasn't right. What Vassell had said about summoning the demon and performing a ritual sacrifice seemed too fantastical to be real. But perhaps there was a half-truth in there somewhere.

Erasmo continued to mull over Vassell's claim, desperate to pick it apart. When he'd been trying to narrow down which creature the group worshiped, his focus had been on demons who might make deals in exchange for children. But a cult who sacrificed babies was another thing entirely.

Were there even any known creatures who demanded the ritual sacrifice of a child? He had a vague memory of reading about Moloch, a Canaanite deity who required children be burned to appease him. Then there was Baal Hammon, the chief god of Carthage. Archaeologists had found urns containing the cremated remains of infants, which they believed was strong evidence child sacrifices were made to him. But the statue of the winged creature Vassell and his group prayed to underneath the city looked nothing like either Moloch or Baal Hammon.

Erasmo checked the time and saw it was almost 7:00 a.m. Torres would be expecting him for his statement in an hour and a half. He would tell her every single thing they had discovered tonight. She'd probably dismiss it all as complete bullshit, but that was up to her.

A desperate, urgent need to see his grandmother suddenly overtook him. Even in her current state, just being in the same room as her would calm him, give him strength. Erasmo considered squeezing in a quick visit before his statement, but the nurses usually came in around now to bathe her, so it wouldn't be a great time. Once he was done with Torres though, he'd head straight over.

As he sat in the car, the shock of Vassell's claims still hung around him like a dense, lecherous fog, clogging his thoughts and weighing down every limb. He needed time to think everything through. But the thought of being completely alone at his house while he agonized over all this nauseated him. To make matters worse, he knew this wasn't the only reason he bristled at going home. An alarming truth quickly became obvious and had to be acknowledged.

He desperately wanted to stay by Vero's side.

This confession both confused and disturbed him. Erasmo was unsure as to why his heart sank at the thought of separating from her. Was he so weak that he needed the resolve she so effortlessly carried inside of her? Or was it something else entirely? Either way, this sudden longing to remain close to Vero could only end badly. At that moment, though, he really didn't care.

"I still have over an hour before meeting with Torres, and I don't much care to go home and stew over everything. I think we should go check on Renata, maybe try to convince her to get to a hospital."

"Do you really think that's a good idea?" Vero asked. "She was pretty clear last night about waiting for my aunt. And after what Vassell just said, I don't know if we're in the right frame of mind to—"

"I feel bad about the way we left her. She could barely get into the house when we dropped her off. It wasn't right to leave her like that. And I really need something to keep me occupied until I meet with Torres. I can go by myself if you're not up to it."

The morning sun cast a weak shadow over Vero's face. "You know me," she said after a long moment, "I'm always down for some crazy."

A paunchy man with a puffy face, clearly hungover, opened the door at Renata's house. He peered at them with suspicion when they asked for her.

"I'm her brother, Manny," he said. "She's not feeling very well right now. You'll have to come back another—"

"Is that Alma?" Renata screamed from inside, her voice tinged with desperation.

"No," the brother said. "It's just two teenagers."

"Hijo de puta. Let them in!"

Manny shrugged and pushed the screen door open. He led them through the house, its walls covered with various crosses and depictions of the Virgin Mary. They entered a dim hall-way and stopped in front of a dirt-smudged door, which had a large, fractured indention in the middle of it.

"Just for a few minutes," Manny said as he motioned them in. "The light hurts her eyes."

As the three of them entered and Erasmo scanned the dim room, Erasmo saw only a vague outline lying in bed. Then Manny shut the door behind him, and Erasmo couldn't even see that. The four of them breathed in the dark, each waiting for someone to speak.

"Where the hell is Alma?" Renata finally asked, her voice wet and raspy.

"It was too late for her to come last night," Vero said. "She'll be by a bit later."

"We just wanted to come by and see if you were feeling any better," Erasmo said. "Maybe give you a ride to the hospital if you weren't."

"I already told you, I don't want to go to the hospital! What I *want* is for you to make that son of a bitch Hector take this curse off me."

"You know we tried that already," Vero said. "We got nowhere."

Despite his best effort to focus on Renata, Erasmo found his thoughts drifting back to Vassell. To the baby. Could those sick bastards really have done such a thing to an innocent child? It was hard to believe, but why would Vassell lie? There was no reason to admit to such a horrific act if it weren't true. His stomach clenched again, but thankfully nothing rose from his throat.

Then, perhaps because it was looking for a distraction from these dismal thoughts, his mind suddenly gifted him with a promising idea.

"Instead of focusing on Hector," Erasmo said, "maybe we should focus on who hired him. If we find that person, then we can ask them to take the curse off. Hector would surely remove it if his client told him to."

"That's not a bad idea," Manny said, his words floating in the darkness. "It's worth trying."

"Is there anyone who might have a particularly bad grudge?" Erasmo asked.

"The first person who comes to mind," Manny said, "is Carmen Espinoza, our sister-in-law. She married our brother Frank fifteen years ago and did a real number on him. Carmen was very possessive and forbade him to see the family. Frank was a kind man but very weak. In the fifteen years they were married, we saw our brother maybe twice. The rest of us gave up on having a relationship with him, but Renata kept trying, and this made Carmen furious. There was some . . . extreme unpleasantness between the two of them. Unfortunately, our brother died earlier this year. Heart attack."

It certainly wouldn't hurt to talk to this sister-in-law, Erasmo considered. Maybe if Carmen swore she had nothing to do with this, Renata would consider going to the doctor. Besides, just because a curse was unlikely didn't mean that every option shouldn't be explored and investigated.

And he still needed a distraction until he met with Torres.

"We'll go talk to Carmen," he said, "and let you know if we find out anything."

After putting Carmen's address in his phone, they hopped into the Civic and headed over. As they drove, mild annoyance spread over Vero's face.

"Is this really necessary?" she asked. "I think we can say with a fair amount of certainty that their sister-in-law didn't have a curse put on Renata over a family grudge."

"I just think we should check out every possibility," he said. "Renata is clearly a very sick woman. If talking to Carmen can help at all, even if it's just to set Renata's mind at ease, we should at least try. Besides, we both know your aunt is going to ask if we pursued every possible avenue."

"Well, that part's true at least." Vero shrugged her shoulders. "If you want to waste your time, knock yourself out."

The drive to Carmen's was quiet. He spent most of it stewing over what Vassell had said, still trying to convince himself the old man had lied. Soon they pulled up to a small, weather-beaten house that had seen better days. No cars sat in the driveway, and no lights shone inside the house.

"So," Vero said, "we're just going to waltz in there and accuse this woman of hiring Hector to curse Renata?"

"Not at all," he responded. "I just want to hear her side of it."

Vero nodded but said nothing more.

They exited the Civic and trudged down the cracked stone walkway to the front porch. He rapped on the door, which had been completely stripped of paint, but no sound approached from inside. He tried again but the house remained silent. Clearly no one was home.

"Well at least we tried," Erasmo said, but as he turned to leave, the front window caught his eye. There was a small gap in the dingy curtain. Just big enough to peek through.

Won't hurt to at least take a look.

Erasmo moved aside a rusted aluminum chair and peered in. The living room was dim, but he could make out some worn furniture and a small television in the corner. At first glance, everything appeared perfectly ordinary. But he then noticed strange discolorations on the walls that stopped him cold. He stared, a chill spreading through his gut, not entirely believing what he saw. But the longer Erasmo looked, the more he was certain.

Every wall in the room was smeared with blood.

Erasmo whirled around, grabbing the aluminum chair.

"What is it?" Vero asked.

Erasmo threw the chair as hard as he could, and the front window shattered. He moved the chair aside and climbed in, a shard of glass slicing his left shoulder open. Remnants of the window crunched under his feet as he trudged through the room and took the scene in.

The blood on the walls took various forms. Some areas were sprayed with a fine red mist. Some were covered with long, thin drips, as if a wound had been opened and left to bleed. And still other parts of the walls were coated with thick crimson smears. To Erasmo, it appeared as if someone had reveled in this mess, spreading the blood to their heart's content.

"Carmen!" he yelled. "Are you in here?"

No response.

Erasmo walked up to the closest wall and touched the blood, which was dried and flaky. Whatever happened here, it hadn't been in the last few hours. Probably not even in the last few days. He jogged through the house anyway, looking for Carmen, heart pounding, afraid of finding something he'd never unsee. When he was satisfied no one was in the house, Erasmo walked back to the living room, where Vero stood studying her surroundings.

"Well, this doesn't look great," she said.

"What the hell do you think happened here?" he asked.

"God only knows," Vero said. "Some kind of violent fight maybe?"

"Seems like a lot of blood for just a fight. It had to have been something more."

"Speaking of blood," she said, gesturing to his arm, "you're losing some yourself."

Erasmo glanced at his shoulder and was dismayed at what he saw. The shard of glass still in the windowpane had sliced his shoulder badly. The wound was deep, and now that his adrenaline was wearing off, it was starting to become painful. He should've been more careful crawling through that damn window.

"Let's get outside," Vero said. "There's nothing for you to do in here except keep bleeding."

They let themselves out, and Vero immediately headed for the backyard.

"Where are you going?"

"Need to go play in the dirt for a bit," she said.

"What the hell are you talking about?" He almost followed her but his shoulder hurt too damn much. So he just stood there under the mild morning sun and wondered what horribleness had happened inside that house.

A few minutes later, Vero returned, a clumpy mixture in her hands.

"Hold still," she said, smothering it all over his shoulder.

Erasmo yelped, his eyes locked on the substance covering the wound.

"It's just a simple poultice," Vero said. "One of the first things my aunt taught me. Let it sit for a few minutes."

As they waited, both of them guessed a bit more about what might've happened in there, but were no closer to coming up with a theory that made any sense. After about five minutes, Vero reached over and scooped off the poultice. Erasmo grimaced, anticipating pain but none came. He glanced down to see he was no longer bleeding, and to his shock, the wound seemed to have closed quite a bit.

"That's amazing," he said.

"Nothing amazing about it. Just nature, if you know how to use the right ingredients."

"Damn impressive though," he said, meaning it.

"Oh, this is nothing according to my aunt. She told me once that a bruja, a real one, can make a poultice that closes any wound, out of nothing more than spit, dirt, and the right combination of words."

Erasmo checked the time. This had taken longer than he'd wanted. "We need to get going."

They walked over to the Civic, climbed in, and drove to Alma's. When he dropped Vero off twenty minutes later, Erasmo was hesitant to leave her but had little choice. Torres was surely waiting for him at the station.

"Don't forget to make sure your aunt gets over to Renata's as soon as possible. I'll tell Detective Torres about the scene we just found at Carmen's."

"Sounds good," Vero said, giving him a weak smile as she exited the car.

As Erasmo drove away, his phone vibrated. Probably Torres wondering where the hell he was. He slipped the phone out of his pocket and his eyes widened, the name on the screen an impossibility. He checked the name again to make sure he'd read it right.

BRADLEY.

Erasmo's hand trembled as he answered and held the phone to his ear. Breathing, delicate and skittish, greeted him on the other end. He waited but this person said nothing. If by some miracle it really was Bradley, he'd surely have spoken by now. It must be someone else. Someone who had access to his phone, someone who—

"Who the hell is this?" a female voice said, hoarse and raw.

Erasmo was so surprised that he failed to register the caller was expecting an answer to her question.

"Who the *hell* is this?" she shrieked.

"My name is Erasmo Cruz," he said. "Who is this?"

"This is Bradley's wife, asshole. We need to talk."

CHAPTER 25

ERASMO TURNED ONTO Courtland, skin trembling and clammy, the mild sun failing to warm him in the slightest. Bradley's wife had demanded they meet in public as soon as possible. He'd suggested San Pedro Park since it was close by, and she'd immediately hung up.

Courtland cut directly through San Antonio College's campus, and he eyed the various buildings with discomfort as he passed them. The redbrick structure on his right was the Radio, Television, and Film Building. He recognized the local college radio station's call letters displayed out front: *KSYM 90.1.*

Rat had mentioned several months ago that he planned to attend SAC next fall and transfer to a four-year university after he finished his basics. Whenever Rat had talked about this, or the future in general, a writhing mass of nerves formed in Erasmo's belly. Surely because he himself had no plan to speak of. Even if he wanted to go to college, there was certainly no money for it.

He'd done his best the past few months to run away from the hard truth that he'd soon be completely aimless. But as graduation crept closer, reality had muscled its way in. Life as he knew it would soon end. And all of his classmates seemed to have a plan, or at least a destination in mind. Except him, of course.

Erasmo turned left onto San Pedro, passing the park's tennis courts and library before turning right onto Myrtle. He parked along the curb, hopped out, and headed for the park benches.

His phone buzzed. Erasmo already knew who was calling, but glanced down anyway.

Torres. He immediately sent it to voicemail. Her name lit up his phone's screen again, and this time he just let it ring.

Nothing was going according to plan. Torres was surely furious with him. And he still desperately needed to see his grandmother. Erasmo abhorred the thought of her alone in that dreary room. But it couldn't be helped. This woman's child was missing. The least he could do was talk with her.

Erasmo chose a bench by a small stone bridge and a sapling with fiery leaves. He waited for her to arrive, unable to stop shaking in anticipation.

Ten uncomfortable minutes passed with no sign of her. He wondered how much longer she was going to leave him twisting in the wind, when a husky voice spoke from behind.

"You're just a boy."

He turned and saw a slender, black-haired woman regarding him with surprise, trembling with either rage or panic. Probably both. She was exactly what Erasmo had seen in the picture, the other half of a perfect couple. Except, of course, she was disheveled and distressingly pale, the emotional wringer she'd been put through draining her of any light she might've otherwise possessed.

Erasmo thought of Vero's suggestion that this woman could have been involved in her child's disappearance, and he already knew with deep certainty it just wasn't possible.

"Hi," he said, bolting up as he held out his hand. "Erasmo Cruz."

She walked around the bench and stopped directly in front of him but did not take his hand.

"Delia," she said, followed immediately by, "How the hell do you know my husband? I checked Bradley's call log, and the *only* number I didn't recognize was yours. A number that he called right before my baby was taken. Now I show up here, and you're not even old enough to vote?"

"I'm more than happy to explain it to you," he said. "It's just kind of a strange story."

"A strange story? I don't give a *damn* what kind of story it is. My baby is missing! Tell me everything you know!"

Erasmo nodded, wanting her to understand what had happened, but he hadn't the slightest idea how to begin.

"Did you," she said, glaring at him, "take my baby?"

"No!" he screamed too loudly. "I had nothing to do with taking him. In fact, it's the exact opposite. Bradley hired me to help stop the whole thing from happening."

"Well," Delia said, her eyes now igniting in barely concealed rage, "if that's true, then it seems like you did a piss-poor job, doesn't it?"

And with this Erasmo had to wholeheartedly agree. Every inch of his skin burned in shame as she fixed him a withering glare. Screw it. He was just going to have to start from the beginning.

"Did Bradley ever tell you about the time he made a deal with the Devil?"

When Erasmo finished recounting the story, Delia remained silent for a long time, no discernible expression on her face. He'd left out, of course, what Vassell had said about the child being sacrificed. There was still too much he didn't know yet.

"How much of that is actually true?" she finally asked.

"All of it."

"Sure it is. So before I called, you were watching this crazy old man attempt to summon a demon? Oh wait, sorry . . . he was just *pretending* to summon a demon, right?"

"Yes."

"Do you realize how insane all of that sounds?"

Erasmo did. Despite his involvement in everything he'd just told her, the whole thing sounded absurd to his ears, too. A frightful, unnerving question began to coalesce in the outer reaches of his thoughts. A question, he could now admit, he'd been increasingly beginning to wonder.

How much of this whole story had even really happened?

No. He couldn't think that way. Yes, he was sick, and starving, and tired, and emotionally wrung out. But all of these things had happened. They *had* to have.

"I know how it sounds," he said. "And I don't expect you to believe me. But you should also know that I found something on your property. In the toolshed."

"The shed?"

"Yes. I found a symbol, a pentagram, drawn on its window. Would you have any idea why it would be there?"

Even more color drained from Delia's face, although Erasmo hadn't thought it possible. "No, of course not."

Erasmo searched her delicate features, her mannerisms for even the slightest indication she was lying. But all that stood in front of him was a tortured mother, genuine confusion and rage running rampant through her.

"Is there anyone else who lives with you?" he asked. "Or has access to your property?"

"No . . . it's just us and the baby."

Damn. It could've been anybody, then—

"Well," Delia said, "we do have a landscaper we hired several months back. He's on the property a lot. And he's watched the house for us a few times when we've gone out of town. But there's no way that he—"

"What's his name?"

"Francis," she said. "Francis Barrett."

Erasmo's heart picked up speed.

"You're sure his name is Francis Barrett?"

"Yeah. It sticks out to me because it sounds so old-fashioned."

That's because it is, Erasmo thought.

Francis Barrett was the name of a nineteenth-century Englishman who was a devout practitioner of the occult. He'd written a famous textbook, *The Magus,* which was still studied the world over. Whoever had passed himself off as an unassuming landscaper, his real name was certainly not Francis Barrett.

"Do you have a picture of him?"

"No, I wouldn't . . . Wait . . . I did take some photos of the backyard after he cut it one day because it looked so beautiful. He might be in one." Delia took her phone out and swiped furiously at the screen.

"This one," she said, handing him the phone with trepidation. "You can kind of see him in the background."

Erasmo worried that just a tiny portion of this man's face would be visible, or that he'd be deep in the background of the photo. Both of those things ended up being true, but it didn't matter. Erasmo recognized this person immediately. His hand trembled as he passed the phone back to Delia.

"Don't ever," Erasmo told her, "let this man near you again."

CHAPTER 26

THE CIVIC SCREECHED to a halt in front of Francis Barrett's small, neglected house. Now that Erasmo knew of his alias, it was hard to think of this man any other way. A filthy Subaru wagon encrusted in bird crap sat in the driveway. The son of a bitch was home.

A pang of regret struck him at returning the Smith & Wesson to Delia. She'd asked for it back before they parted ways, and at the time, he'd been happy to get rid of it. At least he still had his grandfather's switchblade, which would be all he'd need for this visit.

Erasmo would've expected to feel nervous at breaking in, at walking into a confrontation that would most likely end in bloodshed. But this man had been involved in a child's abduction. In a child's murder. A child that Erasmo had been hired to help protect. No, fear was not what ran through his veins as he sat outside Francis Barrett's house.

He considered calling Torres, telling her the Erickson's groundskeeper was involved. But he wanted to have concrete answers first, to be able to explain exactly what happened and who'd been a part of it. Besides, there was no rush. It's not like there was a race to find the child. He was in all likelihood gone.

All that was left now was to make sure these assholes paid. Every single one of them.

Erasmo reached into his pocket and caressed the switch-blade. He wasn't a violent person by nature. In fact, quite the opposite. But he was beginning to understand a phenomenon that had puzzled him for years.

So often he'd read stories about crazed people committing all manners of horrific acts. He'd never fully comprehended how they'd gotten to that point, what had driven them to that level of depravity. Surely, these people must have at one point thought themselves incapable of such things. But he was beginning to understand how a once unthinkable act first arrived as an almost imperceptible, vague notion, and then slowly grew into a warm and inviting desire, until one day you were in a place you'd never imagined, hungering for something terrible.

It wasn't that he wanted to cut Francis, necessarily. He just wanted to make sure the son of a bitch talked. And Erasmo was going to do whatever it took to make that happen. This was the very least he could do. After all, if it weren't for his own involvement, Bradley's child would still be alive.

Erasmo exited the car and trotted through the stained driveway to Francis's weed-infested backyard. He approached the rear door, desperately hoping it was unlocked as usual. On the few occasions he'd been over, Francis had constantly gone out back to smoke, too lazy to lock the door every time. Sure enough, the knob turned easily in his hand.

He stepped inside, careful not to make any noise, but the floorboard didn't cooperate and groaned underneath his feet. After sneaking through the grimy kitchen, Erasmo stopped and listened. Not a single sound. Maybe he was asleep. This'd be a whole hell of a lot easier if that were the case. He crept through the narrow hallway that led to Francis's bedroom, placing his ear to the thin, scarred door when he reached it.

Nothing. Was this guy even home? Maybe someone had come by and picked him up, which would explain his car in the driveway. Best to at least check the house fully, though. Erasmo slowly pushed the bedroom door open, heart thudding in his ears, and gasped when he saw what waited for him inside.

The robed figure stood perfectly still, lit only by flickering candles scattered throughout the cramped room. He held a copper incense burner in his hands, two upside-down crosses carved into its sides. The figure stared directly forward, a mask covering his face. But not just any mask. A goat's mask, with a ragged pentagram carved into its forehead.

It was him. The Goat. The same one who'd pulled him to safety last night underneath the city.

The Goat was clearly surprised at his sudden appearance, remaining frozen in place, seemingly unsure what to do. The incense burner he'd been holding began to slip from his hands.

Erasmo reached into his pocket, pulled out the knife, and released its beautiful, glimmering blade.

"Take off the goddamn mask."

The Goat continued to stare forward, motionless.

"Take it off now, or I'll call the cops and tell them you've been lying to the Erickson family."

Now the incense burner did fall from the Goat's hands, and he took a quick, shaky step backward.

"Okay . . . okay," a muffled voice said.

The Goat placed his hands on the mask and slowly pulled it off. When he'd finished, Erasmo stared at the man in front of him, shock coursing through him, even though he'd already known who would be underneath it.

"Andy," he said, needing to speak the name out loud.

His friend was sweating profusely, eyes darting around in their sockets, unable to focus on any single point.

"How . . . how did you find out?"

"You don't get to ask questions," Erasmo said. "Not after what you did, you sick son of a bitch."

"I know this looks bad, but—"

"*Looks* bad? You helped them kidnap a *baby*!"

"I know . . . but—"

"*Why?* Why would you get involved in something like this?"

Andy's face splintered, and tears welled in his still-frantic eyes.

"I didn't mean to! All I wanted was to learn from them. To understand their secrets. They said if I proved myself, they would teach me."

"You did all of this," Erasmo said, molten rage flooding his veins, "just so you could learn a few bullshit parlor tricks?"

"You don't understand, man. They know how to do things. Things you wouldn't believe. You of all people—"

"I don't want to hear any *bullshit*! Just tell me the important stuff. From the beginning."

"Okay," Andy said, every inch of his excess flesh trembling, "but there's really not much to tell. A while back, I got a DM on Twitter."

Andy ran several occult and paranormal social media accounts. Erasmo thought they were silly and inconsequential. Maybe not so much, as it turned out.

"The message said that if I wanted to learn about real occult practices, about true and lasting power, they were willing to consider me for membership in their group."

"And this bizarre offer, from a complete stranger no less, sounded like a good idea to you?"

"Yeah, it did," Andy said, an edge now in his voice. "I wanted to learn, and—"

"And what?"

"And," he said, glaring at Erasmo, "you sure as hell weren't offering to teach me."

"Wait . . . are you blaming *me* for this?"

"No," Andy said. But the pained look on his face screamed *YES.* "It's just . . . I'd *told* you how much I wanted to learn about these things. I kept hoping that you'd include me, or at least point me in the right direction. But it was like you and Rat were this impenetrable team, and I was a wannabe third wheel. I only ever got to hang out a few times. And an occasional visit at the hotel when you wanted to use me for a free room. So yeah, their offer actually sounded pretty damn good."

"We weren't using you," Erasmo began but then stopped. Andy was the last person who deserved an explanation. "Keep going."

"It started off slow at first. They asked a bunch of personal questions. Although, it seemed like they already knew most everything. After a few visits, they asked what I was looking for, what exactly I wanted to learn from them. And then one night, they said if I committed to being a loyal member of their group, they'd show me the true source of their power."

"And then what happened?"

"And then . . . they did." Andy paused, lost in the memory. "But that's not important right now. Not for what you want to know."

Erasmo resisted the overwhelming urge to press him on this. The baby was all that mattered right now.

"After a few months," Andy continued, "they said my first assignment was to gather information on the Ericksons. To report back about their home security, their schedules, all that stuff. And later, I . . . I had to write that message on the baby. You know, to freak out Bradley to make sure he complied with our demands. But my main job, the reason I spent so much time on those people, was to make sure everything went smoothly when the baby was taken. But after all the planning, all the monitoring of their schedules, the weeks it took to learn about their security system . . . you came along that night and everything got screwed up."

The rage engulfed Erasmo all at once, igniting every cell in his body. At first, its intensity scared him, but then it quickly provided a sense of comfort, of purpose. He was going to use this rage. Use it for what needed to be done. Erasmo gripped the knife so hard it felt like a part of him, an appendage ready to serve its only function.

"Your plan got *screwed up*?" he roared, the words barely audible over the thudding in his head. "That's what you call a dead child? A *screwed-up* plan?"

"Dead? Wait . . . what—"

"I need the name of every sick asshole that was involved in this. *Every* goddamn one."

"You don't understand. We never see each other's faces. That's part of what the masks are for, to keep our identities a secret. We never meet without them. Only the elders know who everyone is."

"You're *lying*!" Erasmo lunged forward, the knife aimed at Andy's face. "Tell me the goddamn truth!"

Andy's eyes widened at the sight of the approaching blade.

"I . . . I haven't seen any of their faces. Just the old man, Vassell. I don't know who anyone else is. I swear!"

As Erasmo got closer, he kept telling himself he wouldn't actually hurt Andy. He just wanted answers, that was all. But then he thought of the child, and what had happened to him, and knew this was a lie. Part of him did, in fact, want to hurt this son of a bitch.

"They're stealing babies!" he screamed. "And you helped them!"

Erasmo placed the tip of the knife against Andy's right cheek. Andy's eyes grew wide, staring at the blade resting against his flesh. After a few moments, Andy proceeded to do something Erasmo hadn't expected. He drew a long, wavering breath and began to sob, deeply and unrestrained.

"Please," Andy said, his entire body trembling. "You don't understand. I only did it because I want to talk to my mom again. I miss her *so* goddamn much! They said they could help."

"Then why the *hell* were you asking me if I could sense her in the motel room?"

"Because they haven't shown me how to contact her yet. But I know they will soon. They keep promising that they will."

Erasmo pressed the knife forward slightly, and a tiny stream of blood ran down Andy's cheek.

"Tell me their names. Now."

"Don't!" Andy shrieked. "I saved you! I risked everything to get you out of there when I saw you in the tunnel. Do you know what they'd have done? You'd be dead right now!"

He pressed the knife harder into Andy's skin, a thicker flow of blood now spilling from the cut.

"It was you, wasn't it? Who trapped us in the shed?"

"I . . . I had to. When you showed up at the hotel right when my shift started, I got nervous. You were obviously still investigating and I didn't want them to hurt you. So I followed when you left the hotel and saw a chance to slow you down for a few hours."

"Give me their names, or I'll slice you open."

"Please, don't! The children are all fine. The ones whose families didn't pay are being raised by the group now. They're perfectly safe."

"Those babies were taken from their families! They don't have their parents anymore!"

Erasmo's rage burned so hot, he could no longer see clearly. The room's drab colors melted away until only a haze of shimmering white floated in front of him.

His hand squeezed the knife harder as he thought of how these goddamn people had ruined so many lives. He seethed at their indifference to the suffering they'd caused to those families. To the children.

Erasmo slowly slid the knife from Andy's cheek to his jaw, the blade loosening flesh on its way down.

Andy screeched, producing a strangely inhuman sound. He swallowed a large, silent breath, like a child, and screamed again. For the briefest of moments, Erasmo almost felt pity, but then he thought of Bradley's terrified baby and slid the blade even farther down Andy's face, all the way to his chin. A large flap of skin now hung open, exposing raw, pulsing flesh.

"Wait!" Andy shrieked. "I . . . I don't have names, but I'll tell you something you don't know."

Erasmo slowly pulled the knife away, despite his rage's insistence he continue.

"And what's that?"

"Earlier. You said that the baby was dead. But . . ."

"But what?"

"But he's not. Vassell must've just said that to get rid of you. He's very much alive. They have plans for it . . . for him, I mean."

Erasmo's heart jumped. Was it possible? Was there any way this could be true? He tried to tamp down his hope but it overtook him anyway, immediately snuffing out his rage.

"What kind of plans?"

"I'm not sure. All I know for certain is it's happening tonight. At midnight. And it's elders only, no rank and file."

"Where? Under the Soul Center?"

"No, we only meet there to initiate new members and for general worship once a month. All of the larger, more important ceremonies happen at some place called the Sanger House. Only the elders know where it is."

The Sanger House. He'd never heard of it. The wall clock told him it was almost 11:00 a.m. now, which meant he had thirteen hours to find this place. He flipped the blade down and pocketed the knife.

"You better hope that baby is okay."

Andy began to blubber, tears mixing with his blood and exposed flesh, still holding the goat mask in his hands.

"I'm scared," he whimpered, his loose flap of skin trembling.

"It's a little late to be scared of going to jail. Should've thought about that before."

"I'm not scared of going to jail," he said. "I'm scared of what Vorax is going to do to me. You don't understand his power . . . what he's capable of . . . the things I've seen him do."

Erasmo's skin prickled, not because of what Andy had said, but because of the pure, unadulterated fear in his voice.

"You deserve whatever the hell you get," he finally said, and turned to leave.

"Erasmo?"

"What?"

"You," Andy whispered, "should be scared, too."

CHAPTER 27

ERASMO HAD GONE straight home, greeted by a mail-box stuffed with more medical bills. A surge of blistering heat scorched his bones at the abject unfairness of it all. He stood there shaking until finally forcing himself to walk inside.

For the next ten minutes, he scoured the internet for any references to Sanger House. There was a town called Sanger outside of Dallas, and a bed-and-breakfast in Milwaukee called Sanger House Gardens, but that was about it. He thought about asking Ashley to put the name through her databases, but that seemed like a stretch at best. Damn. He hadn't antici-pated coming up dry so quickly.

It made sense, though. They probably only called it Sanger House among themselves. And a new recruit like Andy wouldn't be trusted to know where or what it was. Which led to a question that caused flickers of panic to dance around Erasmo's heart.

If not even all of the cult members knew the location of this place, then how the hell was he supposed to find it in less than twelve hours?

His phone vibrated on the nightstand. Torres again. Damn. He'd get to the station soon to give his statement, and get to the hospital, too. But he had to focus on the child right now.

This would be so much easier if he actually knew who these people were. The only member of the group he knew besides Andy was Vassell. He considered staking out the Soul Center, but Erasmo would be shocked if the old man showed his face there today. Not after just getting shot, and not with this mysterious event going down tonight, whatever it was.

Erasmo's breath caught at his own cowardice. *Whatever it was.* He'd been furiously dancing around what they planned to do to Bradley's child since the moment Andy had mentioned it. *Whatever it was.*

He knew goddamn well what it was. The facts all pointed to the same thing. A secret event tonight attended only by the elders. Held right at midnight. Involving the baby. Vassell had been telling the truth, he'd only lied about *when.* They hadn't done anything to that child last night. No.

They were planning on sacrificing him to their blood demon tonight.

His heart skipped several beats at this thought, and the unnerving knowledge that he didn't have the first clue how to stop it. In truth, he had no idea if this demon they worshiped was even real. But it didn't matter. All that mattered was *they* believed he was real.

Erasmo wondered what specific ritual they were going to conduct tonight. The group certainly seemed to be obsessed with blood, so surely it would be part of the ceremony.

He reached for the shelf above his bed and took down *A Practical Guide to the Supernatural and Paranormal.* If he remembered correctly, Dubois had written about the uses of blood in various rituals. It didn't take him long to find the entry.

On the Transformative Properties of Blood

Of the many items used in occult rituals, the blood which flows through our veins is the most prized and sought after. Of course, it's also the hardest to obtain as very few part with it willingly. Perhaps this scarcity is what gives this precious liquid its power.

Ancient civilizations believed they needed to feed their gods blood to appease them. It is well known that the Aztecs provided their gods sacrificed human blood, believing this gift would ensure the sun would continue to follow its course.

There are also countless accounts of those seeking to use blood to grant youth, power, or even life itself. Pope Innocent VIII was said to have drunk the blood of young boys to rejuvenate himself after suffering a stroke. And Countess Elizabeth Báthory was accused of bathing in the blood of young virgins to gain immortality. Many such stories are known in almost every civilization.

When it was clear that my daughter Emma's illness was eating her alive, my desperation got the better of me. If so many throughout the course of history utilized blood rituals to obtain what they wanted, why shouldn't I at least try?

So, one evening, I ventured out into nameless streets and visited disreputable establishments that I'd only heard spoken of in whispers. I am unable to divulge specific details, but I returned home in the morning carrying several buckets of blood.

I roused my daughter from a deep sleep and carried her to the bathtub. Emma panicked when she saw its contents, begging me to take her back to bed. But instead I lowered her in, even as her weak body struggled against mine. She lay half submerged in the rapidly coagulating *blood, screaming. I slathered blood all over her face and body, assuring Emma I was doing this for her benefit.*

In the middle of a long shriek, I poured a thick stream of blood down her throat and closed her mouth until she swallowed. I found myself screaming, begging the universe, God, any deity who would listen to have mercy on my child.

Eventually Emma fainted, and I watched over her as she soaked in the blood awhile longer. My hopes had been so high for this treatment, but when I removed her from the tub, cleaned her up, and laid her back in bed, she appeared just as frail as ever. Perhaps even more so.

But in the morning a curious thing occurred. Emma appeared rejuvenated, her entire demeanor changed. Her mother claimed Emma was acting differently because her mind had been broken, because of what I'd done to her. But I knew this was utter nonsense.

The effects were short-lived, as Emma passed a few months later. But I now know the following to be true: Blood is power. Blood has power. And most importantly, blood gives power.

As long as you believe it does.

Erasmo closed the book, disappointed this entry wasn't more helpful. His worries about finding the baby continued to swarm over him, feasting like frenzied piranhas devouring a carcass.

If only he knew more about these people, knew members higher up the chain than Andy, then maybe he could—

Wait. Of Course. Erasmo chastised himself for not thinking of this sooner. He did know someone who might be able to help.

Surely it would be better to take someone with him though. He made the call, and Vero answered right away.

"Hey, want to go for a drive?"

CHAPTER 28

"YOU HAVE A strange habit of getting into weird shit," Vero said after he'd briefed her about Andy. "Not judging at all. Just an observation."

Despite his unease at where they were headed, and the suffocating sense of dread enveloping him, Erasmo had to stifle a slight smile. There was something about the way she teased him that loosened the ever-present knot in his gut. He needed to be careful. Pining over someone who'd never have him was the last thing he needed right now. But the sight of Vero soothed his burning nerves, and for that, he was grateful.

"Kind of comes with the territory," he replied, making a concerted effort not to look over.

"Fair enough," she said. "In all sincerity, I'm glad you asked me to come along. Gets me out of the garage for a while. And . . . I'm not sure how to say this exactly, but I feel like a part of this whole bizarre situation now. Although the entire thing is crazy for sure, it feels good to be a part of something. You know?"

An image of Rat, smiling at him with excitement, tiny eyes glimmering in the moonlight, flashed through his head.

"Yeah. I do."

The rest of the drive was uneventful but went by far too fast for his liking. As he pulled into the store's sparse parking lot, he was more than a bit disappointed.

"You really think she's going to help?" Vero asked as they exited the car, her pinched expression suggesting she was doubtful.

"Truthfully, my hopes aren't very high."

"I bet," Vero said as they entered the antiques store, a bell on the door announcing their arrival. "They usually aren't."

Erasmo expected Gemma to run off to the back when she saw him enter the store. Or perhaps to get angry and remind him of the promise he'd made just yesterday. But to his surprise, neither of these things happened. Instead, Gemma froze behind the cash register when she saw them enter Finders Keepers. After eyeing them a few moments, expressionless, she stepped out from behind the counter and trudged over.

As Gemma approached, Erasmo noticed she didn't appear as fearful or rattled as last time. But there was still something about her that seemed off. She stopped in front of them, looking older than her years, dull hair matted against her skull.

"Who is this?" Gemma said with a waver in her voice, staring at the floor but clearly addressing Erasmo.

"Hi, I'm Vero," she said, extending her hand. Gemma didn't take it.

"Vero's a friend of mine," he said. "You can trust her."

Gemma gave a subtle nod but remained wary.

"Look," Erasmo said, "I know what I promised yesterday, but this is important."

"It's okay," Gemma said, her voice a little steadier now. "I actually don't mind. After you left, I started to feel bad. Like maybe I should've helped you more. I just . . . you scared me showing up the way you did out of the blue."

"Sorry," he said, meaning it. "I'm just trying to help Bradley."

"I know you are. It's about time for my break. Y'all feel like taking a walk?"

Erasmo tried to hide his surprise. She must've really felt bad about running him off yesterday.

"That'd be great," he said.

"Taking fifteen!" Gemma yelled to whoever was in the back.

As the three of them exited the store, she gestured to a building and a basketball court farther down the road.

"That's American Legion Park. There are some benches over there we can sit on while we chat."

As they walked over in silence, a busy parking lot came up on their right. He estimated at least 95 percent of the vehicles were pickup trucks of various colors and ages. Small-town life. Something about the insulated nature of towns like this had always instinctively repulsed him, although he couldn't even say what, specifically. As he'd gotten older, though, Erasmo began to better understand their appeal. Everyone knowing each other's business. Seeing the same people day in and day out. Neighbors and friends going out of their way to help each other.

It was almost like having a family.

He hated thinking about this subject of course, which is why he so often didn't. His mind had grown vigilant over the years, poised and ready to distract him when these uncomfortable thoughts surfaced. And they always did, no matter how hard he desperately shoved them down, trying to drown them. He may as well have been using his finger to plug a leak in a dam.

Just hearing the words *family*, *abandoned*, or *addict* was enough to send his thoughts scurrying, searching for a safe haven. Surely this was one of the reasons he'd latched on to the supernatural as much as he had. A safe, fascinating topic, far away from the other kids asking why his parents weren't around. So many lonely nights, up well past his bedtime praying for them to come home, only his books to keep him company.

His parents never did show up, of course. He'd found out their ugly truth years later. And when he'd learned they had abandoned him for nothing more than cheap fixes of heroin, it had irreparably damaged him.

Perhaps his grandmother was right. She'd told him more than once that he had trouble facing hard truths, that he ran away from them. Erasmo thought he'd made progress in that regard just a few short months ago, but was now discovering another ugly truth he couldn't run from: in life, you take one step forward and three stumbles backward.

They reached the benches and sat down, a large oak overhead providing an abundance of comforting shade. He wanted to get right to asking about Sanger House but thought it might be safer to ease into it. Besides, maybe she'd accidentally spill some other useful information.

"Do you mind," he started, "if I ask how you fell in with them?"

Gemma reached into her pocket and slid out a small cigarette case. She pulled one out and lit it, taking a long drag before answering.

"My mother was hard on me," she said, small puffs of smoke accentuating each word. "If she ever showed me an ounce of love, then I somehow must've missed it. And my dad . . . well . . . he was no walk in the park, either. I honestly spent most of my childhood wondering why they even had me." She stared at Erasmo, right eyebrow raised. "I strike a chord or something?"

"Sorry?" Erasmo said, his skin suddenly burning.

"Oh, just the look on your face is all."

Damn. Could he be any more transparent? Vero slid her hand over his and squeezed. This gesture only lasted for a moment, but it was enough to steady him.

"I'm fine."

Gemma took another long drag from the cigarette, her eyes never leaving Erasmo.

"By the time I got to high school," she continued, "I was pretty screwed up. Spent most of my time engaging in assorted self-destructive behaviors with some pretty awful people. I didn't know it at the time, but what I was out looking for every night was acceptance, and love, and family. And then . . ."

"What?" Vero asked, curious, but with an edge in her voice.

"And then . . . I found it."

Gemma stopped talking, her eyes lost in whatever memories this story had conjured. A smile flickered over her lips, only to quickly disappear.

"Well, I thought I had at least."

"How did they approach you?" Erasmo asked. This was something he'd been wondering about quite a bit.

"Vassell," she said, eyes narrowed, "can be damn persuasive. One night, I was staggering home drunk from a party in my neighborhood. He pulled up in his Oldsmobile and offered me a ride. Of course, I thought he was just some creep. I told him to get lost, but then he said something that stopped me in my tracks."

"What?" Vero asked.

"He said"—a single tear rolled down the side of Gemma's face—"that he knew why my mother didn't love me. I know it sounds completely insane, but that's all it took for me to get into his car. We talked for hours, until morning. I don't remember all the details, but it was like . . . he knew the *exact* nature of my loneliness, of my deepest unsaid fears and desires. And at the end of our conversation, he offered me what I wanted most in the entire world."

Gemma peered at him, her eyes somehow both wistful and brimming with intensity.

"A family that would accept me, and never, ever leave."

A chill shook Erasmo's bones. Not because of the ease with which Gemma had been recruited. But because he suspected this very tactic might have worked on him as well.

"In the days after, Vassell began to slowly teach me what their group was about. I learned about the elders, the masks, their belief system . . . stuff like that. Of course, deep down, I thought it was all crazy. But the whole thing seemed completely harmless. I didn't want to upset these people who seemed to genuinely care about me by pointing out how ludicrous some of their claims were. After all, every religion has their illogical silliness.

"And I was well aware of the reputations these so-called cults have. But Vassell taught me how mainstream religions vilify groups like theirs while turning a blind eye to their own horrors. Like the old saying goes . . . religions are just cults with political power. All I knew was that these were the only people in my life who truly seemed to care about me. And you know what?" Gemma stared up at the overcast sky, a sad smile on her face. "I sure loved being a part of something.

"Anyway, this introduction went on for a few weeks, until one day they started sending me on errands. Small things at first, like recruiting people to come to our gatherings. It wasn't until a few months later, when I'd done enough to prove my loyalty, that Vassell showed me the sacred text their beliefs are derived from. This book shook me to my very core. The ideas it contained, the historical scenes it depicted, its description of the god they worshiped and His power. After that, I understood Vassell's ideas weren't so crazy after all."

Gemma took another drag of her cigarette as she sat motionless on the bench, lost in memories.

"Fast-forward a few years, and . . . let's just say things ended badly."

"Why specifically did you leave?" he asked, leaning forward.

"If you don't mind," Gemma said, grimacing, "there are some things I don't feel comfortable discussing. Don't let the modest appearance of the Soul Center fool you. Their power spreads far and wide. To be honest, I spend most days looking over my shoulder. I really shouldn't even be talking to you."

She took another drag, considering how much to say.

"Do you know how they keep everyone in line? How they prevent anyone from leaving? Whenever anyone tries to separate from the group . . . they're given to the Master."

"Given?" Vero asked. "What do you mean?"

"You know," she said. "Their blood is drained and gifted to him to feast on."

"Bullshit," Vero said.

"It's true. Don't get me wrong. It's *very* rare anyone ever wants to leave. But it's happened enough so that every member knows what will happen if they go, or if they talk too much. So, yeah, I'm hesitant to answer some of your questions."

"Just to be clear," Vero said, "you're telling us that this demon the group worships is real. Not a statue, not a set of philosophical beliefs, not a creature they made up to scam people, but a living, breathing monster?"

Gemma glanced up at the sky, exhaling a long plume of smoke as she studied a smattering of clouds. She then turned her attention back to them, staring directly in their eyes as she took another long drag.

"Yes."

Vero opened her mouth to respond but then thought better of it.

"I should probably get going," Gemma said.

Erasmo's heart pounded against his rib cage. It was now or never. If she didn't know the answer to what he was about to ask, or flat out refused to help, then there'd be no way to prevent what was going to happen tonight. This was his last hope.

"I really just came out here to ask you one thing. During your time with them, did they ever mention a place called Sanger House?"

Gemma appeared confused for a moment but then recognition slowly spread over her face.

"Yeah . . . Sanger House. It's a property the group has owned for a long time. They use it for larger gatherings. It's a little bit of a drive to get to, out in Kendall County."

Erasmo almost fell over in relief.

"Do you know the address?"

Gemma remained silent for a moment before answering. "Yeah, I do. I'll never forget it, unfortunately." She then recited the address, her voice monotone, and he saved it to his phone.

"Well, I better get back to work," Gemma said, putting out her cigarette on the bench. "But I should warn you . . . that house isn't somewhere you want to go."

Erasmo wanted to pepper her with questions, beg her to tell them what else she knew. But Gemma was clearly too scared to tell them anything more, and he didn't want to waste precious time badgering her for information she wouldn't give. Gemma rose from the bench, flashed them a sad smile, and walked back toward the store, not once turning to look back at them.

CHAPTER 29

THE RIDE BACK to San Antonio was uncomfortably quiet. Vero seemed lost in thought, occasionally muttering unintelligible phrases to herself.

Erasmo considered calling Delia and giving her an update. But what was he going to say? That an ex-cult member gave him an address at which her son might be involved in a demonic ritual tonight? That would just make things worse. He'd call her when he knew a little more.

Vero muttered again, still seeming out of sorts.

"You all right?" he finally asked as they approached the curandera's store.

"Yeah," she said, her face scrunched up in a way he found terrifyingly endearing. "Just trying to guesstimate how much of what she told us was complete bullshit. What do you think? Eighty percent maybe?"

Erasmo was taken aback. He thought Gemma had seemed pretty damn believable. In truth, he was grateful to her for even talking to them.

"Well, she gave us an address at least," he said. "That's something."

"An address that she just happened to have memorized? C'mon, man. None of this rings any alarm bells for you?"

"Doesn't really matter," he said. "It's the only lead we have. What else am I supposed to do? Not even try?"

"Oh, I don't know . . . I mean, this is just off the top of my head, but how about *not* walk into a clearly dangerous situation just because some screwed-up lady gave you an address. Didn't you see all her flinching and complete inability to make eye contact? She reminded me of a dog that's been beaten its whole life and is afraid of its own shadow."

He didn't want to get into a debate over Gemma's sincerity, so changed the subject to one he was more interested in.

"Can you talk something out with me? I'm still trying to wrap my head around how this group might work."

"I guess," Vero said after a lengthy silence, clearly unenthused.

"The way I see it, there are two possibilities as to how they operate. I'll start with the one you're most likely to believe, which is this: Despite what they claim, there is no actual demon.

"I've seen them worship a statue of this demon, so they clearly believe this creature exists. But like any other religion, he's more of an idea and a belief, not an entity they physically interact with.

"Vassell told me that the group needs money to survive, to recruit people, and to buy more properties to expand their influence. So at some point, they must've stumbled onto this scheme to convince some of their congregants they'd really made a deal with the Devil. And then their victims gladly paid the money, both to get their children back and to prevent further punishment from the demon."

"So," Vero said, "they worship this deity and steal money from true believers in order to spread its word?"

"Does that sound so different from a lot of other religions?"

Vero nodded, still mulling it over. "But why go to all that trouble? What do they get out of it?"

"During the underground ceremony," Erasmo said, "Vassell read from a book. It said something like: *Worship unto me, and receive an eternity of everlasting pleasure. Youth shall be our lifeblood, Youth shall light our way.*"

"'An eternity of everlasting pleasure,'" Vero said. "So they believe after they die, this demon will allow them to live forever and indulge in their basest desires?"

"Sounds like it."

"And that second part," Vero said, "about youth. That must be why they sacrificed that baby pig . . . and steal children."

"Yeah," Erasmo said. "They either get money, or they get a child whose blood they can offer to the demon during their worship. Either way, they win."

"I'm sure there are more moving parts," she said, "but that generally makes sense to me."

"The other possibility," he said, "which you won't like, is that there's an actual demon the group summons and interacts with. In this scenario, the entity *actually* makes deals with those who attend the Black Masses. These people then go out into the world and reap the benefits of the demon's gifts. Then when it's time, Vassell and his people make sure the debt is honored, and the demon receives what's owed to it."

"I in no way subscribe to this possibility," Vero said, "but just for the sake of argument, why would the demon want money from these people? The children, I understand, for their blood. But why the money?"

"The same reason Vassell already gave," Erasmo said. "If there really is a demon, surely he'd want his servants to have the resources to spread his word. But I think it's more than that. Vassell said that a deal with the creature extracts a great price. Maybe taking back everything he's given them—money, children, happiness—is what this demon does. After all, I've never read a book or seen a movie where making a deal with the Devil actually ends well."

"Could be," Vero said. "Or maybe Vassell and his people just got greedy, and while in the process of serving their Master decided to line their own pockets to indulge in their deepest desires. Happens all the time in other religions."

Erasmo nodded. That made sense, too.

"Demon or no demon," she said, "these are some dangerous people. All the more reason not to take what Gemma said at face value."

"I don't know," he said. "I still think it seemed like she really wanted to help."

"Erasmo . . . she *barely* talked to you last time. And now, all of a sudden, she's eager to help out? I think someone got to her. And they told her exactly what to say if you ever showed up again."

"Even if that were true," he said, "I still need to go. I have no other leads. If there's even the slightest chance—"

"Then I'm going with you," Vero said, steel in her voice.

"No," he replied, pulling into the parking lot. "Not for this. It's too dangerous. These people are at a minimum kidnappers and extortionists. Possibly murderers. If something happened to you, I—"

"Look, it isn't your responsibility to keep me safe, Erasmo. And I don't want to be a jerk, but you seem to be under the impression that it's your decision if I go. I can tell you with certainty that it's not."

He knew everything she said was true, but his heart still convulsed at the thought of Vero in the same room as those masked psychopaths. Erasmo barely knew her, except for the few intense situations they'd spent together. But that had been more than enough to understand she was a giver of light, and hope, and power. Not just to him, but anyone who might cross her path.

And there were so few souls emanating light in the world. Certainly not enough to counteract the vast majority, of which he was a part, who secreted only sludge and darkness and misery. Vero was one of the rare pinpricks of light scattered throughout a bleak landscape. He knew deep within his bones that allowing harm to come to her would be an unforgivable sin. So Erasmo said the one thing he knew would keep her away from all this madness.

"You told me earlier that you felt like a part of this," he began, his gut churning uncontrollably. "Well . . . you're not. I didn't ask you to show up at my hotel room. And I only wanted you to come along on this trip so I wouldn't fall asleep on the drive. You could *never* be a part of what I'm doing, Vero. How could you? Someone who doesn't believe, who doesn't at least entertain the notion that some of this might be true, could never truly be a part of this."

Vero's face betrayed no reaction to his words. But when she grabbed the door handle, her fingers trembled from either rage or hurt. Maybe both.

"You're a lost soul," Vero said as she got out of the car. "But I hope that one day, you're able to find your way back from the darkness." She closed the door and strode away, stone-faced, as she entered her aunt's store.

He sped off, head swimming. This was the right thing to do but goddamn it hurt. Erasmo disliked many facets of his life, but he particularly hated that he never had any people to spare. As opposed to those lucky assholes who always had plenty. When someone like that, always flush with friends and romance, lost a person who truly cared about them, it was just a minor loss. A blip on the radar because they had ten others lined up. He always had a hard time wrapping his head around this. That for some, losing a person in your life *wasn't a big deal.*

For Erasmo's entire existence, there'd never been more than two or three people at a time who gave a shit about him. So when he lost even one, it was an earth-shattering event. There was never anyone else to take their place. He was just one person poorer, and worse off for it, left to beg the universe for someone else to one day miraculously enter his life.

This was how Erasmo felt now, splintered and broken, like a web of freshly cracked glass. He tried to ignore the sad and utterly pathetic fact that he was distraught over someone he'd just met, but this proved impossible.

He still had one person to turn to, though. His constant. The one soul who had loved him from the moment he'd been born. And he yearned for her comfort, and wisdom, and guidance, and acceptance, even if she couldn't provide it right now. Just seeing her would be enough. It would have to be. Erasmo gunned the engine, not bothering to wipe the tears slipping down his face.

CHAPTER 30

ERASMO STARED AT the doctor, unsure how to respond, trying in vain to subdue his rising rage toward this man. He'd never seen this particular doctor before, with his weathered face and deep-set wrinkles. The fact there'd been someone new looking over his grandmother when he'd walked in had immediately set alarm bells off. The doctor confirmed there was ample reason for panic when he'd uttered a horrific question, which he now repeated.

"Has anyone talked to your family about signing a DNR?"

Erasmo again stared back in silence. This couldn't be right. Just yesterday they'd been talking about the next steps in her treatment, going over the types of antibiotics they were administering to fight the infection in her mouth. He wanted to scream at this doctor, tell him he didn't know what his grandmother's medical team had planned, that he didn't know what the hell he was talking about.

But the thick medical file in the doctor's hand suggested otherwise. There were only two conclusions to draw. The first was that this outcome had always been inevitable and everything that had come before was a charade, solely to give the appearance of hope when there had, in fact, been none. The second was that she'd had a real chance to survive, but while he was off playing investigator, her body's breakdown had crossed a threshold from which there was no return. He should've goddamn been here.

"DNR stands for 'do not resuscitate,'" the doctor said.

Erasmo knew what it meant from when his grandfather had been in the hospital. But this just didn't seem possible. Every other time there'd been a change in her condition, a new course of treatment had immediately been suggested and implemented. It had seemed like there would always be one more step to try, one more avenue to pursue. But now this doctor stood in front of him, saying this was not true at all.

"I need some time to think it over," Erasmo said, hoping this would shut down the conversation. He just wanted this man to leave so he could spend some time alone with his grandmother.

The doctor nodded with a sad smile, checked her IV drip one more time, and then shuffled out of the room.

His grandmother looked even worse than yesterday, the infection not appearing to have lessened in the slightest. He burst into tears, not caring how abjectly pathetic he sounded. If his grandmother heard or even knew he was in the room, she gave no indication of it.

Erasmo continued to stand over her and sob, almost saying a prayer out of desperation but deciding against it. After all, not a damn one had been answered so far. But there were other options, weren't there?

Yes, there were.

He rose to leave, now knowing what needed to be done. If there was any chance to help his grandmother, it wasn't God he needed to turn to.

As Erasmo pulled out of the hospital parking garage, his phone buzzed. Alma's name flashed on the screen. Shit. Vero must've told her what an asshole he'd been.

"Hey, Alma. I'm sorry if—"

"Where the hell is Vero?" she yelled. Erasmo had never heard her so angry.

"I don't know. I dropped her off at the store earlier. That's the last time I saw her."

"Well, she's not here and my truck is gone. And she's not responding to my calls or texts."

"I really wish I knew where she was, but—"

"I sent you with her so this exact thing wouldn't happen!" Alma yelled. "The only place I can think where she might be is Renata's. That's her only client, so maybe Vero went down there to check on her. But Renata isn't answering her phone, either. You get down to her house right now and see if Vero's there."

Before he could respond or ask why she hadn't been to Renata's herself yet, Alma hung up on him. Erasmo checked his phone. Still plenty of time. He'd just have to make it fast.

When he pulled up to Renata's, Alma's old Chevy was nowhere to be found, which meant Vero wasn't here. Where the hell was she, then, and why wasn't she responding to Alma? Great. As if he needed any more worries right now.

Erasmo rapped on the front door. He intended to get in and out, just ask Renata quickly if Vero had been by. But as the front door swung open, his resolve immediately dissipated.

Manny, her brother, stood in the doorway. Tears streamed down his ashen face, and he wore an expression Erasmo knew all too well: gut-wrenching fear.

"Renata is dying," he said. "She's gotten so much worse just in the last hour. I called an ambulance, but I *know* the doctors won't be able to help her. She's cursed, like we told you from the beginning."

"Can I see her?" Erasmo asked, even though every instinct he possessed screamed at him to leave this place.

Manny nodded and gestured for him to enter.

He immediately smelled the acrid stench of Renata's sickness. As he walked through the hallway, approaching her bedroom, Erasmo's stomach lurched repeatedly. Standing outside the thin door separating him from the festering stink, Erasmo was uncertain he could even force himself to go in.

A loud retch bellowed from inside the room. But it wasn't a noise he'd ever heard a person make before. It was violent and sounded like tearing and ripping and gurgling wetness, as if Renata's insides were being mangled.

When Erasmo opened the door, he saw that wasn't far from the truth.

Long streaks of vomit splattered the walls. Its texture and shape varied at different areas in the room, as if the expelled liquid were a piece of abstract art. He turned his eyes to Renata and immediately wished he hadn't.

She sat in the bed, hunched over, vomit dripping from her lips. Strangely, her eyes had improved, much of the blood now drained from them. But this only served to reveal her blank, incoherent stare.

Renata retched again, her head sinking and shoulders rising. A thick, stinking torrent of red bile erupted from her mouth. It was a grotesque scene. But what disturbed Erasmo most was that she maintained eye contact the entire time, with her dead, vacant stare.

Somewhere within the clumpy liquid expelled from Renata's mouth, Erasmo spotted a brief flash of white. He scanned the bed, searching for what it might have been. It was hard to see in the pools of filth, but then he finally glimpsed a small spot of ivory. And his stomach clenched at what it was.

A single tooth.

Erasmo turned his attention to Renata's mouth and saw with revulsion that half of her teeth were missing.

What the hell was going on here?

A sound came from somewhere deep in Renata's throat, a wet and gurgly moan. It took Erasmo a few seconds of listening to this wretched noise to realize it wasn't a moan at all.

Renata was trying to speak.

He approached her, the stench of bodily fluids making his gut spasm.

"What is it?" he asked. "What are you trying to say?"

Some more wet gurgling, but then he did recognize a few words.

"I'm sorry," she said. "I tried . . ."

"Tried what? What did you try?"

"To . . . to take it back."

His body trembled, overtaken by a bone-deep chill. She'd been lying to them. Or at least obscuring the full truth.

"Shed," Renata said. "Behind the house. Go see."

The strain of speaking must've been too much; her head lolled to the side and she lost consciousness.

As terrible as he felt for Renata, there was no use in staying. He'd done what Alma had asked, and an ambulance was already on the way. He felt a deep stab of regret at not making her go to the hospital yesterday. Erasmo backed out of the room, for some reason hesitant to turn his back to the putrid wretchedness.

Once out in the hallway, he pulled out his phone to text Vero. She probably wouldn't reply, given how ugly their last conversation had been. Wouldn't hurt to try though. He sent her a short message asking where she was, and mentioned that Alma was looking for her. His heart leapt when Vero began to type. He stared at the smudged screen, immensely grateful she was even responding. When the message finally came through, he stared at it, stomach clenched.

Leave me the hell alone.

Damn. What had he expected though? Of course she'd be angry with him. Erasmo sighed and slipped the phone in his pocket, now eager to get the hell out of here. He exited the house and jogged to the Civic, but then a single word drifted through his thoughts.

Shed.

His mind told him that he needed to get going, that whatever was in the shed didn't matter. Renata would be at the hospital soon, and all of this would be resolved.

But his gut told him otherwise. They'd missed something, and he wanted . . . needed . . . to know what. He checked his phone. There was still time.

He turned and crept up the buckled driveway toward the backyard. When Erasmo reached it, he saw there was a single feature that dominated the small square of land.

A large, decrepit wooden shed, sitting at the very rear of the yard.

He walked softly through the patchy grass until he reached it. Had Renata left the shed unlocked? Erasmo tugged on the door's rusted iron handle, and it swung forward. He stepped in.

The planks of wood were in various states of rot and decay. Mold covered the many cracks and crevices, as if it were holding the disintegrating structure together. The shed was almost entirely empty, save for one item that sat in the center: a long rectangular table.

Erasmo approached and peered down at the table, trying to process what lay on it.

Melted candles had been arranged in a complex pattern, and symbols drawn in chalk surrounded them. The symbols were drawn in delicate, flowing lines and formed odd shapes that resembled misshapen eyes and off-kilter triangles.

In the center of the melted candles, a small space had been left bare. Within this space sat an item Erasmo could not make out. He reached for it, hesitated, and then picked it up. He saw right away it was a rudimentary stick figure. But as he inspected the arms and legs closer, he realized with disgust what they were made of: fragments of bone.

At first, Erasmo thought they were tied together by black string, but as he rubbed his fingertips over the surface, it could only have been hair. Human hair. What unnerved him the most, though, was the figure's dark maroon shade. As he glanced around and saw similar colored drops on the table and ground, he understood. This figure made of bone and hair had been dipped in blood.

For the second time in just a few minutes, the same question floated through Erasmo's head.

What the hell is going on here?

He placed the figure down and stepped backward until he was outside again. Was this Renata's work? And if so, what had she been trying to do? Maybe she'd been trying to cure herself and had tried whatever crazy rituals she'd found on the internet.

Approaching sirens filled the air, their wails making his head throb. Renata's ambulance. As much as Erasmo wanted to find out more, he definitely didn't want to get stuck here answering questions. Too much was on the line tonight.

When Erasmo made it back to the Civic, he called Alma and left a voicemail telling her that Vero wasn't here and that Renata was being taken to the hospital.

He released a long sigh and closed his eyes, but his nerves continued to seethe. Erasmo knew where he had to go next, that it was absolutely necessary for what he might have to do, but this knowledge didn't make going any easier. After a few seconds of gripping the steering wheel, his knuckles white, Erasmo finally started the Civic and rolled forward under the late afternoon's quickly darkening sky.

CHAPTER 31

THE SMALL HOUSE, its faded exterior badly in need of a paint job, stood in front of Erasmo. A crooked row of Christmas lights blinked along the roof's edge, reminding him of the many holidays he'd spent here. He shoved those memories away. There was no time to indulge in what their friendship used to be. Things were different now.

Erasmo took a breath and ascended the creaky stairs. He stared at the front door, not wanting to knock but knowing he had no choice. It would be a quick visit, he assured himself, just long enough to get the information he needed. Then he'd get the hell out of here and start preparing for tonight in earnest. Certainly he wasn't going to hang around to listen to any bullshit.

The door produced a dull thud as he pounded on it. At first, there was no movement. But then soft, hesitant footsteps approached, pausing on the other side. Maybe, Erasmo considered, he wouldn't even let him in.

But then the dead bolt suddenly retracted, and the door swung open.

Rat, who until recently had been his only friend in the world, stood in the doorway, eyes wide and jaw open. He seemed in utter disbelief that Erasmo was standing on his doorstep. Neither said a word until Erasmo finally broke the silence.

"I need your help."

Rat's tiny eyes narrowed in suspicion, but he slowly nodded and stepped aside to let him in.

They walked into the cramped kitchen, and Erasmo sat down at the round, scarred oak table where they'd shared meals so many times before. Rat settled in across from Erasmo, fidgeting and uncomfortable.

"Look," he began, "I—"

"Do you remember," Erasmo interrupted, "when you were obsessed with demonology a few years back?"

"I . . . wait . . . what?" Rat asked, incredulous.

"You read all those books on summoning and communicating with demons, remember? You became more of an expert on the topic than I ever did. Look . . . I know things haven't been great with us lately, but I was really hoping to pick your brain."

Rat shook his head, as if doing this would make sense of what Erasmo had just said.

"What the hell are you talking about?"

"It's for a case I'm working on."

"A case? I don't . . . Look, why don't you start from the beginning. Maybe I'll understand better what's going on."

So Erasmo did, describing in detail all the events that had happened since receiving Bradley's email. It felt good to let everything out, to unburden himself to this person who had once been his sole confidante.

"I'm going to make you some tea," Rat said when he was about halfway through the story. "Looks like you could use some." He rose from the table, filled a kettle, and placed it on the stove.

Rat then sat back down and listened in silence to the rest of the story without as much as a head nod. When Erasmo finished, he said nothing, instead rising to pour the tea. After setting a steaming mug in front of Erasmo, he finally spoke.

"Don't you see what's going on here?"

Erasmo took a sip of the tea, immediately feeling better as the warm liquid traveled down his arid throat.

"I do," he said. "That's why I came here. I need to be prepared for whatever summoning ceremony or ritual they might perform tonight. If you can just tell me the most likely—"

"Do you really think these people are *actually* going to conjure a demon and sacrifice a child to it?"

"Probably not," Erasmo said. "But I'm fairly certain they're going to at least try. And if by some miracle they're successful, I need to be prepared."

"Prepared for what exactly?"

"Well," Erasmo said, "what I really need to know is . . . what's the best way to enter into a bargain with a demon? What will it accept in return?"

"You're telling me that you want to make a deal with the Devil?"

"Not *the* Devil, but *a*—"

"Erasmo!"

"I—"

Erasmo wanted to tell Rat he knew the chances of this happening were infinitesimal, but that he'd do anything to save his grandmother. He'd saw his goddamn arm off if that's what it took. And if there was even the slightest opportunity to bargain with a powerful demon tonight, he wasn't going to hesitate.

He wanted to say all of those things but couldn't. His throat was closed somehow, like it had constricted to the size of a pinhole. Now his vision darkened, and a wave of dizziness overtook him. Erasmo felt like he might topple right over, even though he was sitting down. And then, unable to move his limbs, he slid right out the chair.

His face struck the linoleum floor, and the mug of tea came crashing down along with him, shattering. The still-steaming liquid pooled by the side of Erasmo's face, and he now saw tiny grains of white powder floating within it.

Rat rose from his chair and stood over him, glaring down.

"Sorry," he said. "But I can't let you leave here tonight."

CHAPTER 32

WHEN ERASMO WOKE, he had no idea where he was. The stiff bed he lay on was unfamiliar, and it was too dark to make out any of the room's details. He tried to get out of bed but his balance was nonexistent, and clumsily plopped back down. After a few deep breaths, Erasmo tried again, and this time he was able to rise, albeit unsteadily. He stumbled around for a bit before finally managing to find the light switch and flick it on.

The room was sparse. In fact, the only item of note was the twin bed he'd been lying on. There wasn't even a closet to rummage through. The one structural feature it did possess was what Erasmo now stared at, his heart withering into a shriveled husk.

There was nothing special about this window. Faded baby-blue paint peeled from the frame, and no curtain hung from it. More importantly, black burglar bars covered its exterior. But the thick metal rods blocking any hope of escape weren't what set his heart to palpitating. No, it was what this ugly window presented to him, a terrible truth he'd not noticed until now.

The dim, late afternoon light that had shone when he'd arrived at Rat's was now gone, replaced with complete and utter darkness.

Erasmo suppressed a scream. How long had he been out? Was it too late? He took a deep breath, forcing himself to stay in control. Maybe there was still time. For all he knew, it was only early evening, leaving plenty of time to get to Sanger House by midnight. *Or*, a part of his brain insisted on whispering, *you could have been out for days.*

He turned away from the window and studied the room again. Had he been moved somewhere else while he was unconscious? No. Erasmo knew this room. In fact, now that his head was clearing a bit and his eyes had adjusted to the dim light, it was obvious where he was. This was the spare bedroom at Rat's house, one he'd rarely ever come into. As he stood there, considering his current situation, a single, inescapable conclusion settled over Erasmo.

Rat was in on it.

This was the only explanation that made sense.

His once best friend had kidnapped him. And why would he do that? Clearly to prevent him from going to Sanger House. Rat must've joined up with Vassell at some point in the last few months after they'd parted ways. Had the group reached out to him like they had Andy? No. There was a much simpler explanation.

When he found out they weren't a team anymore, Andy saw his opportunity and recruited Rat to join those sick assholes. His bones burned in rage at this thought, and Erasmo felt a twinge of regret he hadn't hurt Andy more when he'd had the chance.

What now? He had to get out of here, but Rat certainly wouldn't let him go until the ceremony was over, when it was far too late.

Erasmo slipped his hand into his pocket but then remembered he'd left his phone in the Civic. There was something else his hand brushed against, though, a potential lifesaver Rat hadn't known to look for. He slid the switchblade out of his pocket and regarded it, overwhelmed with relief. There was still a chance.

Erasmo inserted the tip of the knife between the door and the striker plate, about three inches above the knob. He slid the knife down until it made contact with the bolt, then worked the knife side to side. After several unsuccessful attempts, he was rewarded when the bolt finally slid out of the doorjamb.

Erasmo opened the door slowly, but this didn't prevent a loud creak from echoing throughout the house. He froze, certain that Rat would come running at any moment. When no sounds approached, he cracked the door open a bit more, just enough to slide through, and entered the hallway.

He was surprised to be greeted by his own expressionless face. Erasmo took a moment to study the picture hanging on the wall. It was of him and Rat, standing on the Donkey Lady Bridge, their arms over each other's shoulders. Rat beamed, but apparently, he himself had been unable to muster even the slightest smile.

It was unfathomable to Erasmo how they'd gotten here. This just couldn't be right. How was it possible for Rat to have fallen in with these kidnappers and thieves, for his once friend to have actually drugged and kidnapped him? And now here he was, having to sneak through the house they'd made so many memories in, hoping just to survive and escape. He took one last mournful glance at the friends they used to be, then crept down the hallway toward the front of the house.

As Erasmo approached the living room, he heard Rat's voice, his words too muffled to understand. After reaching the end of the hallway, Erasmo poked his head out. Rat stood in front of the smudged window, peering out as he listened on the phone. Was he expecting someone?

That wasn't important. The only thing that mattered was getting to the baby in time. Luckily, he had the element of surprise. Erasmo slowly crept up behind Rat, balling his sweaty hand into the hardest fist he could.

"I have him," Rat said into the phone, "just like we talked about. Got lucky. He showed up out of the blue. Now all we have to do is—"

Erasmo punched his only friend in the back of his head, watching in horror as he crumpled to the ground. Rat writhed, groaning in pain and shock. Erasmo stepped over his body, unlocked the front door, and ran out of the house, his sobs drowning out every other sound in the world.

As soon as the Civic started, Erasmo stared at the dashboard clock, unable to look away, fearful that what it said would somehow change if he did.

11:02 p.m.

There was still time. It wasn't too late. A desperate grunt floated in the night air. He turned to see Rat, lurching through his yard and toward the Civic, arms outstretched, tears in his eyes. Erasmo gunned the engine and sped away, grateful the screeching tires drowned out the sound of his old friend's cries.

CHAPTER 33

AS HE SPED down I-10, Erasmo grabbed his phone off the passenger seat, horrified to see five missed calls. Three were from Torres, no doubt still wanting his statement on what had happened at Bradley's.

The other two were from University Hospital. His heart froze, slowly sinking to dangerous depths as he continued to stare at the screen. A single voicemail notification blinked in the corner.

Erasmo eyed the message, trying to work up the courage to play it.

His phone then lit up, its screen telling him the hospital was calling yet again. Erasmo's hand involuntarily spasmed and squeezed the phone in a death grip, as if trying to crush it out of existence. After a few seconds, he finally forced himself to answer it.

"Is this Erasmo Cruz?" a stern voice said. "I'm Dr. Weaver. We've been trying to reach you. Your grandmother has taken a turn. You should really come down here as soon as possible—"

Erasmo disconnected the call and placed the phone down on the passenger seat, his hand shaking.

Too many thoughts tumbled together at once, each one vying for their time in the light.

His grandmother was going to die. This seemed a certainty now. Even though every day of her illness had been a step in this direction, he still felt completely unprepared. Erasmo shivered uncontrollably, thousands of icy pricks piercing his skin.

He needed to be there for his grandmother, of course. He owed her everything. The least he could do was be with her when her time ended.

But the child. How could he leave him in the hands of those monsters? They meant to harm him, there seemed little doubt about that. He couldn't just allow it to happen.

Maybe there was a way to do both. To help the baby and his grandmother. Wasn't that what his thoughts had been dancing around . . . what he'd been too afraid to speak out loud? He knew the odds of these people wielding that kind of power was small. But the tiniest glimmer of hope was surely better than the cold certainty of despair.

And then afterward, if he was still in one piece, he'd find Vero and apologize to her.

Erasmo checked the time again. 11:15 p.m. He gripped the steering wheel tighter and again gunned the engine.

When he finally turned onto US-87, dread spilling from every cell in his body, only twenty-five minutes remained until midnight. The fast food restaurants and gas stations that lined I-10 now gave way to open spaces and a smattering of local businesses. He passed an auto repair center on his left, as well as various scattered warehouses, all deserted this time of night. After a few minutes, his phone's navigation directed him to turn left onto a smaller, narrower road, lit only by dim moonlight.

He soon approached a church partially hidden in the shadows, a massive wooden cross planted out front. The road began to feel more and more desolate the farther he proceeded. Each open field, cloaked in gloom and shadows, made him increasingly uncomfortable.

He'd never had reason to drive all the way out here before, down a country road like this. With every sprawling property he passed, Erasmo realized just how far away from town he really was. As if to underscore this, he neared a group of cattle grazing in an open field on his left. They stared at him with dull, vacuous eyes, their curved horns glowing in the moonlight. A sudden, frantic urge to stop and turn back overtook him. But the navigation continued to guide him deeper down this dark, winding road, and he obeyed.

11:40 p.m.

As Erasmo passed a long stretch of rusted iron fencing, an unnerving thought occurred to him. If in fact the baby really was at this house, he wasn't entirely sure how to get him out safely. He'd been in such a rush to escape Rat's and get to Sanger House by midnight, there'd been no time to come up with a plan.

He contemplated calling Torres. But what exactly was he going to tell her? That he was racing out to some mysterious house to stop a cult from sacrificing Bradley's child? She'd never take that seriously. Not to mention this place was at least forty-five minutes away from her.

Still, if he could get proof of what this group was doing in there, maybe she'd come running. All he needed were some pictures, or perhaps some video. It wasn't much, but it was better than no plan at all. And there wasn't time to come up with anything better.

Besides, he had no idea how many of them would even be there. Maybe there'd only be a handful, and he could find some way to sneak in and take the child without them noticing. Erasmo had a brief image of a horde of masked maniacs descending upon him while he desperately shielded a baby in his arms, but he quickly shoved this terrible vision away.

11:43 p.m.

Damn. Each passing minute felt like a nail being pried from one of his fingers. The remoteness of the area wasn't helping his nerves, either. When he'd first turned onto this road, there'd been a fair number of properties and ranches, each one fenced and gated. But the farther he drove, the less frequent they'd become. The land rose steadily around him, waves of tree-covered hills now undulating in the distance.

Of course, there was also the possibility that none of this was even real. How much faith could he have in Andy, who'd been lying to him for months? Or Gemma for that matter. Maybe she'd just given him a random address, and he was about to get his head blown off by some rancher as soon as he set foot on the property.

11:45 p.m.

Shit. This was going to be close. Erasmo willed the navigation to show the house only a single minute away, but his phone continued to tell him otherwise. An open field with a row of rusted-out horse trailers approached on his right. As he passed, several pairs of yellow, ravenous eyes peered out at him, their bodies obscured by darkness. Erasmo wondered for a moment which animals, so greedy with hunger, made their homes in those rusted skeletons.

As he drove, the obvious question continued to gnaw at him. What was he going to find at this house? And what exactly would they be doing to Bradley's child? Despite his suffocating fear and worry, a small part of him was undeniably curious.

Erasmo thirsted to know about their rituals and beliefs and what black magic they believed in. And, of course, he desperately wanted to understand more about this terrible creature they loved so very much.

11:47 p.m.

This thought led to a faint stirring in his chest. At first, he was too much of a coward to acknowledge its nature. But deep down, he knew exactly what it was. Hope.

Of course, Erasmo also knew perfectly well that it was ludicrous to carry hope in his heart. Cold logic told him that. Was there going to be anything inside this house that could help save his grandmother? Almost certainly not. But surely it wasn't a sin to feel the slightest flicker of hope, when hope was all you had left.

11:48 p.m.

He passed another open field on his left. Large decrepit warehouses strangely protected by barbed wire lay deep in this shadow-soaked property. A sick, unreasonable part of his psyche urged him to stop the car and find out what secrets lie inside of them. He ignored it.

Soon, a small dirt road, if you could even call it a road, appeared on his right. The navigation told him the house lay in that direction. Almost there. Erasmo clenched the steering wheel in a death grip and turned onto the path.

As he drove, lush trees surrounding him on both sides, a disturbing thought occurred to him, one he unsuccessfully tried to push away. What if Bradley's child actually was at this house, and he couldn't stop Vassell from killing him? A brand-new life, full of vigor and promise, snuffed out because he was too weak to stop the tragedy from unfolding. He imagined having to tell Bradley and Delia there'd been a chance to save their child, but he'd screwed the whole thing up. The thought made him dizzy, and he shook his head to clear it.

Unable to stop imagining this terrible scene, tears slipped down his face. *Please, let me just get this one thing right.*

And then, as if in answer to his desperation, a chime informed him he'd arrived at his destination.

11:52 p.m.

Erasmo pulled the Civic over, swallowing hard when he saw the tall metal fence surrounding the property. He'd have to ditch the car and try to climb over it. Not only that, but the house itself was nowhere in sight, which meant it must be located deeper into the property. It would take some time to reach the house. Time he didn't have.

11:53 p.m.

He tried to push the panic away, but it flooded every vein, every nerve in his body. He threw the car door open and sprinted to the fence. It was black and wrought iron, around six feet tall. Not insurmountable, but he eyed the sharp spearheads at the top of each post with worry. Normally, he'd have stood there and brainstormed a way to climb over the fence without getting gored. But there was no time. He'd just have to go up and hope for the best.

The black metal was cool and slick as he wrapped his hands around the top rail. Erasmo pulled himself up, feet scrambling to find purchase on the slim fence posts. After much struggle, he finally managed to get the tip of his left foot on top of the fence, in a small gap between the spearheads. Erasmo pushed upward until his right foot was on top of the rail as well, also in one of the small gaps.

He stood straight up, intending to gently hop off the fence, but couldn't find his balance. Erasmo teetered backward and screamed in panic, certain he was going to fall off, right back to where he started. He lurched his body forward, overcorrecting, and toppled over headfirst.

As he fell, his face just moments from colliding with the lush grass underneath him, a deep, searing pain erupted in Erasmo's left calf. He barely had time to register it before his nose and forehead smashed against the ground. For a few seconds, Erasmo saw nothing but shimmering blackness. He shook with relief when the world finally reappeared around him, blurry as it was.

When his vision came into full focus, he glanced down at his leg. A bloody, ragged gash ran the entire length of his calf. From the spearhead, no doubt. It hurt like a son of a bitch, but he didn't have time to sit there and wallow in the pain. Erasmo grunted as he got to his feet and surveyed the land. It was dark, so there was no real way to know where the house even sat on the property.

11:55 p.m.

Panic, true panic, now gripped his heart and squeezed. He wasn't going to get there in time. The Children of M were probably preparing for the ceremony at that very moment, and they were going to take Bradley's child to the summoning circle, and they were going to—

Wait. A glimmer in the distance. It took Erasmo a few seconds to realize he was seeing car headlights. He gaped at the vehicle's silhouette. It must be an elder, late for the ceremony. He ran after the car, willing himself to ignore the excruciating pain in his leg.

Erasmo kept his eyes locked on the car's taillights, afraid that they'd suddenly blink out of existence. He must've only been running a few minutes at most, but his lungs burned furiously, and the muscles in his legs threatened to cramp. To make matters worse, this part of the property ran uphill, and seemed to get steeper by the moment. Just when he was sure his legs were about to give way, the land leveled off, and he finally reached the hill's apex. Erasmo surveyed the land in front of him, and his breath caught at what he saw: a massive two-story stone house, sitting only a few hundred feet away.

He sprinted toward the structure, his calf hurting so bad he dragged his leg behind him. The pain in his right arm was agonizing, the slightest motion setting his tender flesh on fire. Whatever was going on in there, he sure as hell hoped he could stop it with just half a body.

As Erasmo approached the house, he studied it closer. It didn't have much in the way of architectural flair, as it simply resembled a large stone square. The front was covered with windows, thick black curtains blocking any view of the inside. His eyes were drawn to the front door.

The thick slab of wood was large and imposing, and as bright red as the blood now seeping from his leg.

Erasmo briefly considered trying this door, hoping it might be unlocked, but quickly thought better of that plan. Even if it were open, there'd surely be someone posted to greet visitors and he'd be caught immediately. The safer bet was to sneak in through the back entrance. Or a window, maybe.

He headed along the side of the house, searching for an opening. The moon's weak light showed him only old gray stone covered with mold. He kept limping forward, his alarm growing, in disbelief at how goddamn long this house was. Erasmo didn't want to check the time but knew he had to. When he pulled his phone out and glanced down, a soft cry slipped from his lips.

11:59 p.m.

He forced himself to swallow the whimpers bubbling in his throat and kept walking. When Erasmo finally reached the end of the house, he'd already decided that if there was indeed a back door, he would kick the goddamn thing in if he had to. As he rounded the corner and the land behind the house came into view, he stopped, gazing at what lay in front of him.

Cars. At least fifty of them. Which meant there were a lot more people in there than he'd been expecting. He scanned the makeshift parking lot. The cars varied from old beaters to sparkling luxury vehicles. Seemed like the guest list for this gathering was pretty damn diverse. Did these cars belong to those who'd already made their bargain? Or perhaps they belonged to those yet to make one.

Erasmo crept along the back wall, searching for the rear entrance. He breathed a sigh of relief when he finally came across a plain white door, its paint showing the first signs of fading. The brass knob was cool to the touch. He twisted it but then paused. One of them could be standing right behind this door. Or a lot more than just one. He stood there, unsure what to do, but then Erasmo heard a sound that broke his paralysis.

A baby's piercing wail, filled with terror, erupted from somewhere inside the house.

Erasmo just stood there, shocked at the nerve-shredding sound, even though this was the very reason he'd come. But believing something to be true and confirming the actual truth of it were two very different things. He'd been right. This was really happening. Bradley's child was in there, and they were killing him.

Erasmo placed his ear to the door and listened for the slightest sound. Nothing. They must be somewhere else in the house. He turned the knob and slowly opened the door, whispering a desperate prayer to the universe that luck would be on his side just this once. But as his eyes fell upon what waited for him inside, Erasmo's heart stopped, and a strangled groan escaped his throat.

He stared, eyes bulging, attempting to convince himself this was all his imagination. But the longer he studied their hideous contours, and their savage expressions, and their lecherous grins, the more Erasmo knew it was real. He blinked, just to make sure, but when he opened his eyes again, nothing had changed.

A roomful of robed, masked lunatics continued to stare back at him.

CHAPTER 34

THEY WERE ALL here. The demented rabbit; the bird with the long, horrific beak; even the monkey with the gouged-out eye, all standing in front of Erasmo, studying him wordlessly. None of them had moved so much as an inch since he'd opened the door. It was unnatural. In fact . . . it was too unnatural.

He walked farther into the room, legs trembling, and took a closer look at them. Then he understood his mistake. Erasmo glanced around, studying the space, and realized what he was standing in.

A cloakroom.

The robes and masks in front of him were empty, hanging from hooks attached to the ceiling. Relief coursed through him, but it was short-lived as the obvious question now flitted through his head.

Where were the monsters who wore these costumes?

Andy had mentioned that only the elders knew who everyone was. They must've ditched their masks for this ceremony since they already knew each other's identities. He took a quick photo of the cloakroom. This wasn't enough to prove anything concrete, but it was a start.

The baby shrieked again, so long and hard that Erasmo worried the child wouldn't have any air left in his lungs.

He peered around the corner, heart pounding, into a kitchen. A sigh of relief escaped his lips when he saw no one inside. Beautiful maple cabinets lined the walls, and an island with a butcher-block top sat in the middle of the room. But strangely, there were no appliances. Or maybe it wasn't so strange. Gemma had said the house was only used for special gatherings.

Like tonight.

Erasmo kept moving, desperately attempting to stay quiet while his heart roared in his chest. Surely these maniacs would come running if they heard even the slightest sound. And if they caught him, the baby would die for sure. Not to mention, they'd certainly slaughter him as well.

He now found himself in a large dining room. A formal mahogany table, lined with antique, long-backed chairs, dominated the space. But thankfully there was no one sitting at the table, and no food of any kind on it. Were it not for the cars out back, he'd be sure the house was empty.

He tread lightly toward the next doorway, but to his horror, a loud creak suddenly arose underneath him. Erasmo froze, certain a stampede of footsteps would erupt at any moment. *Goddamnit.* He'd ruined any chance to save the baby. And his grandmother. He stood there, teeth clenched and skin soaked in sweat, waiting. But to his shock and immense relief, no one came.

Erasmo gathered himself and gently stepped into the next room, limbs shaking. The first and only feature he noticed was the grand staircase rising from the center of the floor. His eyes followed the wide steps covered in crimson carpeting. When he saw what they led to, his heart spasmed. Erasmo tiptoed up the stairs, terrified a plank of wood would groan and loudly announce his presence. Despite the agony in his calf and arm, he continued upward, afraid to even breathe. After he finally reached the landing, Erasmo stared at what stood in front of him.

A set of massive double doors.

But it wasn't the doors themselves that had sent him up the stairs. It was the symbol scrawled on them. The same one carved into Vassell's stomach. He tried to imagine what atrocities lay on the other side, each image his mind conjured worse than the last.

This was his chance to get proof. If he could open the door quietly, take a few pictures of whatever depravity was happening, he'd send them to Torres. Then maybe he could find some way to protect the baby until she got here.

He grabbed the left door's curved metal handle and was about to gently pull it open, when a sharp pinprick pressed at the back of his neck. It took Erasmo several moments to realize someone was holding a knife to his flesh.

"Mr. Cruz," a familiar voice said from behind. "I am again impressed at what a resourceful young man you truly are. Now, turn around slowly, or I'm going to shove this knife into your neck and sever your spinal cord."

Erasmo did as he was told. Vassell stood in front of him, dressed in a vintage tuxedo, grinning at him wildly.

"So persistent," the old man said, his mouthful of yellow teeth on full display. "I almost feel a bit remorseful that I'll soon slit your belly open and slop around in your guts." He winked at Erasmo. "But I'll get over it."

Erasmo studied Vassell's crazed face and recognized a simple truth. The old man, without question, meant to slaughter him.

"You lied about the baby," he blurted out, hoping to buy some time.

"I lied to you about many things that aren't your concern, Mr. Cruz . . . that are outside of your comprehension level. What, do you think because you might have seen a ghost or two that you understand the true power of what lies on the other side of this paltry existence?"

Vassell ran the blade, which he could see was a dagger of some kind, up the side of Erasmo's face until it rested directly underneath his left eye. All the old man had to do was flick his wrist, and Erasmo would feel the gelatinous insides of his eyeball sliding down his cheek. Vassell pressed the blade forward, and its tip began to penetrate the thin skin of his bottom eyelid. Erasmo's vision blurred as the knife pushed his eyeball farther back into its socket.

"You've never been in the presence of *true* power," Vassell said, breathing erratically now. "You've never seen a being that warps your fragile mind forever, that changes your understanding of the natural universe . . . what wonders and horrors it's capable of producing."

"Everything you've ever told me is bullshit," Erasmo said. "All you do is hurt people."

"You have no idea who we are or what we do. Do you think we're simply some gullible, misguided worshipers of Satan? How feebleminded of you."

Even more pressure built up under Erasmo's eyeball. If Vassell applied any more, the blade would slide into his eye with ease.

"We serve a higher purpose. To spread our Master's word and to gather souls for Him. Spending eternity with Him would truly be a gift, one we are attempting to give to anyone willing to listen. And the best part is, my brothers and sisters and I perform this service as one. This gives us something you don't have. A purpose. An existence bound together. This beautiful life we have is what I'm protecting from your interference."

A shriek erupted from behind the double doors. There was no question now. The baby was definitely inside that room. And they were doing something to him. Something monstrous.

"And despite your misunderstanding of our generous attempt to save precious souls, of the sacrifices we make . . . you break into *my* sanctuary and attempt to force *me* to conduct the sacred ceremony? As if I'm some sort of trained monkey? Not to mention *this*."

Vassell held up his left hand. It was heavily bandaged, but blood seeped through anyway.

"Even then, I was going to let it all go. To allow you to suffer in your ignorance and continue the sad, pathetic life you've been trudging through. But now you show up here, and I can only believe you must be a gift. From the generous universe to me."

The old man slid the knife down to Erasmo's belly, his breath quivering in anticipation.

"And now it's time to open it."

Every muscle in Erasmo's body tensed. He didn't fear dying. In fact, he occasionally longed for it. But not like this. Not at Vassell's hands. Not before he could stop whatever horrors were being inflicted on that poor child, right behind those doors.

And not before he found out for sure if there was any possible way to save his grandmother. The slimmest of chances was still a chance.

Erasmo saw the old man's arm twitch, as if in slow motion, the beginning of a deadly lunge that would end with the dagger deep in his belly. He was just about to grab the old man's wrist when a voice spoke from the bottom of the stairs, freezing them both.

"Leave him be," a deep, electronically altered voice said.

Erasmo immediately recognized the voice's cadence. Vassell, in his ill-fitting tuxedo, blocked Erasmo's view of the figure at the bottom of the stairs. But he shifted to the left, managing to peek over the old man's shoulder.

And the cult's leader, wearing his horse-skull mask, stared back at him.

The mask was just as unnerving as when he'd first seen it under the city. Greasy black hair fell around the yellow, elongated skull, and for some primordial reason, this disturbed Erasmo terribly. He wore the same onyx robe as before, with crimson symbols stitched into its rich, black cloth.

"Vorax," Vassell said, a touch of fear in his voice. "This insignificant *boy* was about to interrupt our guests, about to learn things he shouldn't. We need to get rid of him, before—"

"I decide what we need," Vorax said, turning his unblinking eyes to Erasmo. "Mr. Cruz. Come with me. I would like to talk about your future."

"I'm not going anywhere with you," Erasmo said, baffled at what the two of them could possibly have to discuss.

"Oh, but you are, Mr. Cruz. Because if you don't, then I'll allow Vassell to proceed with disemboweling you."

"But the baby—"

"If that's your concern," Vorax said, "I can assure you, no permanent harm is coming to the child."

As if to disagree, the baby erupted in a furious wail, screaming in what sounded like pure agony.

"Here is my offer, Mr. Cruz. Come talk with me. And then afterward I will escort you into that room and you can see for yourself what is transpiring in there. If you choose not to come with me, then Vassell will spill your guts onto the floor, and you'll never get into that room anyway."

Erasmo considered this. He couldn't escape the cold logic of what Vorax had just said.

"Don't do it," Vassell whispered. "Let me put you out of your misery. I can see a part of you wants me to. The part of you that's sick and rotting. I'll make it quick. I promise."

These words, spoken with greedy desperation, were enough to get Erasmo moving. He took a tentative step at first, and then quickly descended the stairs. The sooner they got this over with, the sooner he could get to the baby.

Vorax turned and led him to a mahogany door located behind the staircase, opening it wordlessly. The room was intimate and dimly lit, flickering candles covering most of the floor. A narrow path led from the door to a perfect circle in the center of the room. Erasmo followed to the circle and shuddered when Vorax turned to face him. Cold, unblinking eyes peered at him from behind the mask.

"Do you know who I am?"

"Yes," Erasmo said. "You're the leader of a group that scams people and kidnaps innocent children when they won't pay."

"I meant," Vorax said, "do you know who I am underneath this mask?"

"How the hell would I know that? The only way would be—"

Erasmo's heart ceased beating.

The only way would be if he *actually* knew this person. Not from watching a deranged ritual under the city, but in real life. That just wasn't possible though. Was it? He cycled through names in his mind, frantically searching for someone he knew—or anyone he was even aware of—capable of leading these psychopaths. But not one person seemed to fit the profile of the masked figure standing in front of him.

"You can't figure it out because your thinking is limited. For all your knowledge and experiences you still don't understand the true power of the forces you insist on dabbling in. But I can teach you."

"Teach me? I don't . . . Wait . . . is this some sort of recruitment?"

"You can call it whatever you'd like, Mr. Cruz, but what I'm offering is a ladder out of the sad, broken existence you're currently living. I can show you—"

"You can just stop right there. What on earth would make you think I'd *ever* join you?"

Without warning, Vorax gently pulled up the horse mask, revealing their true face.

"Because," Vorax said, "I used to be just like you."

CHAPTER 35

ERASMO STARED AT the person standing in front of him, only one coherent thought reverberating in his head: he had absolutely no idea what the hell was going on inside this house.

"The first time you came to me at the antique store," Gemma said, her face flush and sweaty from being covered by the mask, "I *knew* it was fate. You'd been sent, from Him, so I could help you. So that you could be a part of all this."

"I don't understand," Erasmo said, his mind struggling to put the pieces together. "You said things ended badly with these people . . . You seemed so scared of Vassell . . ."

"Well, I couldn't exactly be truthful about my involvement, could I? It was all a bit of an act, hoping you'd leave until I could figure out what to do. But you wouldn't take no for an answer. So I mentioned Vassell to get rid of you, and then called and warned him to make sure everything looked okay in case you dropped by. I honestly had no idea you'd be so tenacious. But I'm glad to see it. This resolve will serve Him well."

"I don't . . ."

"I know," Gemma said, "so many questions. Most of the answers simply boil down to this: despite your doubts, the creature we worship is very real, and He's chosen me to lead His followers."

"But you work at the antique store. How is this . . . ?"

"I'll share a secret about us. A substantial amount of money comes into our group through various means. We use the antique store to clean the funds, so no suspicions are raised. The Soul Center serves a similar function, in addition to serving as a recruiting ground."

"But Vassell, I thought he was the—"

"The old man is a genius at gathering followers and taking care of the ugly work, which is sometimes required. I couldn't ask for a better number two. But he's impulsive and has a reckless temper, so our Master chose me to lead. Our Master doesn't tolerate lapses in judgment. Vassell was quite surprised at being demoted, I can tell you that. Don't think it's what the old man had in mind when he brought me on."

Erasmo wasn't sure what to say. He had so many other questions, but one in particular burned hottest on his tongue.

"What did you mean when you said you used to be like me?"

"I think you know what I mean, Erasmo. I saw it all over your face when I mentioned my screwed-up parents. The blood drained from your skin, and you practically started crying."

Erasmo reflexively cast his eyes downward, embarrassed at his transparency.

"I looked you up after your first visit to the store. There are some interesting stories about you online. The incident at the Ghost Tracks. The kidnapping several months back. Not one single word about your parents, though. That's what I meant about being like you. I was discarded by my parents, too. I was unloved and walking through this world lonely and alone, searching for even the faintest light to cut through the darkness. Just like you are now."

He listened, trying to understand what she was trying to accomplish by bringing all of this up. But then a sudden and unexpected reaction to Gemma's words swept through him.

And Erasmo began to weep.

His body shook uncontrollably, and he was unable to catch his breath. Erasmo tried to stop sobbing, in disbelief at his own weakness, but found it impossible to do so.

"Don't be ashamed," Gemma said. "It's difficult to hear your entire existence summed up in a few meager sentences. The recognition of its ugly truth is what you're reacting so strongly to. In fact, Vassell said something similar to me when I first met him."

Even through his emotional outburst, Erasmo saw an opportunity to ask Gemma a question he'd been turning over since they'd talked at the park. "Did . . . did he really know why your parents didn't love you?"

Gemma gave a subtle smile at this, just the slightest tick around the corners of her mouth.

"Is that your way," she said, "of asking if we know why your parents didn't care about you?"

"No," he blurted, "I was just . . ." He blinked away tears, now giving in and saying the words writhing on his lips. "Do you? Know why they didn't love me?"

"I don't," she said after a moment. "But I'm sure He does, as He knows all. And I have no doubt He will bestow the gift of this knowledge upon you. And that is *exactly* what it is . . . a gift."

"How could knowing such a thing possibly be a gift?" he asked.

"Because knowing is freedom. Knowing is letting go. Knowing is understanding that what happened to you was the result of their weakness, not yours. When I found out what kind of pathetic creatures my parents truly were, my life changed forever. All you have to do is join us, and I promise that an entirely new life will be yours."

Whether by accident or design, Gemma had said the magic words. A new life. Wasn't this what he craved . . . an entirely different existence than the one he'd stumbled through for the past seventeen years? Even though Erasmo knew Gemma wasn't to be trusted, he couldn't deny her offer was intoxicating. The idea of being free from all the bullshit that constantly plagued him . . . its gravitational pull was undeniable. Maybe he could agree to stay for a while. Just to gain a better understanding of how—

No. He couldn't consider this. He couldn't. He'd never find his way back. Erasmo shook his head, as if to dislodge the ideas that were at that very moment perilously close to gaining purchase.

"I'm not joining you," he said.

Gemma sighed and nodded, a slight grimace on her face.

"I understand your doubts. I wish we didn't have to resort to such methods, but they're necessary evils. Our Master has very specific needs. And in truth, those people did enter into the bargain willingly."

Erasmo opened his mouth to retort but snapped it shut. Even by Bradley's own account, he'd said yes on that stage eighteen years ago.

"There is so much to gain by joining us," Gemma said. "We've learned much about you. For example, we are aware that your grandmother is gravely ill. Don't you want her to live? He has the power to save her. It would be nothing to Him."

Erasmo tried to wrap his head around Gemma's claims. Did she truly believe all this? This question, though, just obscured what he was really wondering.

What if Gemma's claims *were* true?

Sure, her story seemed too fantastical to be real. But so had other stories he'd heard that turned out to be much more than what he'd expected. Perhaps if he saw evidence of this creature, he could help them learn ways to worship it without committing atrocities. Surely there were ways to placate this demon without hurting anyone.

No. He was trying to talk himself into something insane. All because he was too scared to be alone.

"I could never join a group that would bring harm to a child," he said, focusing on the one act above all others that made them so monstrous.

"Is that what's bothering you?" Gemma said softly. "If so, then let me assure you, no harm is coming to Zevelek upstairs. A minor discomfort at most."

"Zevelek?"

"Oh, that's his new name. Everyone who joins us starts fresh, as if their previous life never even existed. That's how He demands it."

"A baby can't willingly join anything. You stole him."

"We did not," Gemma said. "Erasmo, please, you cannot seriously think that imbecile Bradley obtained his perfect life on his own, do you? Our Master held up His part of the deal. Now the baby is ours. And as Vassell told you, we were going to give Bradley a chance to get his child back, but . . . well, the best-laid plans and all that. To be honest, I'm glad it ended up this way. My strong preference is always to keep the children."

"But if you're not harming him, then what are you doing—"

"I'll show you. I'll take you upstairs right this very moment and you'll find that he's perfectly safe."

She approached him and placed her delicate hand on his shoulder.

"You have every reason to join us. Don't you want your grandmother back home with you and in your life for many years to come?"

Erasmo marveled at Gemma's ability to stoke his most fervent desire. His recognition of her tactic, though, did little to mute its effectiveness. Even now, as a muffled cry from the baby floated down, he ached to say yes to her, to beg for his grandmother's life. As long as they weren't hurting the child. And she promised they weren't.

"I see the struggle on your face," Gemma said. "I'm offering you a new existence and knowledge you would never unearth on your own. But let me end my proposal by acknowledging what the true offer is. It's what you value above all else. The only thing you've ever really wanted."

Gemma paused, and Erasmo said it for her, a barely audible whisper.

"Family."

"That's the only reason," she said, "I joined this group. And the same reason you'll join, too. I see now this must have been His plan all along. He clearly set the wheels in motion that led you directly here. You can't think this was all accidental."

Erasmo didn't want to give credence to what Gemma said, but the timing was hard to ignore. On the exact night his blood family was slipping away, a new family was offering to take his grandmother's place.

As if it were meant to be.

"After you pledge yourself to Him, His followers will be your lifelong brothers and sisters. They would kill for you, and you for them. You will never, ever be alone in this world again."

As these words echoed in his ears, Erasmo felt a tension inside of him, a tension he'd never lived without, suddenly loosen and release. Gemma had said the words he'd been longing to hear for so very long.

Ever since his grandmother's health had spiraled downward, he'd been plagued by so many worries. Some were minor, and some never left his thoughts. Every night he'd lie awake, terrified of his impending graduation. Erasmo imagined the many families around him in tearful embraces after the ceremony, while he desperately searched the crowd in vain, knowing full well there wasn't anyone there for him.

And what about after high school? He had no money for college. Was he just supposed to just keep doing this? Walking into absurd, dangerous situations in the hopes of scraping together a meager existence?

His grandmother had once told him that if anything ever happened to her, he needed to go out into the world and find his own family. It had been impossible, though, to imagine that anyone would ever accept him. Not after the two people who'd created him threw him away.

But now his grandmother was on death's door, and a new family had found him. It couldn't be a coincidence. Perhaps this was fate. Maybe this was the universe—after all the disappointments it had inflicted—finally offering him a way forward.

Erasmo couldn't deny that he yearned to know what secrets lay behind those doors, to discover how much of what Gemma said was true. Was it so bad to want to find out if they could really help his grandmother?

Besides, this was the only way to know for sure what was happening to the baby. He had to accept her offer to get back there. For the baby's sake. Right?

"Okay," he said, fresh tears now streaming down his face. "Okay."

"Great," Gemma said, a genuine smile gracing her face. "You won't regret your decision. Now, let's go see what's happening upstairs, shall we?"

CHAPTER 36

ERASMO HELD HIS breath as they stood outside the double doors bearing the demon's sigil. A strange combination of relief and trepidation coursed through him. Relief that he'd possibly found what he had spent his entire life looking for. But trepidation that what he was about to see would incinerate that hope into nothing but dying embers.

"Remember, keep an open mind," Gemma said, her hand wrapped around the door handle. "What you see might be a bit . . . distasteful at first. But I'll explain everything, and you'll come to understand that it's not so bad at all."

Erasmo's stomach convulsed. If she'd meant for this to soothe him, it hadn't worked.

"Here we go," she said, the door creaking as she pulled it open.

He sucked in a deep breath, released it in a trembling exhale, and slowly stepped in.

Erasmo's first thought was that he'd somehow walked into the wrong room. None of what he'd imagined was actually in here. No robes, or masks, or summoning circles. The room wasn't dimly lit with flickering candles. There were no writhing masses of cult members chanting in a lost tongue.

Instead, it appeared as if he'd entered a posh gala of some sort.

Erasmo watched in shock as refined gentlemen in tuxedos casually wandered the room, making jovial conversation. Women in sultry ball gowns sauntered throughout, also in great spirits judging by their buoyant natures and wide, frozen grins. Light jazz music played softly in the background.

"Some of these people have come from all over the country," Gemma said. "On special occasions like this, I insist that everyone dress up. It's good to celebrate once in a while. Especially when good fortune shines upon you."

"What are you celebrating?" he asked.

An infant's wail erupted from the back of the room. Erasmo stood on his tiptoes and craned his neck, but a cluster of bodies blocked his view. He walked toward the shrill screams, now feeling the attention of the room turn to him. Eager, grinning faces nodded in his direction, welcoming him.

He studied them, his potential new brothers and sisters. They were a true blended family. Every age range accounted for, and multitudes of skin tones and nationalities. As Erasmo nodded back, he studied their faces, wondering if the portly middle-aged man in front of him was the person under the bird mask. Or if perhaps the elderly woman who now waved at him shyly was the Boar. They stepped aside as he passed, as if he were Moses parting the Red Sea.

And as Erasmo moved through them, he tried his best to ignore what was smeared all over their faces.

Soon, he reached the group in the back that had been blocking his view. They didn't move for him as the others had. Instead, their attention was solely focused on the baby, although Erasmo still couldn't see him through the mass of bodies. A balding man in his mid fifties emerged from the group, eyes rolled back in his head. He wiped absently at his mouth and shuffled away, rejoining the party.

There was a sliver of an opening now. Erasmo squeezed in and pushed his way forward. If anyone around him minded, no one said so. They all seemed too focused on what was happening up front to pay him any mind. His heart thrashed violently as he approached the front. When Erasmo finally emerged from the eager group, he stopped, eyes wide at what he saw.

A white bassinet sat against the back wall. It clearly contained the baby, as the full force of his cries now reached Erasmo's ears. He should have been relieved. No one was harming or even touching the child. His worst fears slowly dissipated. But then he saw the long, thin tube snaking out of the bassinet. His eyes followed its short path to the elderly man a few feet away, holding on to the other end. The old man looked at the end of the tube with delight, his pale tongue flicking in and out of his mouth. It took Erasmo a few moments to understand what the thin tube was, but when he saw what flowed through it, knew without a doubt.

It was an IV line.

He watched in growing horror as the baby's blood flowed through the tube. The old man smacked his lips, and Erasmo could see he had no teeth. The old man tilted his head back, raised the end of the IV line, and held it over his open, quivering mouth. Fat drops of blood fell onto his tongue, and the old man convulsed in delight. He continued to smack hungrily at the end of the IV line, until his face was smeared crimson, like everyone else in the room.

After a few moments, he finally appeared satiated, and Erasmo was relieved the disturbing scene was at least temporarily over. But in fact, it was not. The old man now held the IV line over his right eye, and Erasmo watched in disbelief as two drops of blood fell directly onto his pupil. He then did the same with his left eye. The old man blinked several times, appearing as if he were crying tears of blood. He then grinned, showing off his bloody gums. The next person in line, a young gaunt woman with the same eager look in her eyes grabbed the IV from him, her mouth widening into a gaping maw as she desperately shook the IV.

A firm grip took hold of his shoulder, and a whisper tickled his ear.

"See," Gemma said. "The baby is not being harmed in any way. He barely even cried when we put the line in his arm."

Erasmo was shocked at the nonchalant manner with which she'd said this.

"His blood loss is carefully monitored by one of our doctors," she continued, "to make sure we don't take too much."

Gemma's lips parted in a smile, revealing perfect, red-stained teeth.

"After all," she said, her grin growing even wider, "we wouldn't want anything to happen to the little guy."

His legs felt weak underneath him and came close to giving way.

This was wrong. All of it. Every cell in his body reverberated with this truth. The plan. He needed to stick with the plan. Surely these blood-smeared faces, the baby screaming in the background, would be enough for Torres to at least be curious about what was happening here.

"But . . . I don't understand," he said. "Why on earth would you do this?"

"I know it seems a bit strange. But that's just because you don't understand the immense power it gives us."

"Is this something your Master requires of you?"

"Oh, no," Gemma said, shaking her head. "Not at all. But He's responsible in a way. At least once a year, He requires the blood of a child."

She turned and gestured to the baby. Here was his chance. Erasmo slipped his phone out, opened the camera app, and hit Record. He slipped it back into his pocket, making sure the lens remained outside. He then slowly turned to different areas of the room, trying to capture as much as possible.

"But if the blood is for him, then why are you . . . ?"

"Well," Gemma said, turning back to him, "a few years back, I watched with reverence as He drank heartily of our offering. And I had an epiphany."

Erasmo watched as the gaunt woman eagerly lapped up the fat crimson drops falling into her mouth.

"Why not have a taste for ourselves?" Gemma said, grinning.

Erasmo's stomach lurched.

"It's only fair. Think of it as payment for the invaluable service we perform. Plus, we like to think that drinking the same blood as our Master brings us closer to Him. As close to being His children as we can get."

Erasmo peered around, sickened at the unbridled glee in all the crimson-stained faces. So much blood in this room . . . in this house. A sudden realization struck him. Maniacal laughter built in his chest, even though nothing about this was at all funny. Andy had misunderstood. Sanger House. That's what he'd thought they called it. But Andy knew very little Spanish. It was, in fact, *Sangre* House.

Blood House.

A fleeting image of grabbing the baby and making a run for it flashed through his head. But where would he go? So many bloody-faced true believers surrounded him. He'd never get through them all. At least he had some video now. Gemma's back was again turned, so he slipped his phone fully inside his pocket so she wouldn't see it. All he needed now was a chance to send the message.

"You were right," he said, "when you told me that I would find this distasteful."

"Oh, my dear boy," she said, a note of pity in her voice. "This isn't even the distasteful part."

CHAPTER 37

GEMMA TOOK HIS hand and led him past the blood-drunk patrons to a tall door in the corner of the room. The demon's sigil was carved in its aged wood.

"This leads down to the basement where you'll prove your loyalty to your new family," she said.

Gemma pulled the door open, revealing a dank stairwell. He stepped in, the warped floorboards creaking underneath his feet. The cramped passage was unlit, every trace of light disappearing as the door closed behind them. He felt around, using the narrow walls to guide him as he descended into the darkness.

After a minute of stumbling down the stairs, it seemed to him they should've reached the basement already. Perhaps this underground structure was particularly deep, suited for their unique purposes. After another minute of descending into the dark, though, the obvious question rang through his head.

Just how far down were they going?

Finally, right when his nerve was on the verge of dissipating, Erasmo's right foot left the last stair and landed on bare dirt. They were here . . . wherever *here* was. It was still too dark to see anything. As he proceeded forward, the thick rustle of

Gemma's robe grew quieter until it vanished entirely. She'd left his side and was now nestled somewhere in the darkness.

"Gemma?" he called. "Are you there?"

The silence and absolute darkness combined to unnerve him. Had she abandoned him down here? Had this all been a ruse to lure him to an underground chamber where he'd be at their mercy, left to starve and rot?

This was his chance though. Erasmo slipped his phone out, praying to the universe there was at least one bar of reception. He almost cried when two bars glowed in the top right corner. But before he could even touch his finger to the screen, both bars disappeared.

"No . . . no . . ." Erasmo stared at the phone, willing the reception to come back, when something even worse happened. He hadn't charged his phone all day and watched in horror as the screen suddenly blinked off. Shit. The video must've drained the last of the battery. And now, tears did slip down his face.

Erasmo turned in the direction they'd come from, hoping to at least see a shadowy outline of the stairs. But there was nothing, only darkness, still and complete. He could wander around, hope to stumble across the stairs or an opening of some kind. But there was no way to know what resided down here, or what he might accidentally fall over or into. But what choice did he have? Gemma had clearly abandoned him. Just like everyone else.

Erasmo turned to try and find the stairs, when a ball of flame erupted to his right, twenty feet away. The chamber was partially visible now, and he could see that the flame came from a torch, lit by Gemma. She again wore her horse-skull mask, its greasy black hair shimmering in the weak light. Gemma walked along the now visible stone wall and lit another torch, and then another, until the edges of the chamber were clearly defined. She then placed the torch down and faced the middle of the room, which remained in complete darkness.

It was this pocket of hungering black that Gemma approached and was soon consumed by. Her voice, however, escaped the pull of the dark vortex and reached his waiting ears.

"State your name."

This was it. Was he really going through with this? Cold logic told him no, that this was insane. The black void inside of him whispered a different answer.

"Erasmo Cruz."

"This will be the last time you think of that name as yours. Our Master will bestow a new name upon you. But first, you must prove your loyalty to Him, and to your new brothers and sisters. Can you do that?"

He thought of his grandmother lying in that hospital bed, the image of her skeletal face and withered body making his heart spasm. Two words slipped from Erasmo's lips with shocking ease.

"I can."

"Excellent."

"What oath shall I recite?"

"Oath?" Gemma said, almost laughing. "There is no oath that must be spoken in order to join us. There is only what you must do."

"And . . . what is that?"

Gemma did not respond, allowing his words to linger in the stale air.

"What is it I have to do?"

"This place is called Sangre House . . . Blood House . . . for many different reasons," Gemma said. "Its history, how we acquired it, what lives down here, what we do within these walls, all of it contributes to the name it's acquired. You asked what you have to do? It's simple. You must give it some."

"What? Blood? Okay . . . I can do that. Just give me a knife and I'll slit my palm or my chest—"

"No," Gemma said. "Not from you."

A small ball of flame erupted from the center of the room, which had been consumed by darkness until this very moment. Erasmo could see Gemma now, holding the torch that had produced the flame, except she wasn't alone. A figure sat next her, bound to a chair, a hood over their head. Gemma grabbed the top of the hood and slowly pulled it up.

In the dim light, Erasmo at first had trouble recognizing the grim, dirty face staring back at him. But soon his eyes adjusted and made out the shimmering black hair and fierce, trembling eyes. The identity of this person was inescapable.

"Vero," he whispered.

"We caught her wandering around the property. Guess she was trying to help you, the stupid fool."

"Let her go!" Erasmo screamed, the words sounding desperate and shrill.

"Let her go?" Gemma asked. "Oh, that's not possible. Then how would you prove yourself to your new family? Understand this: no matter what you say, no matter what choice you make, she's *never* going to leave this basement. Either you kill her, or we will drain her blood for our Master. He finds the taste of young ones like her quite delectable. Either way, her flesh will be rotting underneath our feet the next time we come here to worship."

"I can't hurt her. I could never . . ."

"You'd rather continue to live a pathetic existence? I see the fear in your eyes. I'm not sure if it's fear of me, or fear of your friend dying. But do you know what true horror is, Erasmo? It's facing this world with no one by your side. Family is supposed to protect us from this sick, depraved world. They're supposed to share and rejoice in our best moments on this earth. And when we lose them, or never even had them at all . . . well, that's real horror. The fear flickering in your heart for this girl is *nothing* compared to that."

Gemma produced a curved blade from her robe and held it out to him.

"Don't fret, Erasmo. There is so much to gain. You will never walk this world alone again. You will gain multitudes of brothers and sisters. You can save your grandmother. Isn't this what you want?"

It was. Of course it was. Every word she said rang true in his heart. Gemma's offer was an answer to his most desperate prayers. But as he stood there, watching Gemma caress the curved blade, a single question burned within him.

Was any of this even real?

For all of the rituals, and masks, and outlandish claims, he had yet to see one true shred of proof this creature even existed. Not a single one.

"Why do you serve Him?" he asked. "What is it that you receive in return?"

Gemma sighed, as if she were a mother disappointed with an underachieving child.

"We have titans of industry within our ranks. And those who live on the streets. And everything in between. He bestows different gifts to each of us. Riches, love, good health . . . even children, when doctors said such a thing wasn't possible."

"That's it?" Erasmo asked in disbelief. "Those are all just events that happen in the course of everyday life. People make money, and have children, and recover from illness. How can you possibly attribute those things to some demonic power?"

"Oh, Erasmo. That's your problem. You don't have enough faith." Gemma paused, head tilted to the ground, as if mulling something over. "Clearly, I haven't been persuasive enough," she finally said, placing the curved blade on the ground and reaching into her robe. She produced a slim, weathered book, holding the text with reverence, almost as if she were afraid of it. "Perhaps a glimpse of our Master's true word will convince you."

She approached Erasmo slowly, holding the book out to him. It appeared to be a leather-bound journal of some sort. His first instinct was to tell Gemma to get away, that he had no interest in seeing it.

Except . . . there was something familiar inscribed on the front cover.

No. It couldn't be.

He reached for the book, hands trembling, the aged leather smooth and supple under his skin.

He stared at the words, his body shaking at their impossibility.

John F. Dubois.

CHAPTER 38

HOW COULD THIS be? He'd searched far and wide for any other books by Dubois, and had never come across even the hint of one. But this wasn't a published book. It looked to be his personal journal. One of a kind. Vassell said he'd spent years hunting down a text that claimed to know the secrets of a powerful being. This must be it.

On the last page of *A Practical Guide to the Supernatural and Paranormal*, Dubois said that he'd ventured off to meet a man who claimed to know how to summon spirits. Was this his account of what had happened afterward? Of what he'd found during the rest of his travels?

Erasmo held his breath and turned to the first page. It was filled from top to bottom with densely packed sentences, the penmanship crisp and perfect. He read the first few paragraphs.

> *At long last, I've finally discovered a genuine opportunity to make contact with Emma's spirit. I learned of a man in Germany who'd gained a reputation for performing minor miracles. I sought him out, and after much persuading, he finally divulged the source of his powers. He claims that during a moment of great personal turmoil,*

a winged demon appeared to him. The creature offered a deal: the power he wished to possess in return for either a life of servitude or his first child. This gentleman chose his future child, as he had no desire to ever be a parent.

I have no child to offer, but would gladly serve this creature for the rest of my days if it meant the chance to hear Emma's voice again. To tell her again how much I love her. But I know not how to contact this demon, as he appeared unbidden to this gentleman. So now I must scour the earth for this creature, and make my own deal with him.

Erasmo quickly flipped through the pages, stopping at certain sections that jumped out at him.

I have immersed myself in research, hunting for a piece of information that might lead to this creature who makes bargains. Unfortunately I have felt unwell as of late, and this has hampered my efforts. I've managed to compile some information though, particularly in regards to the most famous example of selling one's soul: Dr. Faust. The demon Mephistopheles, who is said to have acted as the Devil's agent when making his deal with Faust, fascinates me. Is this just lore, a myth built upon in later works of fiction? Or is there an element of truth to this story? Perhaps if I can't communicate with the Devil directly, I can make contact with one of his servants.

A few pages later: *My research indicates that Mephistopheles is an exceptionally powerful demon of trickery and hatred, responsible for making deals with mortals, and bringing nothing but eternal suffering to those who accept the bargains. While they are not condemned to Hell, they are instead cursed.*

Erasmo thought of Bradley, locked away in a cell, his child taken from him, his entire life upended. Cursed indeed.

Several pages later, Erasmo noticed Dubois's sentences becoming sloppier, often not even written in straight lines.

Nothing has worked so far. Despite my every effort, despite my exhaustive research and many attempted rituals, neither this deal-making demon nor its servant will appear to me. To make matters worse, I fear I am becoming severely ill. My head aches constantly, and my body is wasting away. The opium I've been medicating with has not helped in the slightest. Progress must be made before it's too late. I have now turned to lesser known texts, written by some who are thought to be disreputable, but who claim to know great secrets. I've also heard whispers of a group in Prague said to consort with a demon. I hope to make contact with them soon.

Erasmo flipped ahead. There weren't many pages left. He stopped on a page in which Dubois's words were now barely legible scrawls.

I did it. My search is at long last over. The majestic creature finally appeared to me in the middle of the night, black wings unfurled, and offered a grand bargain. He promised to make me well and allow me to speak to Emma in return for a life of servitude. I wept and wept and wept as I screamed yesyesyesyesyes until my throat was so raw I spit blood.

I inquired of my Master how I'd be serving him. He spoke not with words but as a growling voice in my head. He explained that I would offer deals on His behalf and ensure that the participants fulfill their bargain. I was to

extract coin, blood, and other payment from these unfor-
tunate souls once the deal ran its course.

    Yes! I screamed at Him in jubilation. Yes! I shall serve
as your very own Mephistopheles. It will be an honor to
find those who call out for you. I had but one question for
Him before beginning my new journey.

    Are you the Devil? I asked. If not, then what demon
are you? He did not answer at first, but then finally
said . . . my name has never been uttered by human lips.
I was born into royalty, not so long ago. As you are my
servant now, I will share a secret with you.

    Demons breed.

    Yes. What a beautiful thought. Demons breed. There's
no doubt so many of them now, all around us, watch-
ing, waiting, fornicating with each other and producing
more beautiful monstrosities. The words continued to float
through my head and then rolled off my tongue.

    DEMONS   BREED   DEMONS   BREED
DEMONS BREED DEMONS BREED DEMONS
DEMONSBREEDDEMONSBREEDDEMONS-
BREEDDEMONSBREEDDEMONSBREEDDE-
MONSBREEDDEMONSBREEDDEMONSBREED-
DEMONSBREEDDEMONSBREEDDEMONS

Erasmo's hands shook so badly he almost dropped the book.
This was too much to process. Dubois had been his hero growing up. He'd read through *A Practical Guide to the Supernatural*
and Paranormal countless times. In fact, much of what he'd
learned about the supernatural came from that book. But now
seeing what had become of Dubois—an ill, deranged junkie
unable to tell truth from fiction—it was sickening and heart-
breaking and incomprehensible. But a horrifying understanding of his current situation now began to overshadow even this.

The Children of M. Erasmo had never understood the meaning of their name, but now did.

The Children of Mephistopheles.

They thought of themselves as His successors, agreeing to and enforcing deals on behalf of their Master.

This thought was disturbing enough in and of itself. But what truly sent cold dread slithering through his veins was a realization that unnerved him even more.

Every single one of this group's beliefs were based on nothing more than the ramblings of a madman. The demon, the bargains, the rituals, the kidnappings, all the result of deluded writings from long ago.

"None of this is real," he said to Gemma. "None of it. Can't you see that? The person who wrote this was *clearly* sick and delusional."

"So quick to dismiss," Gemma said. "I know you feel the power emanating from those pages, Erasmo, just like we all do. But you choose to ignore it. That's okay. It takes time to let go of childish understandings, to comprehend our Master's word fully. In fairness, I also had my doubts when I first read the sacred text," Gemma said. "Until Vassell demonstrated its power to me. He used the instructions within it to summon our Master, and then I understood its words were real and true."

Erasmo hurriedly flipped through the rest of the pages, each more disturbing than the next. Crudely drawn pictures of horned demons fornicating. Scrawled instructions on how to conduct ceremonies of worship. Guidance on how to find and assimilate new servants. There were faded, blotchy stains on each page, some covering whole passages. He imagined Dubois's hands, stained and dripping, smearing blood everywhere as he fervently filled these pages. A familiar passage then stopped him cold.

My Master whispered more instructions to me last night:

Worship unto me, and receive an eternity of everlasting pleasure.

Youth shall be our lifeblood, Youth shall light our way.

Vassell had read these words during their underground ceremony, before they killed the piglet. His eyes lingered on the sentences, his stomach dropping out from underneath him.

"*This* is why you take children?" he screamed at Gemma. "Because of these two lines? They could mean anything! He might have meant just to recruit new people into your group. Not to literally take the blood of a child, you sick, deluded fuck!"

"The blood is a necessity, Erasmo," she said. "You have no concept of the power it gives Him . . . of the power it gives us. But everything will become clear once you join." She removed the book from his hands and placed it back in her robe.

Gemma walked back to the curved blade and stood next to it.

"Now . . . no more stalling. You must decide. Are you going to prove your loyalty and save your grandmother?"

Erasmo glanced at Vero. Her eyes looked different now, drained of their usual self-assurance. It took him a moment to recognize what alien presence he saw in them, but then understood.

Vero was scared.

"All you have to do is sate his thirst with this ignorant creature's blood. Such a small price to pay for your grandmother's life."

Gemma gestured at Vero, who now looked even more distraught than before. "She's going to die anyway, Erasmo. Is it even much of a choice?"

Logic told Erasmo there was no choice to make, that everything Gemma and her group believed was wrong. Dubois's demented journal was clearly proof of this. His gut, though, whispered soft but insistent doubts. Bradley's life had changed completely since he'd agreed to the deal. Erasmo had seen monstrous creatures with his own eyes, both at Bradley's and in the alleyway. This group was *so* convinced the demon was real. And Dubois, who'd been a light to him in an ocean of darkness, believed it, too. Wasn't there still a chance the demon really existed?

He eyed the curved blade, its razor-sharp edge glimmering in the torch's fluctuating light. It would slice Vero's skin with ease, separating flesh from bone without having to apply an ounce of pressure. All he'd have to do was place the tip to her soft skin and let the knife do what came naturally.

If there truly was a creature, his grandmother could be saved. Isn't that why he came here? In truth, isn't it why he even took this goddamn case in the first place . . . because a small part of him had heard what Bradley claimed, and immediately wished he could make a deal, too? And now here it was, being offered to him.

"Such a small sacrifice," Gemma prodded, "for gaining so very much."

Erasmo allowed his eyes to wander over Vero's face again. In the shock of seeing it was her underneath the hood, he hadn't had time to fully process what this meant.

She'd come looking for him.

This person whom he barely knew had risked her life coming to this madhouse. To help him. This seemed impossible and yet there she was, staring at him, waiting for his decision.

The idea that Vero would do this grated against every notion Erasmo had about himself. It meant that Vero thought his life was worth something, that it was worth protecting. And if that were true, then wasn't it possible she might not be the only person who would ever feel that way?

An image of Rat lurching through his yard, sobbing, arms outstretched, formed in his thoughts. Why had they been fighting the last few months? Even now, it wasn't quite clear in his head. But Rat had cared for him once. Maybe he would again. Maybe there was a chance to go out into the world and fulfill the wish his grandmother had for him.

"I'm not going to hurt her," he said, tears slipping down his face. "I don't need you. I'll find my own family."

"Oh, Erasmo," Gemma said. "Whoever you find will just abandon you. Don't you see there's an inherent flaw, deep inside of you, that repels others? Why do you think your parents never wanted you? No one will ever stay with you. Except us."

"Maybe that's true," Erasmo said, "but I have to try."

"Very well," she said, sighing. "That's too bad."

Then, in a quick, smooth motion, Gemma picked up the knife and slid behind the chair. She stared at Erasmo with dead eyes while she slowly drew the curved blade over Vero's throat, splitting it wide open.

CHAPTER 39

HE SHRIEKED SO loud that a high-pitched tone now rang in his ears. Unable to convince himself this was real, Erasmo continued to stare at the gaping maw in her neck, blood spilling from it in waves. Vero wore an expression of shock, of incomprehension, as the color drained from her face and down her neck.

Erasmo fell to his knees and screamed again as Vero's body slipped off the chair and landed face-first in the dirt. He was about to crawl to her when a flicker of motion caught the corner of his eye. After scanning the room, he stopped breathing entirely.

Robed figures lined the walls of the chamber, each one wearing their horrific mask. The movement he'd seen was a demented chicken with bloodstained teeth, leaning over to whisper to the elephant beside him, its trunk amputated and ragged. A footstep whispered behind him. Erasmo turned to see the one-eyed rat looming over him, holding a metal pipe over his head. The last thing Erasmo saw before darkness overtook him was the gleam of excitement in the Rat's single, unblinking eye.

The chanting roused him from unconsciousness. Erasmo's eyes opened to see Vero's lifeless body lying next to him, facedown. He wanted to unleash another shriek at seeing her like this, but didn't have the strength. His throat was all screamed out.

He was surrounded by masked, sadistic murderers. They sang in a reverent monotone. The language flowing from their lips was foreign, one he didn't recognize and was certain few would. No, these words fell out of common usage long ago, kept alive only in late-night gatherings, mingled with blood and prayer. And even though he didn't know the meaning of the words, it was clear to Erasmo what these believers chanted so wide-eyed and savagely for.

They were summoning their Master.

And despite himself, despite everything that had happened, despite the very situation he now found himself in, Erasmo couldn't escape an undeniable truth: A part of him was curious if this demon would actually appear. In fact, a part of him desperately wished for it.

The chanting suddenly stopped. In unison, each of them pulled open their robes. Like Vassell, thick scar tissue in the shape of their Master's sigil covered their bellies. They produced daggers and began carving the ragged symbol into their flesh, using their scars as a guide. Grunts of both pain and pleasure filled the chamber.

When the skin carvings were finished, crimson was splattered all over the walls and dirt floor. Blood House indeed. But they weren't done yet. Apparently, defiling their flesh and maiming themselves was not quite enough to persuade their Master to grace them with His presence.

"Who here would like the honor of calling forth the Creature of Wishes?" Gemma said.

A deafening cacophony erupted from the group, each one pleading to be chosen, fingering the open wounds on their stomachs as they did so. Gemma strolled in front of them, studying each one, as if she were appraising livestock. Finally, she stopped in front of a mangy dog, its long, diseased tongue hanging from a slobbering mouth. The Dog whimpered in delight when she reached out and felt his sliced flesh.

"You," Gemma said.

The Dog wasted no time. He made a beeline for Erasmo, straddling his chest while producing a still bloody dagger. Erasmo tried to resist, to buck him off, but between his gouged calf, burning right arm, and the blow to his head, he had nothing left. The Dog ripped off Erasmo's shirt and immediately set himself to the task of carving his master's sigil.

Just minutes before, Erasmo had thought his throat was out of shrieks. He'd been so very wrong.

The pain was blinding and absolute. The Dog was not content to simply slice his flesh on the surface, which would have sufficed for his assigned task. Instead, the Dog used enough strength to force the dagger bone-deep. Erasmo was certain the sound now reaching his ears was that of the blade grinding against his ribs. He screamed for his grandmother. He screamed for Rat. And then he just screamed.

But then Erasmo saw something unexplainable. His eyes remained on this impossibility, unable to take them away despite the savagery being inflicted to his body. The more he looked, though, the more his disbelief faded, until Erasmo became absolutely certain.

Vero was moving.

Subtly at first. A slight shift to the side. A twitch in her shoulder. But now she slowly rose from the ground, her face trembling with pain and determination. And, he could clearly see, unbridled rage.

Now on her feet, Vero raised her right leg, coiled it, and unleashed a vicious kick to the Dog, who until then had not noticed her resurrection.

He tumbled to the ground, his mask falling off from the force of Vero's kick. A teen boy, his face pockmarked with deep acne scars, stared back at Erasmo. If they weren't the same age, they were damn close.

Erasmo turned back to Vero. How had she done it? How had she—

Then he saw. The wound on her neck was covered with some kind of dark substance. A poultice, he realized. But the wound had been much too massive. How could she still be alive?

But then her words, words she'd spoken just that morning, echoed in his ears.

"A bruja, a real one, can make a poultice that closes any wound, out of nothing more than spit, dirt, and the right combination of words."

Vero. A bruja. A practitioner of dark magic.

"Well, look at that," Gemma said, eyebrows raised. "So, you know a few cheap parlor tricks. Do you feel special because you can make some simple mud that clots your blood? Our Master will be here soon. Then you will experience what *true* blood magic is. These silly plants and herbs and incantations you rely on are nothing in comparison."

Vero scanned the room, taking in the masked, blood-soaked believers surrounding them, ending with a withering glare at Gemma. Vero reached into one of her utility jacket's many pockets and produced a handful of what appeared to be fine dust. She held it out in her open palm, pursed her lips, and blew.

The powder flew from her hand, as if brought to life by her breath, and quickly spread throughout the room.

"What?" Gemma asked. "Are we supposed to be scared of a ground-up plant you grew in your garden?"

"Yes," Vero said, a glint of violence in her eyes.

"You'll forgive us," Gemma replied, gesturing to her brothers and sisters, "if we're unimpressed." Each member now approached them, blood still dripping from their bellies, daggers in hand.

"That's because," Vero said with barely restrained ferocity, "you don't know my true power, *pendeja.*"

She whispered to herself, the words too faint for him to make out, and then did something Erasmo would never forget. Vero turned to him, gave a slight smile, and winked.

Immediately, a deep bellow of pain erupted from one of the cult members. The Boar, it appeared. The Boar ripped off its mask, revealing the pale, sweaty face of a lithe blond woman. After a few seconds, a mass of liquid erupted from her mouth. At first, Erasmo thought it was vomit, but even in the dim light he could see it was something else. Thick and mucus-like, with another substance floating inside of it. Blood. The other substance was blood.

Now all of them were bent over and heaving, some not getting their masks off in time. The stench of bile and shit and piss filled the room. Gemma staggered backward, holding her stomach and jerking wildly.

"No," she grunted. "No . . ."

"Now are you scared?" Vero asked.

The robed figures, including Gemma and vomit-spewing Vassell, scattered, stumbling into the darkness, no doubt desperate to get out before Vero could harm them further.

Amid the chaos, for just a second, Erasmo saw a face he thought he knew. It took him a few seconds to place who it might be.

Ashley.

Could it really be her? It was hard to tell for sure, as this person had been retching violently when he'd glimpsed her. But then Erasmo thought of all her questions that night at her apartment, of how she'd been so eager to help out, how she'd shown up *so* fast to Bradley's to get them out of that hole. Had she been keeping tabs on him the whole time? He tried to get a better look, but the figure he thought was Ashley had already stumbled away. It didn't really matter, though; he had bigger concerns.

"The baby," Erasmo croaked. "We have to get him."

"I'll go," Vero said. "You stay here and rest. After I find him, I'll track down a phone and contact Detective Torres."

And in what seemed like just a few seconds, the underground chamber he'd almost died in went from a chaotic frenzy of screaming and violent retching to absolute silence. The effect unnerved him. But after just a few moments, the quiet was broken by the slightest shuffle floating from out of the darkness.

Damn. One of them must've stayed behind. Maybe they were too weak to get away. Or maybe they'd stayed to finish him. Maybe—

And then Erasmo saw what emerged from the shadows, and every one of his thoughts evaporated. His mind was useless in the face of what stood in front of him, peering down. He tried to speak but no words came, his throat clenched tight. It wasn't until a deep, unnatural voice floated toward him that the silence was broken.

Who is this frail boy that has dared to summon me?

CHAPTER 40

ERASMO STARED UP at the massive creature towering over him. Its onyx skin stretched smoothly over lithe, impossibly long limbs. Leathery wings spread out majestically, but then slowly closed, settling over the demon's bony back and shoulders. The creature glared at him, its yellow irises reflecting the torch's dim light.

"I . . . I didn't summon you. It was them. Your servants."

You claim not to have summoned me, and yet, here you stand, with my sigil carved into your flesh.

"I didn't place it there. They did. It's just an accident that I'm the only one here when you arrived."

There are no accidents in this universe. You were always meant to wear my sigil, and I was always meant to appear to you.

"Are you saying . . . this meeting was fated to happen?"

Predestination is unable to adequately explain why certain events occur and others do not. But you are standing here, bleeding for me, which means only one thing.

"What?"

You wish to make a bargain.

Erasmo's breath caught in his throat. Because despite this creature's clear malevolence, despite the viciousness that emanated from it in fierce waves, this very thought had just entered his mind.

"If I did wish to make a bargain . . . what would you require of me?"

The demon's vertical irises narrowed, studying Erasmo closer.

Nothing you currently possess.

"But something I will one day?"

Yes.

Erasmo considered this. If the creature looming over him was to be believed, he'd have something worthwhile eventually, something tempting enough for the demon to want. But was this true, or one of the many lies that surely rolled off its salivating tongue with ease?

He had no idea what possessions his future self may hold one day. But Erasmo was acutely aware of what he was about to lose right goddamn now. And it was within his power to save her. He didn't even have to hurt anyone to do it. Just his future self. And that price, he was perfectly willing to pay.

"Save my grandmother from dying."

The creature's eyes widened ever so slightly.

This is what you desire above all else?

"Yes."

The demon was silent. Erasmo was about to repeat himself when it spoke again.

What you ask is within my power, but I cannot enter into this bargain.

"Why?" Erasmo screamed, his fear of the demon suddenly giving way to anger.

I cavort in lust, and greed, and selfishness, and regret, and blood, and revenge. These are the wishes I grant. Perhaps there is something else you wish for.

"I don't want anything else."

The demon stared into him, its withering gaze one of either disbelief or disappointment.

Then there is no bargain to be made.

The creature spread its glorious black wings, preparing to return to wherever it had come.

"Wait!" Erasmo screamed.

The demon paused, regarding him with impatience.

"Where you reside . . . do you know if . . . have you ever seen . . . ?"

Say the words.

"Is . . . is my father there?"

The demon said nothing, instead only regarding Erasmo with its pensive yellow eyes. After a few moments, it finally spoke.

So much curiosity over a damaged soul you've never even met.

"I just want to know . . . if he's there."

You are a strange creature, Erasmo Cruz, unlike any other who has dared to summon me. I will not answer your question, as you have yet to pledge your servitude. But I do find your sad, tumultuous soul interesting. Perhaps there is a deal to be made after all. Perhaps.

"I'm willing to pay the price. As long as I'm the only one who gets hurt."

So determined to destroy yourself. Over transgressions that aren't even your own.

"I mean it. I'll agree to whatever you want. But only if I'm the one who suffers."

The terms of the agreement are not negotiable. They were set eons ago.

"Well, if anyone is going to get hurt, then I don't agree to the deal."

Erasmo was surprised when a frail-sounding voice echoed throughout the basement. His own.

I'm willing to pay the price, it said, repeating the words Erasmo uttered just seconds earlier.

"No. I take it back now. I meant only if no one was going to get hurt besides me."

I'm willing to pay the price, his voice said again, echoing from all around him.

"I don't understand," Erasmo said. "Are you saying we've already entered into an agreement? Or . . ."

Everything will happen as it should, the demon said, its voice somehow lighter now. In fact, the creature almost sounded happy. *I promise.*

"I don't know what that means!"

Perhaps we will meet again, Erasmo Cruz.

And with that, the demon retreated into the darkness and faded out of existence, leaving only an unnerving silence behind.

Erasmo crumpled to the floor, the pain in his skull and limbs growing more severe by the second. The torches burned low, what little light there'd been retreating rapidly. The dark grew emboldened, reclaiming its territory inch by inch. Soon, he couldn't tell if the waves of blackness undulating in front of him were from the chamber's all-encompassing darkness, or from his consciousness slowly drifting away. Perhaps it was both, joining together to carry him away to a void he might never escape.

CHAPTER 41

ERASMO WOKE TO the sound of violent, urgent ripping. What was being torn apart with such glee? His flesh. It must be. The scars on his stomach, and forehead, and the newly born wounds on his stomach, those were just the beginning. More of him was being torn apart this very second. It was true . . . it was . . .

It was his jeans. Erasmo opened his eyes to a young, burly paramedic cutting and ripping his pant leg off.

"Hold still," he said. "Need to get your calf patched up before you lose any more blood."

Erasmo glanced down and saw that his stomach had already been cleansed and bandaged.

"I gave you something for the pain," he said. "We'll get you to the hospital once I finish dressing this wound. Can't take you up all those stairs with you bleeding like this."

"No," Erasmo said. "I can't go to the hospital right now. Just clean me up and I'll stop by there later."

"Check him for a concussion, too," a voice said from behind. "I can see a huge lump on his head from here."

"Will do, Detective Torres," the paramedic said.

She stepped into his field of vision and stared down at him, pale as a ghost.

"The baby . . ." Erasmo said. "Vero . . ."

"Both fine," Torres said. "Upstairs being checked out. Vero already briefed us on what she knows. Damn crazy story. I'll need your account of it, too, when you're feeling well enough."

"Derrick Vassell and Gemma Stone. You need to find—"

"Already scouring the area for them, along with anyone who might be wearing a robe or have vomit or bloodstains on their clothes."

"Please," Erasmo said, "find them."

After the paramedic finished with him and he drank some much-needed water, Erasmo explained to Torres how everything went down. He selectively edited out details that might be problematic. Confessing to a cop that he'd shot someone, for example, seemed like a bad idea. She was silent and reacted little to the bizarre story, save for an occasional arched eyebrow. After he'd finished, Torres released a long sigh.

"Anyone ever tell you that you have a knack for getting into weird shit?"

"Actually, yes."

"I'm still a little confused," she said. "All of this was just for money?"

"As far as I can tell, yes, they took the baby for money. To ransom him to fund their group. But this"—Erasmo gestured to the chamber and to his mutilated stomach—"this was all because they're true believers. And there's nothing more dangerous than a true believer."

"So these cult members really believe they have a reciprocal relationship with a demon? A demon they occasionally summon and make blood sacrifices to? That's pretty far out there."

"You left out the part where they convinced themselves that drinking babies' blood makes them powerful, like their Master."

"Wild," Torres said. "Did you see anything else in the house, or down here, that we should know about?"

"No," Erasmo said after a moment. "Not going to lie, though. Had one hell of a delusion right before I passed out. But I was in so much pain and shock, it's no surprise my brain malfunctioned before putting me to sleep."

"Speaking of your physical condition," Torres said, "I really wish you'd let us take you to the hospital."

"I'm fine. It's just a few scratches."

"Bullshit. But I can't make you go if you don't want to. At least get home, then. I'll let you know if we make any arrests, or if we have any more questions."

Erasmo turned to leave, every part of his body hurting in one way or another.

"Hey," Torres called out, "do me a favor. Get some rest, will you?"

"Maybe later," he said. "There's somewhere I need to be."

Erasmo stared at his grandmother, shifted his gaze to the shrugging doctor, then set it back on her again.

His grandmother's face was no longer lopsidedly swollen. In fact, just the barest of inflammation remained. The doctor raised his bushy eyebrows and sighed.

"It was the damndest thing . . ." he said. "Last night her infection was out of control, and her fever had spiked to unsustainable levels. The situation was as dire as it could get, which is why we called. But then all of a sudden—"

"She got better," Erasmo said.

"And in a hurry, too. Don't often see such drastic turn-arounds like this. You must've done a lot of praying."

"Something like that," he said after a long pause.

"Just to temper expectations, your grandmother is still very ill. But at least this crisis has been averted. Oh, there is more good news. Just got some test results back, and every one of her numbers is much better. Hopefully this is a good sign. Like I said, it's the damndest thing . . ."

"Thank you for taking such good care of her," Erasmo said.

He nodded. "Well, I'll leave you two alone, then."

Erasmo stood in front of his grandmother's bed, still numb from the shock of her appearance. She hadn't looked this good in months. Her skin actually had color . . . it was almost vibrant.

Perhaps there is a deal to be made after all.

No. That wasn't possible. The whole thing had been a hallucinatory delusion. It had to have been. Brought on by shock and lack of food and sleep, not to mention all the blood loss and the blow to his head. There'd been no conversation with a demon.

And yet there his grandmother lay, breathing peacefully.

"I owe you nothing," he whispered. "Nothing."

Perhaps it was best not to think too much about the reason for his grandmother's recovery. At least not right now. All that mattered was it had happened, and for this he was eternally grateful. Erasmo took a seat on the chair next to her bed, gently took hold of his grandmother's delicate hand, and waited for her to awaken.

CHAPTER 42

LATER THAT AFTERNOON, after the nurses had shooed him away to run more tests, he pulled into the curandera's parking lot. Instead of entering the store, though, as Erasmo had so many times before, he trudged over to the small garage out back. He was just about to rap on its battered aluminum door when it suddenly swung open.

Vero, her neck bandaged and black bags under her eyes, gestured for him to come in.

"I was wondering how long it would take for you to come by."

The garage reminded him of his own room. It was a cramped space, dimly lit, and stacks of books lay everywhere. But Vero was much more organized than he was. And there were qualities in this room missing from his own: life and warmth and energy, somehow suffused from her essence into these bare walls. Erasmo soaked it in, grateful to be in its presence again.

He settled into a folding chair in the corner, while Vero plopped down on her unmade bed. She caught him staring at her neck.

"I'm fine," she said. "There will be a scar, but it'll add some much-needed character to my overall look, don't you think?"

"What I think," he said, "is that your sense of humor leaves something to be desired. Are you really okay?"

"I will be," she replied.

"Look . . ." he said, the words in his mouth not feeling nearly large enough. "I'll never be able to repay what you did for me down there. What you did for the baby. Thanks for caring enough to come. Even after what I said to you."

"No sweat," she said. "It was out of selfishness really. Can't have you dying on me so soon. We're just getting to know each other."

Tears momentarily threatened, but Erasmo forced them back.

"I'd have headed to the house sooner if I'd known you were there," he said. "But I had no idea. When I got your text, I assumed you were just mad."

"Vassell had my phone and saw your message," Vero said. "I guess he didn't want you to suspect that I was missing. He used my face to unlock the phone and sent that message to throw you off."

Erasmo felt his face grow hot, ashamed at how easily he'd been fooled.

"What you did with that powder," he said, wanting to turn the focus back to her, "it was amazing."

"A simple but effective compound," she said. "It's mostly worn off by now, but they won't fully recover for several weeks."

A sharp knocking interrupted them. The door swung open and Alma walked in, her face pale and grim.

"I thought that was your car outside," she said to Erasmo. "I'm glad to see you're still in one piece."

"Thanks. Sorry about dragging Vero into everything. I didn't mean to—"

"We're definitely going to have a discussion about your decision-making, but right now I'm just glad the two of you are okay." She glanced over their various injuries. "For the most part anyway. The bottom line is the child was saved. The two of you did a good thing."

"It was mostly her," Erasmo said. "I was pretty damn useless there at the end."

"You helped plenty," Vero replied.

"Since you're here," Alma said, the tone in her voice shifting, "there's something we need to talk about. Something that—"

"Actually, I'm pretty tired," he said. "I should really get home and rest. I'll be back to visit soon though."

"Wait, Erasmo—"

He let himself out, feeling a twinge of guilt at leaving so abruptly. It was true though. He really did need to get some rest. It had been a hell of a few days, and all he wanted was a little well-earned oblivion.

Shortly after arriving home, Erasmo's phone buzzed in his pocket. He glanced at the name, surprised to see it.

"Erasmo," his client said, voice shaking. "It's Bradley. My wife's on the line, too."

"Hi," Delia said, sounding completely different than she had in the park. Her voice was weary, but content. "I understand we have you to thank for finding Eric."

"It wasn't only me," he said. "I'm just glad we were able to find him and get him back to you."

"Well, to hear Detective Torres tell it," she said, "you and your friend went through quite an ordeal to save him. I'm forever grateful. I mean that. You're like family to us now."

This was just an expression, Erasmo reminded himself. But the words still spread a comforting warmth through his chest.

"How about you, Bradley?" he asked. "Are you doing okay?"

"Yeah," he said, "for the most part. The police just processed me out, and we're going to the hospital now to be with the baby. They're going to keep him a few days for observation."

"They should've never arrested you in the first place," Erasmo said.

"It was those damn bloody rags," he replied. "Detective Torres said they were left behind by those bastards who wrote the message on Eric's forehead. They must've just ditched them in the closet once they were done. Apparently, tests showed they used pig's blood. Can't be that mad really. I understand how it looked suspicious."

"Well, at least you're free now," Erasmo said. "I'm grateful that it all worked out."

"We need to get going," Bradley said. "The both of us just wanted to call and express our gratitude for what you and your friend did. But, uh, one quick thing before I go. Did you find out the answer? About my original question? Do I owe everything I have to . . . ?"

Bradley let the question linger, not wanting to utter the last few words. Erasmo stayed silent, mulling over the events of the last few days.

"No, Bradley," he finally said after a long pause. "It was all you."

CHAPTER 43

THAT NIGHT, A writhing knot in his gut refused to let him rest, despite how badly Erasmo wanted to give himself to the darkness. He lay in bed tossing, unable to ignore his blistering thoughts.

It doesn't matter. Everything is over now.

Except it wasn't. Deep down he knew that. And desperately trying to pretend it was over didn't make it so.

Let it go. Please. Just this once.

But he knew this was an impossibility, no matter how much he wanted to leave it alone. Erasmo forced himself out of bed and checked the time. Just past midnight. He got dressed and staggered out into the chilly night, a shimmering moon guiding his way.

He drove by the most obvious location first, but no one was there. This really just left one other place to try. When Erasmo arrived, he retraced their steps until he found the right trail. He carefully tread down the steep portion, almost falling a few times. After reaching the bottom, he approached the hulking structure and searched the darkness within it, but saw nothing.

"Are you here?"

Erasmo again strained to see if anything lay inside, but nothing moved.

"Please. I just want some answers."

"Are you sure?" a voice drifted from behind one of the concrete pillars. "You might not like what you find."

"I'm sure," Erasmo said. But in truth, he wasn't sure at all.

Hector Valles stepped out of the shadows, wearing the same black cowboy hat and long leather coat as when they'd first met here. The clink of jewelry and thud of his biker boots reverberated through the night air.

"Some secrets are better left unknown," he said. "They have a way of diminishing who you think a person is and showing who they actually are. And who they actually are can be quite ugly."

Erasmo took a breath and said the words trembling on his lips.

"You may as well come out here, too."

After several seconds, a person who Erasmo would give his life for slipped out of the darkness.

"I wish you hadn't come here," Vero said, her eyes reflecting pale moonlight.

He stared at her in disbelief, despite having known full well she'd be here.

"What you did to the cult," he said. "Their symptoms were almost identical to something I saw earlier that evening."

Vero said nothing, staring blankly at him. She was going to make him come out and ask.

"Do you know what's wrong with Renata?"

"Of course I do," Vero said. "I'm the one who made her sick in the first place."

A bitter cold spread over Erasmo's skin, even though he'd already suspected this to be the truth.

"But how did you even learn to do such a thing?" Although the answer was now obvious, he wanted to hear her say the words. "Alma would never—"

"My mentor taught me how to use nature for . . . destructive purposes. To even the playing field." Vero walked over to Hector and beamed at him. "My *real* mentor."

Hector tipped his cowboy hat to Erasmo and gave him an amused wink.

"But what about not wanting to be a curandera like your aunt?"

"That is one hundred percent true," Vero said. "I went in a different direction and studied another discipline behind my aunt's back."

"Brujería."

Vero nodded, her hair reflecting stray rays of moonlight.

"Aren't you scared? Of its power . . . of its darkness?"

"No," she said, but flinched at the question. "I can control it. Hector is teaching me how."

"But why did you curse Renata? I still don't understand."

"Oh, don't feel bad for her. She left out an important detail when she came to us." Vero grimaced at the memory. "That woman is a murderer."

"A murderer?"

"Well, she *tried* to kill someone. Her lack of success doesn't make her any less guilty."

"Carmen Espinoza," Erasmo said.

"Yes. Renata hated Carmen for keeping her brother away for so many years. When he died, it sent Renata over the edge. So she came to Hector, begging him to curse Carmen. The worst kind of curse, too. I watched from the shadows as Hector refused and sent her away."

"That's why she was so sure Hector had cursed her," Erasmo said. "Renata thought Hector was punishing her . . . for what she'd tried to hire him to do. She lied to us so we'd come down here and get Hector to take it off."

"Right," Vero said. "But she shouldn't have been worried about Hector. She should've been worried about me. I figured Renata would still try to hurt Carmen, so I went to check on her a few days later. Sure enough, I found Carmen in her house, vomiting blood everywhere."

"Renata found a way to curse Carmen herself," Erasmo said, recalling the grotesque scene in her shed.

"Yes. She must've found another brujo who taught her how. I brought Carmen to Hector, and he cleansed her of the black magic. She's fine now, recovering in El Paso with some relatives."

"But that wasn't the end of it."

"Of course not. I took it upon myself to . . . teach Renata a lesson."

Hector nodded and grinned, clearly proud of his student.

"I had no idea she'd call my aunt for help. Imagine my shock. I really should've known though. My aunt is the best curandera in San Antonio. Who else was Renata going to turn to?"

"You never even bothered," Erasmo said, "to tell Alma how sick Renata was. That's why she never went over to help."

Vero nodded. "I just told my aunt everything was under control."

Damn. How could he have been so wrong about everything? How could he not have seen all this unfolding right in front of his face?

"Why didn't you tell me any of this when we met?"

"I don't usually make it a practice to share my deepest secrets with a practical stranger."

"What you did was wrong," he said. "It's not up to you to punish Renata."

"Are you sure? Because that's not the lesson I learned from my father. His death taught me that evil needs to be dealt with. Sometimes tumors have to be cut out to prevent further spread. I was just trying to stop her from ever hurting anyone else."

"But what you did crosses a line," Erasmo said.

"After my father died . . ." Vero's breath hitched, and she hurriedly wiped at her eyes. "After my father died, I came to realize the only way to fight evil is to go right up to the edge of that line and cross right over if that's what it takes. When pure malevolence exists, the kind that leaves a child waiting up all night for a parent who's never coming home . . . it's worth sacrificing a bit of yourself to stop it."

Vero's words were assured, but her trembling face betrayed the turmoil underneath. Maybe she wasn't so sure of the path she'd chosen. Maybe she was scared of the dark magic she'd been studying.

Maybe she was just as broken as he was.

Erasmo then forced himself to ask a question he was scared to know the answer to. A question that would determine if Vero would be in his life anymore.

"Is Renata going to die?"

Vero stayed silent, as if she were trying to make that determination at this very moment.

"Take the curse off," Erasmo said. "I understand why you wanted to punish her. But Renata has suffered enough now. When I saw her last night, she said she was sorry. Said that she tried to take it back."

"It's easy to be sorry when you're vomiting your insides out."

"Please, Vero. I was so wrong when I said you could never be a part of this. I'm the one who'd be lucky to have you around. We can help people. But I can't be a part of letting Renata die. Please. Don't throw this away."

Vero mulled his words over for a few moments, then walked up and placed her hands on his shoulders.

"Renata was never going to die," she said. "I'm not like those people who killed my father. I just wanted to give her a warning she'll never forget. The curse wore off a few hours ago."

A mixture of relief and embarrassment settled over him. He slumped down, suddenly overcome with exhaustion. But then Vero enveloped him in a hug, and momentarily, all was right with the world.

She released him and locked her eyes onto his.

"There are limitations to turning the other cheek, Erasmo. I wish light could fight darkness. In a better world, it would. But sometimes darkness needs to be met with darkness."

He nodded, wanting to object to most of what she'd just said, but was much too tired to find the right words. There was plenty of time to reason with her. This was at least a start.

"We were just wrapping up our lesson for the night," she said, looking exhausted herself. "How about a ride home?"

A short time later, Erasmo trudged to his room and sat on the edge of his bed, preparing to finally indulge in a well-deserved respite from the world. He closed his eyes and allowed the rhythm in his veins to carry him away to a dream so dark, there wasn't the faintest memory of light.

CHAPTER 44

VOICES. THERE WERE voices in his room. No. That couldn't be possible. He'd locked the doors. Hadn't he? Someone had broken in, then. Not just someone. Them. Gemma . . . or Vassell . . . or one of those other sick bastards had come for him. Or maybe it was even—

Wait. He wasn't lying in bed, where he should've been. He was in a chair. And his arms were paralyzed. His legs, too. They wouldn't move a goddamn inch. Who had put him in this chair, and why couldn't he move?

Erasmo strained his limbs in every direction and now understood why they didn't respond. He was tied down, the ropes against his wrist and ankles coarse and tight.

No. No goddamn way. How could this have happened again? It wasn't possible. It wasn't. He must be dreaming.

But then, as if to prove the reality of it, a single footstep shuffled behind him. He turned his neck, but the intruder remained just out of sight.

"He's awake," a voice said. A familiar voice.

Light from above flickered on, and Erasmo was shocked to see that he was still in his room. They'd broken in and done this to him while he slept. How the hell had he not woken up?

Footsteps now approached. He would see who they'd sent to finish the job. Just please, whoever it was, please don't let it be . . .

"Rat," he croaked, now seeing the person he'd once considered a brother standing in front of him.

He looked pale and haggard but had a determined look in his eyes. It was obvious he intended to go through with whatever he had planned.

"Hey," Rat said, "sorry about the restraints. But it's the only way."

Erasmo noticed Rat held a hunting knife in his right hand, which trembled slightly.

"Do it if you're going to do it," he said. "I can't believe you're with them. At least make sure my grandmother doesn't see any of the mess."

"What?" Rat said. "You think . . . ?" He shook his head. "We're not here to hurt you."

He looked sincere, but Erasmo knew better. Besides, the knife in Rat's hand told a different story.

"Then why are you in my room? Why am I tied up like this?"

"Because," a different voice said, "it's the only way to make you see."

A new figure approached from behind. Erasmo's jaw dropped when she took her place next to Rat.

"Alma," he said, unable to believe it. The curandera had been involved with them the whole time? This made no sense. But then a memory surfaced, of his late-night visit to her shop. There had been voices behind her door. Whispers. They'd been there that night, plotting. Maybe it had even been Rat on the other side of the door. Wait. If Alma was involved, then that meant . . .

"Vero," he said, tears slipping down his face as she stepped forward from the shadows. "You too? This isn't possible."

"Do you know why we're here?" Rat asked.

"To hurt me."

"No," Alma said. "We've all been trying to help you. But the lies you whisper to yourself are too powerful. You are not thinking clearly."

"Why wouldn't I be thinking clearly?"

"You know goddamn well why," Rat said.

"I don't."

"Really?" Alma said. "Well, let me ask you this. Have you been falling asleep lately . . . waking up confused?

"No," he said without hesitation. "Not at all."

In Ms. Jenkins's basement . . . a voice from deep inside whispered . . . *in the Soul Center parking lot . . . in the alleyway before you saw the emaciated creature.*

"Have you seen yourself in the mirror lately?" Vero said. "Have you seen what you look like?"

"I've had a bug. And haven't been eating or sleeping very much. That's all."

"Take a better look," Rat said, and held a small mirror up to Erasmo's face.

He tried to avert his gaze but eventually had to glance at the reflection. True, his skin was a bit yellow, and he'd lost some weight, and the bags under his eyes were black and purple, but it wasn't so bad. Not really.

"Haven't you wondered why certain parts of your story don't add up?" said another voice from behind him.

No. Please. Not her, too.

Detective Torres stepped in and joined the others. She'd been lurking behind him the whole time, observing.

"What do you mean?"

"You told me a demon stole the baby from Bradley's . . . that you saw this creature with the child in its arms. But, Erasmo, why would a group kidnapping a baby for money send a demon to take it, if such a thing were even possible?"

"I . . . I don't know."

"The answer is that it wasn't a demon at all. We caught Vassell. He said that it was just one of their members dressed in a robe who took the baby. Why do you think you saw a demon instead?"

"I don't know."

"And the creature you claimed you saw in the alley . . . does that make any sense to you? Do you really believe this monster, that didn't even look like a demon, appeared out of nowhere and attacked you?"

"It's what I saw," he said, tears slipping down his face.

"It's almost as if . . ." Torres said, "you were having some kind of hallucination. What would cause something like that to happen?"

"I don't know what you're talking about."

"Has your right arm been bothering you?" she asked.

"No . . . not at all."

"Really? Go ahead and take a look at it, then."

Erasmo remained still. His arm was a bit sore from the fall he took in Ms. Jenkins's basement, that's all.

"You have to look," Rat said, his eyes red and tear-filled. "You have to admit what's happening."

He stared straight ahead, his neck muscles tensed. They couldn't make him if he didn't want to.

But they could. Rat slid behind the chair, grabbed Erasmo's head, and tilted it downward. He struggled, but it was useless. His body was too weak. After a few moments, he gave in and finally set his eyes on what they so badly wanted him to see.

Erasmo was both surprised and not surprised, which was the essence of lying to yourself, he supposed. The skin on his right forearm was a mess. It was black and purple, his veins bruised from overuse. A pus-filled abscess sat in the middle of this tender flesh, leaking even now as he glared at it. Not to mention the track marks.

So many goddamn track marks.

"She was dying," Erasmo said, the words catching in his throat. He said nothing else, as if this were the only explanation necessary. In a way, it was.

Erasmo thought he'd be prepared when the worst came. But a few months ago, as the news kept getting progressively worse, the suffering had overwhelmed him. The impending certainty of a life without his grandmother had shattered whatever semblance of control he'd once had.

Even now, he wasn't sure where the idea came from. Well, that's not entirely true. His parents, of course. He'd long been curious about the poison they'd chosen over him. In fact, he'd been born with it coursing through his veins. And he'd been so desperate to soothe his blistering nerves. It was almost as if the thought were always there and needed just the slightest nudge to present itself. In truth, it hadn't been the first time he'd considered doing this. The drug had whispered to him, offering a single, delectable promise.

I'll ease your pain.

Just once, he'd promised himself. Just to see what it was like. Just to get a good night's rest. Just to calm himself after hearing the worst news of his life.

But those were all just lies he'd told himself . . . his specialty.

What he'd really wanted was an occasional taste of oblivion. Or to take the edge off by having a quick snort, like in the alleyway. And that's exactly what he got. It wasn't a big deal. He'd done it just a few times at *most*.

Right?

No. His arm screamed a different truth. Erasmo turned to each of his captor's faces, spending a few seconds to study their expressions. And another truth bloomed, as clear as the marks on his arm: they were terrified for him.

This realization dislodged something inside, allowing a stray beam of light to shine on his darkest delusions. And what it revealed was monstrous.

"I need help," he heard a wavering voice say, as if it belonged to someone else. In fact, it did. It was a voice that had been trapped and buried underneath a mountain of grief and lies and abandonment, but now had the slightest sliver of space to call out through. It was the voice of the person he once was. A voice of the person he could still be. "I need help . . . please."

Rat, his tiny eyes trembling, approached with the hunting knife. He slipped the blade underneath the ropes and released his arms, then his legs. Erasmo rose unsteadily and almost fell, but each of them stepped forward and caught him.

They all embraced at once, with Erasmo in the middle, sobs filling the room.

"We've got you," Rat said. "We've got you."

Erasmo's legs gave way, but he didn't fall, held up by the people surrounding him. Was this possible? Was it too much to hope that the very thing he'd been so eager to sell his soul for was in this very room, attempting to save him from his own self-destruction? God, he hoped so.

Who else but family would do that?

Erasmo closed his eyes and, despite the reason they'd gathered here, enjoyed the feeling of their embrace, even as he continued to beg them for help.

CHAPTER 45

THE THREE OF them rolled down I-10, a sense of anticipation building in the Civic. As pleasant as the ride had been so far, a lingering doubt nagged at Erasmo. Was he ready for this?

Three months in a rehab center that Torres had gotten him into had certainly helped. He felt a lot better and hadn't touched any of that garbage since the intervention. But of course, it wasn't that easy. The oblivion called to him every night, pleading and incessant.

In rehab, one of the treatments they suggested was journaling. After the craziness with Nora and Billy and Leander awhile back, he'd already started one, mostly to document what he learned from his cases. Erasmo had written in this journal every day for the full three months, but he'd written only one entry about Bradley's case. He'd read that entry over and over during his stay there, somehow finding it therapeutic, until he'd accidently memorized every word. Erasmo thought of it now as the three of them rode in silence.

The Devil's Promise

Looking back over the last few months, especially the last few days, I'm not sure how to process everything I saw. Everything I did. Both to myself and the few people who care about me. I thought I had everything under control but was too blind to realize I was in a frantic dance with the Devil. It's so tempting to blame Him, but it takes two to tango, doesn't it?

Part of what makes the Devil so cunning is that His promises are so simple and yet so seductive. He eagerly agrees to dull your never-ending anxiety, your doubts, your fears, give you a taste of sweet oblivion. For a price. And it's a price I'll be paying for a long time.

As far as Bradley and his case, I'm still not quite certain what to make of it all. Somehow, I ended up in the exact same situation as him: unsure if I've made a deal with the Devil. If I did, then He's already upheld His part of the bargain by saving my grandmother. Perhaps this means one day He'll come to collect what He's owed. This frightens me terribly, but that's a problem for another time.

I still think a lot about Gemma's offer to join her group. It would've been so easy to slip into the life she offered, to ignore the part of myself I was destroying in the process. Perhaps self-destruction was what I was actually looking for. Seems like most people usually are.

And what exactly did I see down in that basement? A drug-induced hallucination or an ageless evil? My mind gives one answer, but my heart tells me another. And I'm scared that what my heart whispers to me every night as I drift off to sleep is true.

I tell myself that I'd wanted to make that deal only to save my grandmother, to give her more years to shine her light on this earth. But now I'm not so sure. Seeing my grandmother wither away, the suffering she endured, pushed me to the edge. Beyond the edge. I couldn't bear it. My seething heart told me to do anything to save my grandmother, commit atrocities even. Which makes me wonder if I sought out the Devil for her benefit, or for mine.

Was a demon really summoned that night? I'm not sure, but I do think Vassell was right about one thing. Love is what's necessary to summon a monster, the essential ingredient. After all, you must love something a whole lot to promise your soul to the Devil for it. And surely He smells the desperation on you, the eagerness to gut yourself for what you love. It's probably what draws Him to you in the first place.

Is this what happened to Vero? The world took the love she had for her father and crushed it, transformed it into a lust for vengeance, a temptation to harm other damaged souls. I worry for her, scared that one day her need to inflict hurt will overtake her entirely.

Despite the pitfalls of love, it can also banish the monsters, can shield you from their sick charms. Love is what is pulling me through as I sit here writing this. And if I can get right with myself, love is what will sustain me.

I want to tell whoever might read this to run from the Devil, to flee as if your skin is on fire. That would make me a hypocrite, though, as I myself ran toward Him. But I'll also spend the rest of my life looking over my shoulder, and that's an ugly way to live.

If anyone ever does read this, please be wary of seeking out the Devil. Because if you make a promise to a monster, you might accidentally become one.

When Erasmo finally got out of rehab, he'd often caught Vero and Rat glancing at him nervously, as if he were just seconds away from making a run for the nearest dealer. This didn't aggravate him though. In fact, it made him love them more. And the ugly truth was, there were plenty of times when he was in deep contemplation of making that very run.

What made Erasmo the most nervous was that he'd felt cautious optimism before. And look what happened . . . what depths he'd sunk to. But he now understood a simple truth that he hadn't before.

Life will knock you down twice as hard, just for the sin of having hope.

Books and movies always make it seem like once you've had a fundamental realization of your own nature, once you've accepted that your life has worth, you have made it through the rough part. What they don't tell you is the rough part is just beginning.

Erasmo knew his recovery was not going to be a straight line. All the complications, of course. And he was uncertain if during his darkest nights, he'd be able to ignore what his veins cried out for even now. But what he did know was that a throbbing mass that had sat in his gut for as long as he could remember was now gone. Or at least temporarily away. He no longer felt alone or feared the looming specter of solitude, and this quieted his veins' incessant pleas.

"So, anything in particular we need to know?" Vero asked from the passenger seat. "Or is our normal modus operandi going to be just flying by the seat of our pants? Because honestly, I could get behind that."

"Yeah, preparation is totally overrated," Rat chimed in from the back. Erasmo had noticed lately that Rat always eagerly agreed with every utterance Vero made. He wondered if this was going to become a problem.

"No," he said. "If you two don't mind, I'd like to take the lead on this one. Since I've already dealt with her, and this is our first case since . . . you know."

"You have at it, dude," Rat said. "Besides, she sounds like a tough one. Better you than me."

Soon after, they pulled into their client's driveway. Well, she wasn't their client exactly. In fact, she didn't even know they were coming. Erasmo's heart thrummed in his chest as he approached the door. He stood in front of it for several moments, not quite able to bring himself to knock.

Erasmo then felt a hand on each of his shoulders. He could tell the slight, reassuring one on his right was Rat's, and the one bristling with power on his left was Vero's. They both infused him with the strength he needed to lift his hand to the wood and knock.

Almost immediately, footsteps approached the door. They were slow and deliberate, but they neared nonetheless. Finally, the door opened, and a familiar face stared back at him.

"Well, look who it is," Ms. Jenkins said. "You come to take another nap on my property?"

"Hi," Erasmo said. "I . . . I came to apologize for what happened on my last visit. I wasn't in great shape, and I'm sorry that I wasted your time and didn't get the job done."

The old woman was silent as she appraised him.

"Well, that's okay," she finally said. "It takes a big person to own up to their mistakes." She paused for a moment before adding, "I'm glad to see you looking so much better."

"Thank you," he said, unexpectedly moved by this.

"Too bad, though," Ms. Jenkins said. "That house is still scaring the hell out of whoever goes in there."

"Well, speaking of that, there's something I wanted to ask. I'll understand if you say no."

"And what's that?"

Before Erasmo answered, he turned to Vero, comforted by her reassuring glance, and then to Rat, who grinned at him with excitement.

"If you don't mind, I'd like to try again."

"Is that so?" she said. "Think you'll have better luck?"

"Well," Erasmo said, "I'm not alone this time. And that makes all the difference in the world."

Ms. Jenkins nodded in agreement, and invited them inside.

Before he entered, Erasmo turned back and glanced at the beautiful afternoon sky. His heart swelled in gratitude for this second chance, which was all he'd wanted. And with his family by his side, Erasmo was going to do everything he could to get it right this time.

ACKNOWLEDGMENTS

This book wouldn't have been possible without the help of so many of you.

Thank you, Lynda and Gracie, for the constant support and for picking up my slack when I needed time to write.

Thank you to all my friends and family. This whole endeavor is a lot easier when you have amazing people in your corner encouraging you.

Thank you, Layla, for all the hugs and for making sure I took plenty of writing breaks.

Thank you, Marcos Viera, for suggesting one of the cult's attributes early on, which was immensely helpful.

Thank you, Jay de la Cruz, for suggesting the Devil's Den location, which was perfect.

A big thanks to Adam Gomolin, both for continuing Erasmo Cruz's journey with me and for helping to shape this book.

Thank you, Noah Broyles, for your many insightful suggestions.

Thank you, Ryan Jenkins, for another fantastic copy edit.

Thank you, Joey Solis, for the amazing handmade figure of Erasmo Cruz. It's so damn cool.

And lastly, thank you to all the great folks in the horror writing community who've helped in so many ways. Preston Fassel, L. P. Hernandez, Johnny Compton, Agatha Andrews, Max Booth III, Debra Castaneda, Cynthia Pelayo, Lydia Peever, Danger Slater, Patrick Delaney, Miguel Myers, R. C. Hausen, Ryan C. Bradley, R.J. Joseph, and so many more. Whether it was an encouraging word or offering a great piece of advice or just being fantastic people, you've made a tremendous impact on me. Thank you.

INKSHARES

INKSHARES is a community, publisher, and producer for debut writers. Our books are selected not just by a group of editors, but also by readers worldwide. Our aim is to find and develop the most captivating and intelligent new voices in fiction. We have no genre—our genre is debut.

Previously unknown Inkshares authors have received starred reviews in every trade publication. They have been featured in every major review, including on the front page of the *New York Times*. Their books are on the front tables of booksellers worldwide, topping bestseller lists. They have been translated in major markets by the world's biggest publishers. And they are being adapted at the biggest studios and networks.

Interested in making your own story a reality? Visit Inkshares.com to start your own project, connect with other writers, and find other great books.